STAR LIGHT, STAR BRIGHT

STAR LIGHT, STAR BRIGHT

Marian Wells

BETHANY HOUSE PUBLISHERS

MINNEAPOLIS, MINNESOTA 55438

A Division of Bethany Fellowship, Inc.

Published by Bethany House Publishers
A Division of Bethany Fellowship, Inc.
6820 Auto Club Road, Minneapolis, Minnesota 55438

Printed in the United States of America

Library of Congress Cataloging-in-Publication Data

Wells, Marian, 1931-
   Star light, star bright.

   (The Starlight trilogy ; bk. 2)
   Sequel to: The wishing star.
   I. Title.   II. Series: Wells, Marian, 1931-
Starlight trilogy ; bk. 2.
PS3573.E4927S73   1986   813'.54   86-6102
ISBN 0-87123-883-7 (pbk.)

Introduction

In the first book of this trilogy, *The Wishing Star,* Jenny Timmons, "nearly twelve—come January," is living in South Bainbridge, New York. Her family is poor, and except for the green book, life holds little excitement or interest.

Then Jenny's best friend, her brother Tom, introduces Jenny to his new friend, Joe Smith, a fascinating youth whose ideas about life seem to parallel the discoveries she has made through reading the forbidden green book. Intrigued by the mystery surrounding Joe and Tom, Jenny is determined to insert herself in the middle of their fascinating enterprises. While Jenny struggles with her world, Joseph Smith provides South Bainbridge with a new touch of excitement. Even from those early years, people either loved or hated Joseph.

Within the year, Jenny's father gives in to his yearning to go west. The family moves to Manchester, New York, the first leg of the westward trek.

That year, Tom becomes a stable-hand, working for a man named Martin Harris. After one happy year, Pa's feet begin to itch again, and in the process of packing the wagon to move, Pa finds Jenny reading his forbidden book. When the wagon leaves, Tom and Jenny remain behind, both working for Martin Harris—Tom in the stables and Jenny as the hired girl. And Pa's green book stays behind as well—stolen by Jenny and hidden away for safekeeping.

Manchester is a small town, nestled close to Palmyra, New York. At school, and at the Presbyterian church on Sunday, Jenny becomes acquainted with the Smith youngsters and their parents. She develops a fondness for Lucy Smith. Once again the threads of life stretch between Jenny and Joseph Smith.

But one of those threads has been snapped. When Jenny had first met Joseph Smith, she had vowed to marry him. Now her girlish dreams of romance are terminated when Joseph Smith takes Emma Hale as his wife.

For a short period of time, Joseph and Emma live in Palmyra, New York. During this time, Martin Harris becomes involved with Joseph, and the rumors grow. Talk of the Gold Bible Company and other mysterious events surround the lives of the Smith family.

Jenny's life in Manchester becomes filled with excitement and trauma. Martin Harris' strange beliefs and uncontrolled anger rise to a climax. When he sells his farm in order to finance the printing of the gold bible, his wife Lucy resists him, and he responds in rage, beating both her and Jenny.

Thus Jenny and Tom Timmons find themselves without employment.

Befriended by Mark Cartwright, a young man Jenny and Tom first met in South Bainbridge, New York, at the time of Joseph's first trial, the brother and sister go to eastern New York State. But soon Tom's restless feet lead him after his friend, Joseph Smith.

Jenny stays behind as a hired girl, and finds security and the promise of power in the forbidden green book she took from Pa.

Her fascination and curiosity with the book send her delving into the occult. Jenny still believes herself in control of her life, but desires born back in South Bainbridge days begin manifesting themselves in strange ways.

As Jenny matures, the choices she makes include a search for secret power, leading her to Kirtland, Ohio, to a prophet, her old friend, Joseph Smith.

Jenny becomes a follower of this new church. In time she learns that Joseph's control over his people extends even into their personal lives. Joseph instructs her to ask Mark Cartwright to marry her. And she obeys.

CHAPTER 1

The buggy was finally moving along rapidly. Since Mark and Jenny had left Kirtland early in the morning, every buggy and wagon in the Cleveland area seemed to conspire to bog them in traffic forever. Each mile that brought them closer to Cleveland had added more vehicles to the road.

Now they both breathed a sigh of relief as their path turned away from the wharf and meandered down country lanes. Overhead trees sheltered their way with shade. With the absence of shouting men, clanging bells and snorting horses, they began to relax. Bawling peddlers and angry wagoneers behind them, Mark sighed with relief and settled back to allow the horses to pick their own pace.

Now Jenny felt his warm glances, and saw the pleased grin. But the high tide of emotion she was feeling kept her silent. It had been early dawn when they self-consciously faced each other. There had been a moment of panic as Mark helped her into the buggy; just knowing this was *the* day made Jenny pause, fighting the impulse to run and hide. How badly she wanted once again to hear Mark's assurance that his mother would *really* be pleased that they were marrying! Still trying to hide the tumble of strange new emotions, Jenny was only shy, while Mark was proud, rightfully possessive.

Through the silence Jenny was doubly aware of the rhythm of the horses' hooves clicking against the hard-packed earth; it was the only sound on this quiet road. At the start of the day, Jenny had been full of chatter and laughter. She guessed Mark knew that her mood was designed to hide her real thoughts.

9

Not all of those thoughts were to be shared, though, and eventually they had lapsed into the present silence.

Jenny studied Mark out of the corner of her eye. The sun picked out copper glints in his hair and illuminated the broad shoulders of the well-tailored suit. A gentleman. Jenny looked down at her dress, one she had made herself. *Kitchenmaid.* She winced painfully, suddenly wondering if she shouldn't be back where she belonged. Surely that was anywhere but here!

Abruptly, scenes from the South Bainbridge days filled her thoughts: the shabby shack, Pa and Ma, all the young'uns, and not enough milk to go around. She thought of Jenny and Nancy, of their faded dresses lined against Prue's daffodil yellow. And she remembered Joe Smith, the diggings, and the green book of Pa's. How could she have dared involve Mark Cartwright in all this?

She chewed at her lip, trying desperately, even now, to find an excuse to run away from it all. But even as she thought that perhaps Mrs. Cartwright would take one look and send her packing, Jenny realized how badly she wanted to marry this man.

She was taking a deep, shaky breath when Mark reached for her hand and gave it a gentle tug. "I'm glad I don't have to meet *your* mother today. She'd probably say I'm not good enough for her daughter."

"Oh, Mark!" Was he guessing how she felt? Suddenly she could face him, and the expression in his eyes was reassuring.

He teased, "There's not another person on this road; please prove you are real, not a pretty dream to vanish when I blink my eyes."

"Mark, you are silly, not the least like a dignified attorney at all."

"It's taken this long for you to discover the fact?" Now she saw his eyes were serious, but he was still tugging at her hand. "Since we left Kirtland this morning, you've been as wide-eyed as little Jenny with her nose pressed to the window of the candy shop."

Jenny winced. How it hurt to be reminded of those South Bainbridge days. Looking up at him she said slowly, "Mark, I am. I'm even fearful. What am I doing to you?"

"What will your mother think of me?" It was a whisper.

"You'll find that out in less than an hour." His voice was confident, "I don't think she'll be disappointed." Mark studied her for another moment before he turned to point the whip to the north. "You'd never guess, but just beyond that line of trees is the biggest body of water you've ever seen."

But Jenny would not be distracted. Her voice was brooding as she said, "There are disadvantages to marrying a man who has known you since you were a little tyke. Mark, you needn't remind me there will be no surprises in our marriage. You know me too well."

For a moment his face was still, and then she saw a hint of shadow in his eyes. "I only wish I did. Jenny, I sense I'll never be certain of knowing you completely. Life will always be full of surprises with you, I'm guessing. I hope I prove nimble enough to keep up with you." He was teasing again, and his smile was warm. With a quick grin his mood changed, "Little owl eyes, look yonder—that is the beginning of the Cartwright acres."

"All of this?" Jenny turned wondering eyes back to Mark. He saw again that expression, the little-kitchenmaid one.

"Jenny, don't forget, you are now a part of the Cartwright family—at least you will be just as soon as we can get that preacher to come listen to us promise to love and honor each other for the rest of our lives."

He brushed his lips across her cheek, and she blinked tears out of her eyes as she smiled up at him. "Mark, I will love belonging to you, but not because your family has more acres than I've ever ridden across." Her voice was wistful as she touched his face. "It's all like a dream. And I didn't really think I'd ever be in the middle of the dream."

Later, Mark's mother held her face and kissed her. When she felt Mrs. Cartwright's tears, Jenny, with a shock, saw herself unworthy and guilty; and the emotion had nothing to do with Mark's wealth.

With his mother's words, in one bewildered moment, Jenny discovered herself to be sailing under a false banner. *Strange*, she thought as the woman talked, *never before have I seen my-*

self in just this light. With difficulty she forced herself to smile as Mrs. Cartwright held her away to study her face. Would she guess her averted eyes were more than shyness?

The woman continued, "Jenny, you'll never know how I've prayed for this day." The fragile white-haired woman whispered, "My son is twenty-seven years old, and I had begun to think I wouldn't live to know his wife and children."

Later, over tea in the parlor, Jenny tried to act calm and relaxed. Mark and his mother, pointing to an alcove lined with windows, talked about candles and flowers and music, while Jenny's thoughts churned on. Mrs. Cartwright had *prayed* for a wife for Mark. She, Jenny, was that answer.

He had called her, with a bit of awe in his voice, a fine Christian lady. Right now Jenny was having difficulty swallowing the tea; her thoughts were on the green book of magic, the charms, the talisman she wore hidden in the folds of her dress. She nearly choked on the tea as she visualized the horror on Mrs. Cartwright's face were she to hear Clara advising Jenny to build the waxen figure of Emma Smith and insert the pins.

Mark and his mother returned to the tea table. Sentiment was forgotten now as Mrs. Cartwright, her eyes bright with curiosity, surveyed Jenny over the top of her teacup and asked, "Your parents?"

Jenny was shaking her head and explaining. For a moment she was caught by the picture of her mother in these surroundings. The mental image left her with an aching heart.

But Mrs. Cartwright was moving on. "Tell me about your home. Do you have brothers and sisters? I assume you attended church." While Jenny struggled over the necessary answers, Mrs. Cartwright continued talking, her brow furrowed as if her own problem of explanation was too great. "When Mark was tiny, I gave him to God. See, Jenny, I had a dream of having my son measure up to the best that God expected of him."

Something in her eyes sought confirmation; Jenny was left wondering how she could hope to be that best. Looking into the candid eyes of Mrs. Cartwright, she desperately wanted to reassure her. Jenny searched for words, but the only words she could find were the ones she had already decided mustn't be said around Mark: *power, talisman, charms, grimoire.*

The contrast startled Jenny. She looked at Mark, suddenly realizing the width of the gulf between them. Was she sentencing herself to a lifetime of constantly guarding her tongue? As she studied the face that had become dear and familiar, Adela's words echoed through her: *Anything except Mark.* Jenny's fingers tightened around the handle of the teacup and then relaxed. *Remember, Jenny,* she advised herself, *you've chosen Joseph's way, not Adela's.*

Mrs. Cartwright was still talking about God, and with amusement Jenny decided she was trying to cover life with one cozy blanket. Jenny needn't tell her that she didn't like the blanket, and besides, she had discovered long ago that the blanket of faith had holes in it.

Jenny settled herself to listen to the story. Mark's grandfather and even his great-grandfather were Methodist preachers. "We've always been a Bible-believing and practicing people. I want to see it carried down into your generation." She gave a gentle shiver. "There's so much abroad today that is anti-God. It seems as if in these past ten years people have turned restless, searching for something more than old-time religion. I pray that the spirit of revival will sweep this nation. There is the potential; we're seeing a new breed of men coming into the pulpit."

Abruptly Mark took notice. "Is that so? To whom are you referring?"

She was nodding with enthusiasm as she replied. "I was specifically referring to young Charles Finney. He's advocating a deeper life, deriding the trend toward religion that's all show. He's asking for a heart-changing experience with God. If it will happen, this nation can be changed in every area, from the social to the governmental." She stopped abruptly and Jenny saw the touch of sadness in her eyes as she watched her son stir impatiently.

Before Jenny could leave the room, she had to ask, "You believe God changes hearts? How people think and feel, and even act?" Mrs. Cartwright nodded, but Jenny could ask no more.

The next day Jenny stood at her bedroom window and decided that the Cartwright home was mellow like Mrs. Barton's fruitcake: perfect, opulent. Her troubled eyes swept over the scene, and she remembered her own corn bread beginnings.

Thinking back to yesterday, she breathed a sigh of relief. She might have been forced to give detailed explanations, but Mrs. Cartwright had kindly accepted her fumbling answers without further questions.

The Cartwright home was quiet and green, away from the noisy waterfront and the bustle of town. The estate, from the stately old oak trees to the stone-and-timber home, looked settled and peaceful, as if it had always been part of the landscape.

With a sigh Jenny shook her head and moved away from the window. She still wondered why a man like Mark noticed her, why he had allowed himself to be talked into marrying her.

Briefly she touched the talisman pinned securely into the waistband of her dress. Could that metal be responsible, or was Mark simply too much of a gentleman to say no? She was still pondering her dark thoughts when she heard a tap at the door.

Mrs. Cartwright came into the room followed by a wide-eyed young girl carrying a dress in its dust cover. Jenny found herself studying the awkward, poorly dressed girl, seeing the awe on her face and the expression of defeat. For a moment Jenny pressed her fingers to her eyes. It was like looking at the young Jenny, and the picture was painful.

"Jenny," Mrs. Cartwright said softly, "I know you've had little opportunity to shop for a wedding gown. When I wore this dress I dreamed of the daughter I would have and who would someday wear it. Mark's baby sister died before her first birthday. I don't insist that you wear the dress, but if you would like to wear it, it is yours. If you were to wear it, I would be completely happy on your wedding day." Touching her fingertips to her eyes, she turned and left the room.

Completely? The hard, sore spot around Jenny's heart softened.

The following Sunday Jenny again stood at her bedroom window, marveling at the scene before her. How could this great assembly of people and those tremendous quantities of food have been summoned within a week's time?

Walking gracefully down the curving staircase, wearing Mrs. Cartwright's lace gown, squeezing the cascading bouquet of yellow roses against her pounding heart, Jenny paused on the stairs. The hallway below was a sea of strange but friendly faces tipped upward, smiling and nodding. They clustered after her as she went into the parlor where Mark waited to take her hand.

She faced the solemn, graying man with piercing eyes who would seal her fate with Mark's. For a moment she trembled. Mark's hand, steady and warm, linked her with life and response and reality.

The minister declared, "It is before this group as witness, in the presence of the great eternal God, that we meet together to join this man and woman together in holy matrimony. Marriage, holy, ordained by God, is to be maintained as a sacred trust between these two people."

The vows she pledged under Mark's serious gaze became weighted with meaning that grew, doubling and tripling in strength until she felt the vows amplified to the very heavens. Her whispered promises were, to her, shouts of eternal declaration, binding Jenny with cords of integrity when she didn't know the meaning of the word. Caught up, knowing only that she was partner in a holy act, she faced Mark and murmured, "I pledge you my love, my honor."

Astonished, she watched and listened to Mark. With tears in his eyes, he promised to love and care for her as long as she lived. For one swift second her father's face seemed to rise up between the two of them. Trembling, she knew herself to be at the terrible mercy of this man.

At the reception, she lifted a fragment of wedding cake to his lips, and the glow of the golden wedding ring flashed between their eyes. His eyes were sparkling with joy, and she carefully smeared icing on the end of his nose. Amid the laughter, Attorney Cartwright transferred the icing to her cheek, and the specter of Jenny's father disappeared forever.

"A hurried wedding I will tolerate gladly, lest you change your mind," Mark had said, "but a leisurely wedding trip I will not forego." He had promptly booked passage on a lake steamer for a two-week trip around Lake Erie.

When Mark and Jenny returned home to Kirtland, Ohio, still basking in the glow of their honeymoon, they were amazed to find their previous world unchanged. And while Jenny dreamed about her house and cooked meals for her husband, Mark faced the world to which he had been innocently summoned.

Because Mark was Mark, firmly believing with his lawyer's mind that black was black and white only white, Jenny was called upon to share his feelings and be a sounding board for his questions as he explored the thought and structure of this new world—the Mormons.

During one of those early dinners, after he had remarked on the fine roast, he said, "Just today I found the Prophet has gone to Salem, Massachusetts."

"Whatever for? Salem is a strange place for him to be."

"There seems to be a bit of secrecy involved. Some say it's a missionary trip and that he's taken men with him. Andy is disturbed."

"Oh, you've seen Sally?"

"No, just her husband. Jenny, you smell better than the apple pie."

"Must you go out tonight?"

"No, of course not." Jenny touched his face. *Sally was mistaken*, she thought, *when she said Mark was not good husband material.* But she wistfully admitted that this perfect moment wouldn't last forever.

As the days of September gradually became more golden, their marriage mellowed and became more precious.

Though her happiness seemed a steady and constant thing, at times she felt the frightening edge of uncertainty. Jenny had erected barriers in her life because of the nameless dread. The barrier she was least willing to explain was her reluctance to walk in the woods.

The small stone cottage Mark had purchased for them was separated from the Morgan home by an uncleared strip of timber. Although the forest was warm and friendly, with a rich golden light, Jenny chose walking the extra distance through the center of Kirtland to reach Sally's home.

One day in the middle of September, Jenny piled a basket with apples and started through town to visit Sally. When she passed the printing office, she met Sidney Rigdon just leaving Joseph at the door. Sidney bowed and passed on without a word, and impulsively Jenny turned in at the door.

Oliver disappeared into the press room, but not before she saw the disgruntled expression on his face. She looked up at Joseph. "Of the lot, you're the only one who hasn't been into the sour apples."

He laughed and took her arm. "Then come to my office and tell me all that's transpired in Kirtland the past month."

She followed and took a chair before saying, "I can tell you nothing except that the Thomas family has a new baby. Will that suffice? Tell me about your trip. It was very mysterious. We returned from our wedding to find you gone. Both Andy and Mark are upset. I don't know why they can't juggle funds without your presence."

Joseph shot her a quick look and then concentrated on removing his tie. "Perhaps because there are so few to juggle." He met her eyes and she was caught by the sharp, questioning expression in them. "Jenny, you know that the church is in dire circumstances financially." He got to his feet and restlessly paced the room. "Missouri has great needs right now. You've heard of the specie circular, I'm sure, since you're married to an attorney."

"Pray, sir," she said primly, "I've been on my honeymoon. We haven't discussed finances."

He grinned now, holding her eyes with his own in a way that brought the blood to her face. In another moment he was saying, "The specie circular issued by Jackson forbids the acceptance of anything except gold and silver for the purchase of public lands. Of course this makes the situation in Missouri impossible."

Still watching her, his voice softened as he explained, "It is imperative that we have gold to buy land in Missouri. The Lord has promised; He will provide."

Jenny frowned and said slowly, "I am trying to understand it all, but there's a missing link. Did concern for money relate to your trip to Salem?"

Now he was startled. After studying her face, he said slowly, "I'd thought the gossip had come home before I did. Jenny, I suppose I shall tell you since you've asked, and since the word will be around Kirtland before long." He paused to shuffle through the papers spread across the table.

"Before I left for Salem, I knew what I was doing and where I was going. Suffice it to say that the enemy was working with all his powers to prevent me. Fortunately, the Lord gave me this revelation while I was there; otherwise my companions would have been greatly discouraged. You may read it."

As Jenny read she muttered the key words, *treasure*. Why did He say *folly*? *You have power over Salem, with the wealth of silver and gold belonging to you.* She dropped the paper into her lap and leaned forward, "Joseph," she whispered, "what does this mean? What have you been doing?"

Despite her resolve, she knew that her eyes were sparkling with excitement; she knew it by the answer from his own. Leaning close he said, "Jenny, a fellow came to me and told me about a house in Salem where there's gold and silver buried in the basement. I knew the Lord was giving it to me to pay the debts and to purchase land in Missouri."

"The folly?"

"I went back to the rod and the stone in order to find—"

Like a scolding mother, reacting before thinking, Jenny cut him off, "Joseph, you told me the Lord had forbidden you to use the stone, forbidden you to search for hidden treasures!"

"I know, but this was such a sure thing, and the need was so great. Besides, you've seen the revelation. He's said it's all right."

Jenny was shaking her head in bewilderment. "I don't understand God at all. But since He's told you the treasure was for you, I suppose it was okay to keep it."

There was a strangled noise from Joseph and she looked up. "Jenny, we didn't find any." But when he saw her face he quickly added, "We've retained the house and will go back next spring to try again."

Jenny walked home, still shaking her head in disbelief. When Mark returned home that evening, she was unable to tell him of her conversation with the Prophet. As she hurried about her kitchen, setting the table with the pretty new china and taking reassuring sniffs of the stew, she was miserably aware that she was keeping a secret from Mark, deliberately hiding the conversation with Joseph. During the short walk home, the facts weighing on her mind had become warped and ugly.

The next day Mark brought her a letter from Tom. After dinner she eagerly tore it open, saying to Mark, "I'm so anxious to hear his reaction to our marriage. Shall I read it aloud?"

"Only if you are certain he won't be angry with me for taking his sister," he said with a chuckle.

"Oh, Mark, you know he won't." She spread the sheets and began to read. "It's addressed to both of us. He says:

> Having you married to Mark makes me the happiest man alive. I am grateful, too, that he has joined the church. If I'm called upon to shed blood in Missouri, I'll die happy knowing my dearest kin are part of God's Zion.

She paused and looked up, "Oh, Mark, he sounds so dreary and formal." Looking back to the letter, she brushed at her eyes.

> Yes, things are as bad as you've been hearing. Late June the Missourians in Clay County requested the Saints to move elsewhere, and as you know, the appeal to Governor Dunklin for help was denied. He had received the same complaint given last time, but amplified. They're accusing us of wrong motives in our relations with the Indians. They refuse to consider the red men as Lamanites, or to believe that we, as God's people, have an obligation to bring them into the fold. For the time being, this response makes it impossible to follow Joseph's injunction to marry a Lamanite, and I can't say that makes me unhappy.

When she paused to turn the page, she glanced at Mark. He nodded, "I'd heard about Joseph's revelation."

She waited, but he didn't add to his comment. Returning to the letter, she continued:

> Our spirits were kept high, despite having the people of Clay County turn against us. We remembered the prophecy given by Joseph, appointing September 11, 1836, as the day for the redemption of Zion.

Needless to say, some of us spent the day in prayer and fasting, looking for a miraculous sign that this would take place. Our disappointment when nothing happened was exceedingly hard to bear, and we were forced to prepare for our trek to the northern part of Missouri before more pressure was brought to bear.

The prairie land is bleak, with water and timber in short supply. But we must keep our hopes high, remembering this is our promised Zion. God, true to His word, will in time deliver into our hands, not only the land but also the riches of the Gentiles. For brass we will receive gold; for iron, silver. All the Saints here in Zion are looking forward to the day when Joseph Smith will be able to surrender the reins in Kirtland and move to the Lord's Zion.

For now, nearly all the Saints in Missouri have moved to the new county named Caldwell. We are working hastily to settle ourselves and will be proud to show what we have done when the Kirtland Saints move here. This, despite the fact that we have been short of the needed and promised funds to buy more land. We call our goodly town by the name of Far West. Already our cultivated fields show our industry, and we are proud of them. Until you and my new brother-in-law, Mark, move to Zion, I remain faithfully,

Thomas Timmons

Jenny slowly folded the letter. Tom must have spent days on the writing. It helped explain Joseph's trip to Salem. She wished she dared question Mark about the financial problems being rumored around. But as she studied his somber face, she was uneasily aware that she couldn't endure hearing criticism of Joseph.

CHAPTER 2

As the winter snows began to pile up around Kirtland, covering the landscape and chilling the bones, so did events that most intimately concerned the citizens of the little community. But the new year was well under way before Jenny was aware of the further unrest throwing the town into upheaval.

In the months since her marriage, Jenny had been content in her role as housewife, comfortable with Mark's love. But her isolation had its drawbacks. Jenny knew little of the forces digging at the roots of the community. Her contentment had lulled her into avoiding the gossip and rumors.

As autumn slipped into winter, Jenny enjoyed not only the esteem she and Mark had as a newly married couple, but also the respect Mark's position was earning for him as a financial advisor in the church. She was also becoming aware of the increased demands upon his time.

Early in January, on a glowering day that made her loneliness more acute, Jenny trudged through the snow to visit Sally. As she slowly unwound her shawl and sat down at the kitchen table, Sally's first words pressed her into facing life. As she listened, Sally's worried face and dire news seemed to pick the cotton padding away from her, letting in the unpleasant realities Jenny had shunned. Sally was enumerating the grave financial woes besetting Kirtland.

Jenny listened and watched as Sally paced the room, holding her fussing daughter against her shoulder. "Did you know that Joseph made a trip to New York to borrow money, and has started a bank?"

"That doesn't seem wise." Jenny shook the last of the snow from her frock. "Did he use the borrowed money?"

Sally shook her head, "No, that was to pay off creditors. Andy says the bank intends to print notes, with the purpose of exchanging them for hard money."

Jenny frowned, "I can't understand how that would put them ahead in the game. Sounds like it's closer to—"

"Illegal? Did Mark tell you how worried he and Andy are about the whole situation?"

"He didn't say worried," Jenny said slowly, "and he didn't talk about borrowed money. He did tell me that Sidney Rigdon is president and Joseph is cashier of the new bank. He sounded concerned when he said there's a whole flock of banks springing up around the country, all doing the same thing. He said they were printing notes and exchanging them for anything of value as well as gold and silver."

"The bank was established by a revelation," Sally continued, "and the Prophet has predicted that like Aaron's rod, it will swallow up all the other banks around it. He also said it will grow and flourish to the ends of the earth, surviving when others are in ruins."

"Then I guess we needn't worry," Jenny remarked without looking at her.

"Oh, Jenny, be sensible. Our money is in that bank!"

Jenny stared at her friend. She was thinking not of Sally, but of the money Mark had given her. Back in November she had deposited it in the bank. How proud she had been to make her first transaction as "Mrs. Cartwright"! She winced as she recalled plunking down one thousand dollars in silver and gold, and the way Sidney Rigdon's eyes had brightened.

Now Sally demanded, "Why do you look so concerned? What have you done?"

Jenny straightened and lifted her chin. "Just what any other housewife would have done. Mark gave me a thousand dollars and I deposited it in the bank."

Slowly Sally sat down and shifted Tamara to her lap. "Then you haven't read the newspaper. The Ohio legislature refused to incorporate the bank. Jenny, the bank is operating illegally."

"Oh!"

Sally looked up at Jenny's exclamation and frowned. Jenny explained, "Now it makes sense. Mark said they changed the name of the bank to the Kirtland Safety Society Anti-Banking Company. Mark mentioned it one day as he flew out the door, but he hasn't talked about it again."

"Does he know you've put your money there?" Jenny shook her head. "Then you'd be wise to hightail it right down there and quick draw it out while they are still above the waves."

"What do you mean?"

"Andy says everybody in town's running around with his pockets full of notes. Joseph's paid off all the debts around and even sent bills back east to clear the mercantile businesses in town."

"But why are you so worried about the bank?"

Sally's lips were tightly pressed together, and if the shake of her head didn't convince Jenny her silence was sealed, the expression in her eyes did. Jenny couldn't resist guessing, "You don't think the church has the funds they're advertising they have." Sally didn't answer.

Jenny was nearly home when she stopped and turned back toward the bank. Since leaving the Morgans' house, she had been mulling over the events Sally had discussed.

Jenny began to hurry toward the red-brick building on the corner. A newly painted sign stretched across the face of the building. She stopped just long enough to read, *Kirtland Safety Society Anti-Banking Company.* Inside the door Warren Parrish hurried to meet her. "Well, Jenny—I mean, Mrs. Cartwright—what may I do for you?"

She took a deep breath. "Mr. Parrish, I've come to withdraw my money from the bank."

"And how much?"

"One thousand dollars."

She saw him pale and quickly turn aside. "Jenny, that is rather unusual—at least, such a large sum is."

"You didn't say that when I deposited it in November."

He leaned close and whispered, "If you are doing this because of the rumors, I assure you that they are unfounded."

She whispered back, "How do I know?"

He hesitated and glanced around the empty room. "This is unusual, but since it is you, come with me and I'll prove it to you." She followed his rapid steps through dark corridors and heavy doors. When the last door creaked open, he struck a match and carefully lighted a row of candles. "There!" He waved toward the shelves lining the narrow room.

Stepping forward, Jenny saw each shelf held numerous wooden boxes, each clearly marked as holding one thousand dollars. "Oh!" she exclaimed, "shall I take one?"

"No, no," he interrupted. "I merely wanted to reassure you. I—" He stopped and cocked his head. "Someone has come in. I'll return in a moment."

She watched him disappear and then went to stand on tiptoe beside the shelves. A box just at nose level was heaped with shiny silver fifty-cent pieces. So were all the other boxes she could see. She paced the floor, waiting for Warren to return, amused at being left in a bank vault filled with money. After another trip around the room, she paused beside the nearest box, cast a quick glance over her shoulder and dug her fingers into the box of coins.

"Ouch!" She pulled her hand away and looked at her bleeding finger. Again on tiptoe, she carefully lifted aside the top layer of coins and cautiously probed. Once again there was the sharpness against her finger. Quickly she pulled the box down and peered inside. Beneath the silver coins she saw iron nails and jagged chunks of metal.

Shoving the box into its place, she moved quickly down the length of the shelves inserting her fingers into each box. Some boxes contained sand, others held chunks of lead and the rest were filled with old nails. "Joseph," she murmured, "you rascal!" She almost began to chuckle.

Breathlessly, Warren popped back into the room. "Oh my, sorry to keep you waiting. I'm glad to see you in such good humor. Dark rooms aren't to my liking."

"You are a brave man to leave me with so much money. But maybe not. There's not too much I could carry, since it's all in fifty-cent pieces."

Back in the brightly lighted room, Jenny looked up at the worried, gray face and said, "I suppose for now, I'll just leave the money."

On her way home, she alternately chuckled and shook her head, then abruptly faced the implications of her discovery.

By the time Jenny had prepared Mark's dinner and set her table with the best china, she had decided that as soon as the meal was finished she would share her discoveries with him.

Dinner was a silent affair. Jenny was still busy planning her speech. Just when she thought of a way to broach the subject, she became aware of Mark's preoccupation. Studying his face and his unfinished dinner, she asked, "Mark, don't you feel well?"

He stared at her for a moment. "Oh, my dear, I've neglected you. Sorry. I've been miles away with business problems." He reached out to touch her cheek. "No need to trouble you with them. I do wish I needn't go out again this evening."

"Oh, Mark," she said in dismay, then saw his distress. "I'm sorry. But I'll miss you terribly. It is so cold and I was hoping—"

"I know." He rose to kiss her and reached for his coat. "Don't wait up for me. I must see Brewster about his will. I've promised for weeks, and now I'll need to track him down."

Outside, Mark hesitated beside the barn and then muttered, "I'll be warmer with the walk, and the mare won't have to wait in the cold." He set off down the street, striding rapidly as he headed for the Brewster home.

He was breathing the sweet, winter air, spiced only lightly with the scent of burning wood, thinking what a relief it would be if the fresh exchange of air in his lungs could cleanse his troubled thoughts. He sighed heavily, thinking of Jenny, wishing he could press his head against her softness and unburden all the turmoil he was feeling.

Mark had spent the day arguing with Joseph and trying to juggle impossible figures. Even after facing the hard reality of facts, the Prophet's avowal of faith and confidence had left Mark feeling as if he were battering against an impregnable wall.

As he hurried through the snow to meet Brewster, Mark lashed himself for failure to exercise his newfound faith, at least to the degree of believing in the Prophet. He was also trying to push aside the gossip he had heard and the doubts that assailed him.

Suddenly he threw his shoulders back and breathed deeply of the fresh air. "In new, out old," he called out toward the moon. His usual good humor made him shrug off the binding thoughts, and he found himself free to contemplate his lot. Joseph had gotten himself another church member, and he had his wife. Mark chuckled with delight, seeing himself as the winner after all. For just a moment he shook his head in disbelief over Joseph's suggestion that he would win favor with both man and God were he to invest all of his worldly goods in the betterment of the church.

He was still shaking his head when he reached the small log house where the Brewsters lived. Perhaps old man Brewster had been approached with the same suggestion, and that had promoted the idea of a will.

Mark had barely freed himself of snow and settled beside the fire when a tap was heard at the Brewster door. He recognized the bent, white-haired man coming in the door as the Prophet's father, Joseph Smith, Senior.

When the old man settled himself beside the fire and rubbed his hands, he said, "On a night like this a good nip would help." He twisted his rheumatic body to face the elder Brewster. "But I didn't come to be sociable. There's a task before us." His voice dropped to a low rumble as he pointed his finger at Brewster's son, James. "I've told you before, there's money hid in the earth and it's our duty to obtain it." His voice was slow and shaky as he added, "My friend, to fail to do so will cause the curse of God to fall upon us."

Mark saw the look of distaste cross the elder Brewster's face. In a playful manner Mark said, "Brother Smith, money digging is an old, old scheme of the wicked one to get us to dissipate our energies in running after a dream."

Unexpectedly Smith turned on him and shook his finger. "Now, young man, don't you be disputin' your elders. I know more about money diggin' than any man in this generation, seein' I've been in the business for more than thirty years."

Mark had only a moment for surprise before the man turned to James, saying, "Must I remind you again of your patriarchal blessing? You know the Lord promised power for you to discover and obtain treasures hidden in the earth."

Facing Mark again, he went on, "I know how you fancy young'uns don't hold with usin' the rod and such, but I know the Lord approves. Why, we've even taken the rods and the seein' stones into the temple, anointed them with consecrated oil and prayed over them so that the devil wouldn't be deceivin' the menfolk as they sought the treasures."

"Have they found any?" Mark asked curiously.

With a snort of disgust, the elder Brewster answered, "Nope, no treasure found yet."

Smith got to his feet. "Now come along, James. The rest of the fellows are waitin' at the temple. Beaman and I will stay there and pray while you youngsters get out there and do your lookin'." He paused to glare at old Mr. Brewster. "The Lord rebuke you for your unbelief. You best stay home, lest that unbelief taint the others."

For a moment he fastened Mark with an eagle eye, then turned toward the door without another word.

Mark was whistling as he started for home. For once he had found reason to be glad his faith was very feeble. But as he looked beyond the evening with Jenny, he sobered. Tomorrow, juggling the church's figures would take more faith than even old Joseph Smith possessed.

The following evening when he returned home, Mark found Jenny sitting at the kitchen table, surrounded by newspapers.

She lowered the paper she held and explained before he could ask. "We haven't been getting the papers, so I borrowed them from Sally. Mark, do you realize I've scarcely been aware of what has been going on for months now?"

"And why is that, my dear wife?" He came to nuzzle her neck. "I know, it is because you have been busy keeping house and cooking for me."

"I suspect my husband thinks he is protecting me from uncomfortable news." Jenny's gaze was very serious now. Yesterday's humor over Joseph's money boxes had disappeared and dismay had taken its place. "Since I assume you haven't read the papers either, let me read to you."

He interrupted. "I have read them. I could nearly quote them. Jenny, don't be angry. I know how much you believe in Joseph and his new church, and I couldn't bear to have you hurt. You also know how little I believe. You know why I joined the church." Lightly he added, "I would have walked the nearest gangplank in order to have you. Let's not pretend I believe in religion."

And Jenny looked up at him, sensing the love that was visible more often than spoken. Searching his face, seeing things that had escaped her attention before, she was filled with dismay. Those tired lines on his face—was she beginning to see the consequences of following her flighty heart? Where would it lead her next?

Lifting the paper she stated solemnly, "Well, I don't know the words by heart, and right now I need very much to know what is taking place out there. Please, dear husband," she begged, "don't keep these things from me."

Mark sat quietly beside the fire until she had finished and folded the last paper. "Is there a suggestion that the Prophet isn't entirely honest?" Jenny asked. "Yesterday's *Painesville Republican* sounds cynical. The advice to circulate the specie in order to benefit the community seems sound, however."

"Wife, do I get my dinner now?" Jenny jumped to her feet, but as she folded the papers and hurried to rescue her meal, she tried to hide the irritation she felt. At times Mark seemed to view her as only a child.

Still feeling that irritation days later, she stood at her window one evening and watched the snow fall. It was late and Mark should have been home. She looked down at the newspaper she clutched and read again the words that made her think of a house of cards, stacked and swaying until the last placed card sent them all tumbling. Which word was that final card?

The newspaper was old. It was now February and she knew the events that were rocking the town. This paper, the *Painesville Telegraph,* informed her that the Prophet had closed up shop. His bank wouldn't redeem another dollar except for land.

Jenny tried to feel sorry for Joseph; an amused grin twisted her lips. Like a cat, he would land on his feet and once again triumph.

Joseph was plainly running just one step ahead of them all. He had closed the bank just as the newspaper stories nudged loose a stream of people, running with their bills, suddenly frantic for their money. She also knew that by the first of February the bank notes had been worth only twelve and a half cents on the dollar. Mark had told her that Joseph Smith and Sidney Rigdon had both resigned their positions in the bank.

As Jenny continued to stand at the window and watch the snow, her thoughts were not of the stories in the paper, or even of the loss of her money. She was thinking of Mark's tired, worn face, wondering why he must suffer so deeply over affairs that were not really his concern. She frowned over the contrasting pictures her mind cast: Mark, serious and plodding; Joseph, laughing, running through life a step ahead of everyone else.

In the quiet of the house, Jenny heard the fire pop and the clock chime. A timber creaked and Jenny's heart began to thump slowly and heavily. With that sense she had lately refused to exercise, she was being made aware of the hidden movements in the room. Was it possible that just thinking forbidden thoughts had unleashed the spirit forces?

In her acquiescence to life, was she gaining power that had been denied her before? Her eyes were busily searching the room; she felt herself pushed and twisted by thoughts of Joseph. Were they trying to get her away from home, from Mark? Momentarily, her mind fastened on the warning given by Adela: *Anything except Mark.*

Jenny frowned, and her restless eyes probed the dark corners, searching out reasons for the nameless sounds in the room. Now her thoughts flew to the green book safely hidden in the attic. "Do I no longer control me?" she whispered.

She closed her eyes and immediately saw her fingers turning the pages of the book, underlining those words, tracing those pictures. Now she knew, without a doubt, there was a presence in the room. Not daring to open her eyes, she waited breathlessly for the manifestation.

Her body seemed to lighten, barely aware of substance under and around her. There was a touch against her face, fingers lifting her chin. She tried to move and was powerless; behind her closed lids she saw Joseph's laughing face, felt his hands.

"No!" The scream came from her own lips, and suddenly she was across the room, staring at the spot beside the windows. Empty now, moments before it had been filled with moving, surging spirit life.

Now her voice was low and guttural. "No, never!" Even as she saw Adela's face, her mind was filled with white lace and yellow roses. On that day Mark and their special vows had been carved forever into her heart. But now, even as she stood trembling at her own fireside, she sensed there was a battle going on again, one that had begun in her mind years ago on a wooded trail near South Bainbridge. Her marriage to Mark had caused the conflict to recede to the background, but it was far from over. She thought of the talisman Joseph once again possessed, and her heart sank.

Jenny clasped her hands, lifting her face ceilingward. She prayed like they did in church: "Kind heavenly Father, I beseech You—"

She stopped. Adela's words rolled through her mind. Jenny saw the woman, heard again her musical voice: "There is only one god, and many different ways to worship him."

Slowly Jenny settled in the rocking chair and compared all the pictures of God that were in her mind. In her quest for power through Adela's teaching, the resulting picture of God was frightening. Joseph's image of God was diffused, unclear. Only one clear impression captured her mind, created the moment she and Mark had stood before that pastor and pledged those vows.

She closed her eyes. She recalled a sense of presence on that day, commanding and strong. But there was another element to it, and she didn't know how to define it, except to admit it left her feeling an emptiness in her life. It reminded her of the church, bathed in violet light from afternoon sunbeams through the windows; of Lucy Harris's attempts to help her understand God; of Mark's mother's insistent questions about her own faith.

Jenny sighed over the picture. Then she heard Mark's step at the kitchen door and flew to welcome him. As he held her quietly in his arms, Jenny didn't see the lost expression on his face.

CHAPTER 3

Later that spring Jenny faced Mark across the kitchen table. "No!" she exclaimed, then fell silent, caught by the defeat on his face. How long had she been seeing those sad, tired eyes? And how often had she turned away, feeling only her own helplessness and defeat? Now she wanted badly to go to him, but more than the table lay between them.

Unable to endure his expression, she looked out the window at the newness of May. As the snow had melted and the flowers bloomed, their marriage had seemed to frost and wither. She watched the wild roses pressing across the picket fence and wished she had forced Mark earlier to share the burdens that had been weighing him down.

Now it was obviously too late. When she turned he was shaking his head. "I'm just as caught as you are, Jenny. How can I prove my loyalty to Joseph by less than obedience? Besides, I won't be gone forever. And right now maybe we need a time apart." He paused, and she saw the painful twist to his lips.

"It has been bad, hasn't it, Mark? How miserably I've failed you!" She watched him turn away and nearly ran to him. But she had asked him to marry, and Mark was too much of a gentleman to ignore all that had come before that proposal. Jenny, the kitchenmaid, proposing to Attorney Cartwright! Now her bitter smile mirrored his. How blind she had been!

But she must pretend. She turned from the window with a bright smile and a bustle of energy. "So Joseph Smith has tapped my husband with his reward, the opportunity to go to merry old England to convert the land to Mormonism."

"And the irony is in your voice, not mine." Mark came around the table to face her.

She forced herself to look at him, to search those weary lines. "It has been bad. All these problems heaped on the church simply because of that foolish banking idea." He ignored the hand she stretched toward him, but she continued. "Knowing you, I can guess how you cautioned against the venture in the first place. No doubt it's been difficult charging Joseph with operating the bank illegally when he knew by law it should have been shut down months ago. But you see, Mark, Joseph fails to see himself bound by the laws of this land, and—"

Mark interrupted, "The only thing that has kept him from looking like a complete scoundrel has been all the other banks tumbling down." He looked away for a moment.

"Despite the rightness of the court's decision, it was very unfortunate Joseph had to lose his suit for operating the bank illegally. Some poor Saint's thousand dollars paid his fine," Mark added bitterly, and Jenny searched his face, wondering if he had guessed it was likely her money—their money.

Desperately she sought for something to say. "I'm surprised that Joseph chose you to go now. With all these suits pending against him, I'd think he would need you here more than ever."

"Let's say I spoke my feelings one time too many. He's testing my loyalty. I must obey or I'll lose everything I've worked so desperately to gain." Jenny turned quickly, hoping to see some sign that Mark's words referred to her. But he was fumbling through the papers in his cubbyhole of a desk in the corner of the kitchen.

Jenny's shoulders sagged in defeat. "When must you leave?"

"There's a bunch going in June. He wants us to encourage converts to come with their money and settle among us." When he paused, Jenny reviewed his words, searching for scorn, but there was none. Again she felt his heavy spirit and regretted the past months of emotional strain.

Now Mark was quoting Joseph. "He promised that this place will be built up and that every brother who helps discharge these contracts will be rich."

Since their marriage, Jenny had never inquired into Mark's financial affairs. Timidly she asked, "Did you—"

With an amused smile he said, "Fortunately, even were I so inclined, I couldn't. My father's estate is completely in the hands of trustees as long as my mother lives." Jenny couldn't hide her small expression of relief.

With a grin, backed by an expression so dark she couldn't understand it, Mark added, "Just the other day, Heber C. Kimball stated that he thinks there's not twenty people on earth right now who believe Joseph is truly a prophet of God. But cheer up, my dear, things will smooth out, and you will all get your faith back."

Trying to read the expression in his eyes, Jenny wondered whether Mark blamed Joseph's church for the widening gulf between the two of them. Her heart was heavy with the sense of failure. In the beginning, only love was necessary, she had thought. Now she knew that as deeply as she had learned to love Mark, she still sensed a barrier. One look into his hurt eyes convinced Jenny that Mark was as much aware of the lack as she. Jenny turned away with a sigh.

June came, and Mark and the other chosen ones departed on the first missionary assignment to a foreign land. Jenny was left wondering how one as bitter and disheartened as Mark could hope to baptize converts for Zion.

Despite her loneliness and despair during the weeks immediately following Mark's departure, Jenny found reason to be glad: he was not there to see the turmoil. For a time, it looked as if the entire church structure would crumble. Six of the twelve apostles were in open rebellion against Joseph, and even Parley Pratt threatened to bring suit against the Prophet.

Soon Sally carried another tale to her. Warren Parrish, who had earlier resigned as cashier, had now left the church and was openly describing the Prophet's banking methods.

She added that Parrish was now being accused of absconding with $25,000. Even Jenny was surprised when Sally bit her lip and then let the bitter words burst out. "What rot! If the church has that much money, it's all in bank notes." Her agitated pacing around Jenny's kitchen was her final comment on the state of affairs. Again, Jenny was grateful Mark had escaped this.

On the day after her conversation with Sally, Jenny was pulling weeds and sighing over the sad state of her garden. When she heard the gate squeak, she gladly dropped her hoe and went to sit in the shade with Nettie.

"Seems the Prophet's just having more trouble than goes with the job," Nettie said. "Even Jesus Christ had to contend with trouble, but only one skipped out on Him."

"You're comparing Joseph with Jesus?" Jenny asked curiously.

"Of course; he's the Christ for this time in history."

Jenny thought about that for a moment before saying, "Well, I don't have the grounds to argue the case. It would be nice if the Prophet had a school for the women so we could be learning just like the men are doing."

Nettie sighed. "Most of us are just too busy. Maybe when we move to Zion there will be time for such. I hear some women are a mite uneasy with some of the teaching they hear. Might be our duty to help them along by studying together. What about the Prophet's wife, Emma? She's strong-minded and needs something to do other than tend babies. Might be she'd consent to teach us."

As Jenny searched for words, she remembered the chunk of wax and Clara's advice to get rid of Emma once and for all. Now Nettie leaned close to Jenny. "That reminds me of the real reason I came. I just heard it this morning, and I had to rush to tell someone. The Prophet's neighbor, Alma, said she heard a great commotion during the night and got up to peek out. All the lights were a-blazing at the Smiths', so she put on a shawl, thinking they needed help. When she went out, there stood Emma on the front steps in her nightgown, waving a broom. She had chased Fannie Alger clear outside—in her nightclothes, too. Alma said as she came on the scene, Joseph was trying to quiet Emma down, and she was waving her broom and yelling about getting Fannie out of there because she was in the family way. Joseph was sure nervous, but he took Fannie and headed toward Oliver Cowdery's place.

"This morning I walked past the Smiths'. The Prophet is getting ready for a missionary trip to Canada. I saw the two of them out in front, and Emma was just as nice as pie. Poor girl, I'm not surprised about it all. There's sure been the talk lately. I wonder what's lackin' over there? Oh, well, men will be men, you know." In a few minutes she left to carry her news down the street, and Jenny tarried in her garden, pulling weeds and wondering at the strange churnings inside of her.

Later that week while Jenny and Sally carried their shopping baskets down Kirtland's main street, Jenny said, "It's easy to guess the Prophet's out of town. The whole town feels different, doesn't it?"

Sally's eyes widened as she looked from Jenny to the nearly deserted street. "It is strange, isn't it? Everything is kind of dragging. Andy says there's a heap of discouragement abroad." Abruptly she turned to point down a side street. "Oh, Jenny, look at the crowd! Let's go see what's happening!"

The two women stood on the fringes of the crowd. Jenny stretched to look over the heads. "Why, there's Martin Harris, Oliver Cowdery, and David Whitmer talking to a young woman. Oh, Sally, can you see? She's dancing, spinning around like a top in the middle of the clearing."

"Sounds like one of those strange ones. The men will sure put a stop to that in a hurry. Let's go."

"Wait." Jenny put out a detaining hand and cocked her head. The crowd began to melt away, some with shamefaced glances at Harris, Cowdery, and Whitmer, others with snorts of disgust.

Jenny and Sally watched the three men press around the woman. Sally said, "Look at that silly girl; she's trying to get attention, and those men will give it. I'll bet she's pretending to be a witch or a sorceress."

"Let's go hear what she has to say." Jenny grasped Sally's arm.

"No!" Sally's voice was sharp and Jenny turned to look at her. "I've always been taught that's all of the devil, and my mother says the best way to avoid evil is to stay away from all such things. I'm going shoppin'." She turned on her heel and left Jenny standing in the street.

Jenny's intention was to follow, but curiosity won out. She moved close to the crowd and listened. The girl was still breathless from her frenzied dancing. She shoved aside her black cape and lifted a small dark stone. "Now who wants to hear the future read to him?"

For a moment Jenny teetered, eager to step forward, but she saw Martin Harris pushing his way toward her. Jenny shivered and slipped back into the crowd. She watched his tongue slip out to touch his lips, a symbol of his lust for the new and mysterious. Jenny turned and hurried away. Although years had passed since that last horrible encounter when he beat both her and his own wife, Jenny still found herself fleeing his presence, shuddering with terror.

In the weeks that followed, the young woman attracted further gatherings of Saints, those tired of the winter's problems and eager for a new thrill. Soon it was evident that the church was nearly evenly divided. Excitement swelled through the town like a tidal wave as the stranger gave forth revelations about the future after consulting the seer stone. At the end of July, Joseph Smith returned from his trip to Canada. Jenny settled back to watch him shake law and order back into the wayward church members.

Jenny's satisfaction was complete. Martin Harris was cut off from the church, and the repentant Cowdery and Whitmer were dispatched to Missouri.

Later at church conference time, Jenny listened to Joseph's rebuke, visualizing him wiping the dust of the whole affair from his hands as he talked. Once again Joseph Smith was sustained as president of the church.

Despite Sally's close companionship, restlessness was settling upon Jenny. She staggered under the burden of her loneliness and mourned Mark's absence. When she would come to the end of the labyrinth of her emotions, the anxious faces of Sally and Andy awaited her. And once again she became aware of the troubles around her.

In the golden days of autumn, at the Morgans' dinner table, Jenny heard Andy say, "Surely you've noticed."

"I've scarcely moved from my own doorstep."

"The steam mill isn't even operating. Land values are dropping out of sight, and every merchant in town is ready to go under. Jenny, if you'd walk the streets, you'd see half the houses empty. Families are moving west as fast as they can pack. It isn't just Kirtland; the whole country is in a depression. Soaring land prices no one can afford. Banks closing and shops going out of business."

"Well, at least that keeps Joseph from looking so bad," she said, lifting her spoon. Sally sighed and shook her head.

Andy said, "Joseph is leaving for Missouri. That's a smart move on his part. There are six suits pending against him. He's sent men around to the people to gather money for the church, but it'll have to come in a hurry if he's to save his skin."

As summer slipped into autumn, Jenny's spirits took a deeper plunge. The letters from England were short and businesslike. She eagerly scanned each one, looking for words of love, words which would assure her that the widening gulf was only in her mind.

Disappointed, she read the dutiful catalog of the daily activities of the missionaries. Only an occasional word added detail to the bleak picture, but the words reflected only confusion, questions, and more discouragement.

Eventually the letters ceased coming altogether.

On a dark, cold December evening Jenny took action. She went to Joseph, now back from Missouri.

The print shop was empty, but as she entered the building, she saw the door at the head of the stairs standing open. A light gleamed through the dusk. Quickly she climbed the stairs. Joseph sat slumped forward across his desk, coat discarded, hair rumpled.

All the worst tales Jenny had heard made her rush through the door to his side. When her hand fell on his shoulder, he lifted his startled face. His delighted grin made words unnecessary.

As he brought her a chair, and touched her arm, her shoulder, her chin, the unsaid things became more important. She was aware of his overwhelming manliness and that pleased smile. When he bent over her and she waved him away, they both knew it was not rejection.

As she watched the pulse in his throat settle to a steady beat, her own emotions calmed. But she was filled with dismay. The emotional protection her marriage had given was stripped away, and once more she stood weak and vulnerable before him.

"What brings you out this late?" He waited.

"I haven't heard from Mark for such a long time. The other wives have had letters." She was twisting her hands, and he glanced down at them.

When his eyes finally met hers, she saw the lines on his forehead, lines of concern. He spoke slowly and she read meaning into them. "Jenny, don't worry. We know Mark's a stable young man. You wives always start guessing. A missed letter doesn't mean your husband is chasing some young girl. Our men are dependable, and we must trust them."

His eyes! He didn't believe a word he said. "Why, Joseph! The thought never entered my head. I was supposing he might be ill. He left here tired and discouraged."

Joseph sighed. "Aren't we all."

"What is it, Joseph?" she whispered. "Where's the power? Why is everything suddenly all going awry?"

He leaned toward her. "Jenny, it isn't. Where's your faith? The Lord expects us to keep on plugging away without getting discouraged. For Mark's sake, be brave."

He touched her shoulder, at first timidly, then bravely. "Jenny, despite problems, these are great days for the church. We shall move onward and upward. The Lord plans for us to be the most holy people on earth, and that shall be accomplished as we obey Him. I have things to teach you about the priesthood. I—" They both heard a sound, and Jenny sighed with relief. She recognized she had been rescued.

The dark shop seemed silent again, and Joseph continued, speaking now in a low voice. "Jenny, I need you desperately." He hesitated, and a shadow touched his eyes. "These are difficult days; too often there's no one to listen. I can't understand any better than you why trouble surrounds us and the revelations fail. I do know we need power."

She nodded, momentarily forgetting the whisper of sound. "Joseph, I sense it, too. Once you asked me why I needed so desperately to join the church. The power, Joseph, that's why. But where is it?"

"Right now I'd settle for harmony." His voice held a touch of irony. "Come this Sabbath there will be a meeting in the temple. Be there if you care to see the power at work."

"The miracles, the strange speech, the visions," Jenny whispered. "Joseph, can anyone—"

"No, I mean—"

"Joseph," the woman's voice was tremulous as she swept into the room, "working late again! I need you to—Oh!"

"Emma!" At Joseph's exclamation, Jenny got to her feet, noticing that Emma Smith's expression was not one of surprise. She was busy taking in every detail of the room, including Joseph's discarded coat.

Jenny nodded. "Mrs. Smith, we've never met. I'm Mark Cartwright's wife; I stopped to inquire about him."

Jenny went on her way, feeling as if she had been caught with her hand in the candy jar. Guilt rode her steps all the way home, but looking back at that last scene, she was not without a measure of relief.

That first Sabbath after the new year, Jenny slipped into the pew beside Sally. Since her meeting in Joseph's office, she had made a point of visiting Andy to glean more information.

Sally's husband had been very serious. "More lawsuits, instigated by the faction fighting for control of the church. Jenny, I'm glad your husband isn't here to see this. Some of us old-timers can rock with the punches, but I'm afraid Mark's too idealistic."

Shaking his head, he continued, "Many of the elders, including Brigham Young, have been forced to flee to Missouri in order to avoid being sued. And Joseph is being followed. Just after he left the printing office the other evening, a bunch tried to get in and burn the press." Shame washed over Jenny as she thought of that evening. Did Andy know she had been there, too? His steady expression told her nothing.

Now, sitting in the pew with the Morgans, Jenny mused

over that conversation with Andy and listened to the rustle of the crowd. A line of black-coated men marched into the temple and down to the front pew. Sally whispered, "That's the trouble-making bunch."

Now Joseph Smith and Sidney Rigdon were taking their places. Jenny looked from Joseph's face with its confident half-smile to Rigdon. Sally whispered, "That poor man looks nearly dead." Jenny could only agree as she watched the pallid Rigdon being assisted to the pulpit.

When Rigdon began his talk, his voice was weak, but as he continued, the momentum grew. "Liars, thieves, adulterers, counterfeiters, swindlers!" These were the words of a man who had kept his wrathful silence far too long. And in the end, while quietness gripped the temple, he was helped from the podium, through the auditorium and out the door. Abruptly the dissenters rose to their feet.

Appalled, Jenny watched and listened as charges and ugly counter-charges echoed through the grand edifice.

Suddenly Joseph jumped to his feet. Shouting above the din, he commanded attention and called for a vote on excommunication. One of the black-coated men jumped to his feet and waving his arms, he bellowed, "Joseph Smith, you would cut off a man's head first and then ask to hear him afterward!"

Rising to their feet as one, the congregation watched their prophet stalk from their midst. His face wore defeat like an ill-fitting mask. For the first time, he was unable to regain control of his people, and it was obvious to everyone. Andy watched him go, muttering, "He is a broken man. All he has fought for is gone." Joseph, Jenny remembered, had promised her a display of power.

During the lonesome days that followed, Jenny spent a great deal of time pondering the situation. As she paced the floor in front of her cheery fire, she longed for Mark's calm, level-headed wisdom. She tried to recall his face, even his touch. All the while she was listening to a secret part of her heart advise her that Mark was gone from her life forever.

The January evening was bleak, snowy, and shadowed. Now her thoughts turned to Joseph, the bleakness coloring her picture of him also.

"Power!" she muttered, pacing the floor. "Power!" This time it was a plea. If she wanted power, there was still the sabbat. Jenny felt her spirit recoil in horror as she recalled the trampled cross and the chalice of blood. Momentarily she puzzled over the significance of denying the Christian faith, wondering why these dark promises Adela had tried to extract from her left her trembling with fear. Did it matter that she deny the baptism? Just thinking about it brought the brooding spirit world close, and she trembled at the sense of presence. "I will not!" she declared into the recesses of darkness. But then she contemplated Joseph's failure and found herself nearly ready to give up the church, her final hope of power.

There was a knock on her kitchen door. Glad to flee the gloomy thoughts, Jenny rushed to open it. Though the shadowy figure was covered with snow, she recognized him immediately. "Joseph!" Reaching for his arm, she pulled him in and closed the door. "Why are you out on a night like this?"

The snowy crown of his hat reminded her of the old white one he had been wearing the first time she saw him. He saw her smile and abruptly bent to brush his cold lips across her cheek. She stepped backward and shivered.

"I beg your pardon," he murmured. "Jenny, I'm leaving."

She helped him out of the coat and went to hang it by the stove. He followed. "Would you like tea?" He nodded, and she pulled her shiny teakettle over the fire, the kettle she had purchased for Mark. "Why are you leaving?"

Looking curiously about, he selected Mark's chair and pulled it close to the fire. "Grandison Newell has secured a warrant for my arrest, charging bank fraud."

"Where will you go?"

"Missouri, of course. Remember, we are still looking forward to Zion. Why the Lord chooses to beat us into submission before we go to the promised land, I don't know, but we must trust God." She had poured the water over the tea and he got to his feet. His eyes, curiously light, held hers. "May I depend on you, Jenny? Will you promise me that you will remain true to the church, and that as soon as possible you will move to Zion?"

He waited. Jenny, feeling compelled, trembled. "I promise, but—"

He interrupted, his voice nearly a whisper. "It seems I must again count my followers one by one." He sighed and lifted his head with a smile as if shaking off the somber mood. "I came to tell you good-bye, but also to ask if you had a message for your brother Tom."

She shook her head. "I've just written to him."

After Jenny closed the door behind Joseph, she still pondered his strange visit. She wondered whether the ties of the church or the magnetism of the Prophet had made her promise to follow him to Zion. Why did she feel as if the promise had been pulled from her against her will?

Immediately after Joseph left Kirtland, the dissenters seized the temple. Now the building rang with resolutions proclaiming his depravity.

Deep in the cold of the January night, the print shop caught fire and burned to the ground. The embers were hardly cold before Jenny, standing in front of Warren Parrish, heard him say, "He did it himself. Joseph fired the place to fulfill his prophecy that Kirtland would repent of its wickedness or the Lord would burn it to the ground." He continued, "These men are infidels; they have no fear of God before their eyes. They lie by revelation, run by revelation, and unless they themselves repent, I fear they will be damned by revelation."

CHAPTER 4

Spring sunshine had everyone in Kirtland outside. Nettie had just left, and the familiar lonesome feeling settled on Jenny. She lingered on her steps, watching her neighbors shake rugs and pull weeds. They looked busy and content. Jenny tried to square her shoulders and fix a smile on her face; she failed dismally at both.

Slowly she went down the steps and walked around the house. "So you're disappointed, Jenny," she advised herself. "Stiffen your lip. What's to disappoint you except you haven't had a letter from Mark since Christmas, and now it's April. And you hear today that the Prophet has another little son and his wife is hale and hearty."

"Jenny." The quiet voice came from behind her. For a dizzy moment, Jenny recognized the voice, then rejected it. Again it came, "Jenny." This time she turned. "Mark!" For a moment it was impossible to move. She studied his face. At first he was only a stranger. There was a guarded question in his eyes, but there was also the beginning of a smile. She flew into his arms, stretching eagerly for his kisses. She knew it didn't matter— none of it, not the absence, the lack of letters, the hurts, the silences. Only Mark was necessary.

She held him, straining against him. Were all those tears hers? When she leaned back to look at his face and saw his tears, she sensed a newness in him. Jenny led him into the house, closing the door firmly behind them; she knew she couldn't be away from his touch for a moment until the gap of those long months was bridged.

Not until the next day could they sit together and face questions. Jenny had one question too tender to be probed—and that was *Why? Why wasn't love enough?*

"Jenny, I still don't understand it all." He paced restlessly and she was beginning to see the things Mark could never explain. Those agitated steps hinted at a torment his tired face had refused to admit last June. Momentarily, Jenny recalled the Mark she had glimpsed during their snowbound time in Cobleskill long ago.

She studied the new, tender smile and realized once again she was close to the hidden man. Unexpectedly Jenny was filled with an overwhelming desire to be one with that real Mark, but at the same time she was afraid.

He was ready to talk now, haltingly at first. "Jenny, I know only that I left here in bondage—to myself, to the church, most of all, to Joseph. I went to England trying to believe in all that I had been taught here. I went determined not to come back until I could honestly face your little-girl faith and say, 'I believe in Joseph Smith and his divine commission.' " His voice yearned for her understanding. "Did you sense how tired I had grown of pretending? Jenny, you'll never know how hard I tried to believe. I knew it was necessary if I was to come back here and live in the shadow of Joseph, following his teachings."

Jenny was distant and curious. "And what did you find?" she asked hesitantly. *Why wasn't love sufficient? Why must you have more?* her thoughts raced.

For a moment his glance wavered. And when he spoke, it was to himself. "How can I make you understand? I'm only just now beginning to comprehend all that's happened. I should have waited to come, but I knew I couldn't be away from you a moment longer." His hand was on her cheek, stroking, and his eyes were gentle, remembering her welcome.

Jenny's heart leaped. Surely their love would be all that was necessary! She knelt beside his chair, resting her head against his chest. When he pulled her onto his lap, she was satisfied that she had won. Love *was* sufficient.

Later he recalled his subject. "Jenny, for the first time I was put in a position where I had to understand Joseph's teachings and what his book says. I had to be out there ministering to people. I couldn't just say I had 'a burning in the bosom' like the rest of the fellows were doing. I had to *know*. I studied until my head was swimming. I talked with the brethren until we were all hoarse. Finally, Kimball let me borrow his Bible." He shot her a quick look. "Not the gold one."

She touched his cheek, and he turned his head to press a kiss into her hand. Taking a deep breath, he said, "Jenny, do you know God has promised that when we seek Him with our whole heart, He will allow us to find Him? I've come to understand what His message is."

"What message?"

"The Bible's message of salvation. What God is trying to get across to mankind. Jenny, it isn't as Joseph teaches at all. Before I could understand I had to read the whole book through several times. Essentially the message for man is the same now as it always has been. He's a sinner; from way back in the beginning that's so. There's no way on this earth a man can live good enough or wise enough to be righteous. There's love, too. I was overwhelmed by the message of love in the book."

His hands were holding hers now, pleading for her attention. "The words kept coming back at me. God loved us so much even while we were sinners that He provided a way for us to come to himself, not through doing good things, or being special set-apart ones, but simply through accepting the only possible way to bridge the gap between God and man."

Mark's voice broke. He dropped her hands, jumped up, and resumed his agitated pacing. "Jenny, I was raised in the church. You heard Mother talk about her beliefs. When I was young I heard the Bible read daily, and I heard my parents pray.

"Somehow, during all those years in Sunday school and church, the truth skimmed right over my head. I really didn't understand until I became so desperate that I was reduced to begging God to show me what I was failing to see.

"Jenny, Jesus Christ is God. Not *a* god, like Joseph has been telling us that all we men will become when we choose to accept the Mormon way. This Jesus is God. He came in human flesh, just like another man. But He did what none of us, including

Joseph, has ever done; He lived His entire life without sinning once. He is God."

As he talked, every word Mark spoke became a brick in a wall between the two of them. Jenny's attempt to remain quiet, to hear him out, was knotting her stomach, chilling her hands, and setting her whole body to trembling.

Jenny jumped to her feet and whirled away from Mark. "I don't understand why I am feeling this way, Mark," she whispered through gritted teeth, "but all this talk is churning me up inside. If you say another word, I'll scream."

He came to her. "Jenny, I have no desire to upset you. I only needed to let you know what has been happening to me."

Abruptly he turned to pace the room and when he returned to her, he said, "My dearest Jenny, you know that I love you more than my own life. That's why the step I'm taking now is so necessary. I don't expect you to understand, just trust me." She looked up at his serious face, wondering. His smile wavered slightly as he said, "We're leaving Kirtland and Joseph's church just as soon as I can close up our affairs."

"Leave!" she gasped. "Leave the church and turn our backs on all that Joseph has taught us?" She was trembling, pressing her hands to her hot cheeks. "Mark, I can't begin to understand the strange things you've been heaping on me. I don't want you to quarrel with me about it, but can't you see? I can't leave the church. I—" she gulped and trembled. "I *dare* not. I'm fully convinced that I will plunge myself into the deepest hell were I to do so."

Mark saw the fear in her eyes. "Let's just wait then, Jenny," was all he said.

One Sunday morning Nathaniel Taylor stood to his feet in the midst of Sabbath worship and waved his arm. "I'm for Zion!" he roared. "Everyone of like mind, prepare to go as soon as possible. Let's clear the town and make the biggest wagon train ever seen."

For the first time in weeks, Jenny felt her heart lift. She knew it was impossible to deny the challenge. With a smile, she turned to Mark sitting beside her. She saw his slight frown and watched him move uneasily. Her heart sank and she sighed.

The past weeks had been full of strain. She admitted that the strain was on her part. Mark had been a sweet, tender lover, a patient husband, an understanding friend. Patience and understanding often kept him silent these days when she could see he yearned to talk.

While she couldn't understand this new Mark, the man with the tender smile and infinite patience, she was beginning to notice an underlying strength in him. In the face of her petulance, he was unmoving. Painfully conscious that neither one of them dare yield position, they both skirted the issue Mark had introduced.

Life resumed its old pattern, but there was a difference. Even while laughing together and loving, Jenny found herself desperately resisting this elusive new side of her husband.

On the day Jenny admitted that her church hadn't power to hold Mark, she finally acknowledged that which she had sensed all along. There was only one way she could win the struggle. Using charms and spells, Jenny redoubled her efforts to gain the power she so desperately needed to sway Mark completely under her control. And control him she must, or he would never consent to going to Missouri. With generous impartiality she prayed both to God and Luna, the moon goddess, begging help and favor.

As Kirtland prepared the wagon train for the trek to Zion, Jenny watched the activity of the families around them. She saw the loaded wagons and empty houses. Meanwhile, Mark was bringing his business in Kirtland to a close. Still fearful of facing the issue of leaving, still hoping for a miracle, Jenny began to sort and pack their belongings.

One day Sally Morgan came by. She surveyed the loaded barrels and said, "Mark's informed us of his new beliefs." The dismay was evident in her voice. "Reminds me of that Martin Harris. He's off again looking for another church to join." Jenny was stung by the comparison, but didn't answer.

Sally watched Jenny work, and finally she gave a heavy sigh. "Well, if he's going his way, you're welcome to join up with us. Andy can find a hand to drive for you."

Jenny threw the towels in a heap on the nearest trunk.

"How can two people who love each other be separated by something as petty as religion?"

"Petty?" Sally echoed. "You mean that's the way you see your beliefs?"

"No," Jenny shivered. None of it was petty. At one time, Adela's decree had bound her with paralyzing fear as she searched for power. Now fear entwined her with Joseph and the church. How could an innocent search for power and knowledge bind her in fear? And what did she really fear? Hell?

Jenny thought about Mark and his new beliefs. Was hell the dark something lurking out there which had sent him seeking? If so, no wonder he was acting as he did!

That evening when he came into the house and looked at the trunks and barrels, she saw the questions in his somber eyes. But she must ask him a question first. "Mark, is it because of the terrible fear that you are pulling me away from here?"

"Fear? Jenny, my dear, my fear's resolved. It's because of truth I want this. Fear used to hold me, but not anymore."

She studied his face. He actually believed what he said. Anticipating the pain of further separation, she whispered, "Then you won't mind that we go to Missouri? It is for fear that we must."

"Jenny!" In desperation he grabbed her, digging his fingers into her forearms, commanding attention. "You don't understand!" He paused to steady his voice. "But you will someday. Until then, trust me. We must not go with Joseph."

"Someday," she whispered back. "Mark, there's no time to wait for someday. You've heard Joseph. Christ will be returning very soon and we must be in Zion waiting. There's no time to waste. Joseph's revelations say there will be destruction and death for all who refuse to accept the truth of this dispensation. All of the churches have been polluted; there is no other church with the truth. Joseph has shown us clearly that there is no other way." Mark turned away.

But now Jenny was caught by a clear, illuminated moment. Understanding suddenly dropped into her mind. Only by surrendering Mark would she have all things—and Mark, too. The key was obedience to the church. Before her loomed the promise of power. Joseph had said those words. Without power the dream could not be, and now the dream included Mark. Oh, how desperately it included Mark!

She found herself whispering, "How blind, Mark, how blind can you be! Am I the only one who sees clearly?"

Mark turned his ravaged face toward her. Their eyes met, and in another moment they were in each other's arms. But even as Jenny lifted her lips and held him close, tears were streaming down her face. There was no turning back. The truth was *very* clear.

In the end Jenny, white-faced and rigid in her new wagon with a hired teamster, prepared to leave. Mark, equally white-faced, stood helpless and confused as he watched his wife, ready to ride out of Kirtland with her share of their marriage in the wagon.

And in the final moments, when it didn't seem possible for another word to be said, while Mark leaned against the wagon wheel, a flock of geese flew overhead. The quiet of the dawn was broken as their wings beat the air. Both Jenny and Mark lifted their faces, hearing a note of desperation in that honking as the geese flew on.

They watched the formation disappear into a tiny black check against the dawn. "Mark," Jenny whispered and her face came close to his, "that's just the way it is with me. I can do nothing other than go. I am compelled beyond my own personal desires, even the dearest longings of my heart. I prayed to understand my destiny, and I'm seeing it clearly."

The wagon train had just started to move when Mark walked away. He trudged through the silent streets, listening to the echo of his own footsteps. Old Matthew Lewis hailed him. "You're a fool." Lewis paused to spit contemptuously. "Joseph's taught these women that if their husbands refuse to join them, then their marriages are null and void. For the Saints, there's only one way—it's living up to the laws and revelations given in this dispensation under the Prophet. This new church has the keys to the kingdom; there's no other way."

Mark continued on to his lonely house. Still contemplating the half of his life that was left, he entered the house and witnessed Jenny's final act. She had left food prepared for his first lonely meal. He looked at the bread and milk, the cut of roast beef and the still warm apple pie.

Slowly he sat down and turned his back to the table. The door was open and he saw the shadow before he heard the knock. "I can't believe it—Tom!" Mark's lips moved woodenly as he got up to greet his brother-in-law.

Tom looked around the kitchen with a bewildered expression. "They told me most of Kirtland is gone, that even the troublemakers are headed for Zion." His eyes were wary. "Down at the stables, they gave me the story that my sister Jenny left her husband and has gone to Joseph's Zion."

Mark studied Tom's frowning face and shoved at a chair. "Look, you deserve a decent explanation. Sit down and eat this stuff while I talk."

Tom was eyeing the table as he said, "I met the wagon train just as I pulled into town. Didn't have an idea Jenny was on it, or I'd have looked for her."

Mark watched Tom cut into the roast. "I guess the only way to make myself understood is to start at the beginning." He noticed that Tom was picking at the meat in a half-hearted manner and he hunched his chair closer to his brother-in-law.

"See, in the beginning," he said, "back when Jenny and I were married, I didn't give a fig for any kind of religion. I joined the church because I wanted your sister. Also, I intended to keep it that way. I suppose if this were just another church, I would have."

"What do you mean?"

"I wasn't around Joseph long before I began to notice the blind adoration of his followers. I tried to ignore it, but I began to see an unquestioning obedience that bothered me. Somehow it all seemed wrong. I couldn't reconcile it with what I'd been taught about God."

"Mark, face it. All religions are like this. People are scared to death of losin' out and gettin' kicked out of the church." There was a touch of pride in his voice. "Joe inspires these people to give it their best if they want to make it in the hereafter."

"Is that it? I was beginning to think Joseph had some strange power over these people. Maybe it is fear. Fear of God and hell, of being left on the outside. At least Jenny talked like that. Tom, I'm seeing man's mindless groping. I find myself wishing there could be more than one way to God."

Tom lifted his head and slowly put down his spoon. "What do you mean, Mark? What are you gettin' at?"

"I went to England as a missionary. About the first week out in the countryside, while I was trying to tell the people about the new religion and how this was the latest thing and how the Lord was coming soon and they'd better join up and go build up Zion, it hit me.

"I saw those faces believing me and hanging on to every word. They were wanting what I had to offer. You should have seen them. Dirt-poor, without a chance of improving their lot. Sure, they were ready for anything sounding as good as Zion. But I was feeling bad about it. You see, I wasn't the least convinced."

Tom winced. "So what did you do?"

"I started reading the Bible. After all, the Mormons are supposed to believe that's God's Word, too."

"That's right," Tom nodded. "Brigham Young said he believed there was enough in the Bible to lead a man into finding salvation."

Mark paused and then continued, "Well, I decided to borrow Heber's Bible and have a go at reading it."

"To be fair, you should have read the *Book of Mormon*."

"I have. I've also read the Prophet's revelations and some of the other writings." Mark paused and watched Tom eat Jenny's apple pie. Finally Mark got to his feet and paced the kitchen.

He was thinking about Tom's statement. Confusion and excitement mingled in him and finally he sat in front of Tom again. "So Brig said that. Tom, have you read the Bible?" He shook his head and Mark continued, his excitement growing. "Tom, do you consider me a fairly intelligent person?"

Tom looked up surprised. "Well, certainly, man. I've never doubted that. You know I've always respected your mind. Why do you ask?"

"There's a couple of things I came up with in my reading

that just won't let me alone. One is that God is unchangeable. The *Book of Mormon* says that. Another is that the Bible says Jesus Christ is really God, come to this earth and born just like any other man except that His conception was a miracle from the Holy Spirit—not the result of a union of Adam and Mary. But here's the rub. The Bible teaches that sin caused separation between God and man, and the only way the separation can be bridged in a decent and honorable way is by the blood sacrifice provided by God himself."

Tom's face was thoughtful, and Mark added, "Mormonism teaches Christ's death does not bring righteousness, but instead only another chance at life for everyone. It teaches that righteousness and holiness are to be earned. It says man can work his way into good standing with God simply by following Joseph's new church with its rules and regulations. I don't get the idea from watching people that this church is all that holy."

Tom sighed and sat back, "Now you've hit the nail on the head. There's stuff goin' on that even an ignorant blacksmith like me can figure out as bein' all wrong." His forehead puckered and slowly he spoke again. "If you're feelin' like this, what caused the big fight between you and Jenny that sent her runnin' to Missouri?"

Mark sighed and for a moment he dropped his head into his hands. "Tom, can you believe that I love your sister with all my heart and that I want nothing more than to spend the rest of my life with her?" He paused. "First, I tried to make her understand all I've told you and she rejected it. Then, like a complete dummy, I put my foot down and announced we were leaving the church and Kirtland. That did it. If I'd left well enough alone instead of trying to push my way on her, everything could maybe have been settled between us."

"So what happened?"

"She said she was scared to death of not going. That the second coming of Christ is so near, she didn't dare risk changing her belief. Tom, I could see she was running on account of fear. I just didn't know how to handle it." He looked imploringly at his brother-in-law and waited.

Tom slouched back in his chair and pushed his hat over his

eyes. Mark waited while May's sweet perfume drifted through the door, reminding him that life was moving on. Finally Tom straightened and tossed his hat in the corner. "You say she's scared? I suppose you're just as scared God'll get you for not being in the right place at the right time."

"Tom," Mark protested, "that's not it at all. There's not one thing I can do to earn righteousness, but I don't see—"

"It's simple. Go to Missouri and wait this out. Seems if you're followin' God while the others aren't, you ought to be around to pick up the pieces when Zion falls apart. Besides, Jenny needs you—even if she won't admit it. Mark, she needs you more'n I can let on right now." Mark watched the troubled expression settle down across Tom's face, and as he pondered the heaviness of Tom's statement, new hope made him straighten up in his chair.

He was beginning to grin when Tom stood up and asked, "Gotta horse?"

He blinked, "Well, yes, but—"

"You can catch up with that wagon train if you hustle." He was addressing Mark's back. "Better take your duds. I'll pack up the rest of the furniture and see you in a couple weeks."

The wagon train was curving its way slowly out of Kirtland like a serpent, its tail still touching the edge of town while the head stretched in a cloud of dust south and west toward the prairie. He paused only a moment to measure the line of wagons and pick the one with the billowing top pressing toward the crest of the hill.

Mark rode his horse hard, pushing through the line of wagons and the surge of cattle. Winding out of the trail, spurred by impatience, he cut through the trees and headed for the spot where he knew Jenny's wagon would crest the hill.

He winced as he put the whip to the horse's flanks and leaned into the wind. That billowing top would blow loose before the week was out. What poor excuse for a driver had she found, a tad who couldn't even fasten a canvas?

Now Mark was beside the wagon, shrouded in dust, watching it lurch through the ruts. The driver was indeed a boy, straining at the reins. Jenny, tense and pale, clung to her seat.

Mark's yell was a mixture of triumph and anger. He had the reins in his hands before the youth could move. With one leap Mark was on the seat, dropping down between Jenny and the boy. "Here." Mark shoved some silver coins into the hands of the youth. "Now, get that horse and take it back to the stables. Tell Tom Timmons I sent you."

His hand urged the startled lad into action, and Mark settled into the seat and straightened the reins. He dared not glance at Jenny. "Didn't like the looks of that top. Decided I'd better come along and do the driving myself."

Mark leaned over and carefully wrapped the reins around the seat bracing. There was still no sound from her, but their silence shattered the first stone in the wall between them. For a moment he shivered with fear. What if she wouldn't have him back? When he turned, Mark was conscious only of amazement as he looked into her face. It took a while before he summoned the strength to draw that deep, ragged breath he needed, but when he did, Jenny moved and blinked. Slowly color began to touch her cheeks.

He could only whisper; even then he felt words were unnecessary. And over the creaking and groaning of the wagon, the lowing of the oxen and the crack of the canvas, they both knew the miracle. "Jenny, I'm here to go with you—all the way." Her eyes were speaking back, saying she could accept and there would be no questions. But he must say it. "Remember those words? I promised to love you as long as we both shall live."

Her lips moved stiffly and he leaned closer to hear, "Mark," she was pleading, "I know it is a strange love, but truly I do love you."

He couldn't speak, but when he bent to kiss her, he caught a glimpse of the shadows in her eyes. She didn't know that his lips moving against hers were promising, "In sickness, in health, I pledge you my love."

CHAPTER 5

It was hot in the Cartwright wagon. Jenny brushed at the dampness on her face and shifted on the wagon seat. She glanced at Mark, studying the new beard and the wide-brimmed hat shading his face. Instead of his usual white shirt and silk tie, he was wearing the coarse homespun of a frontiersman. She touched his sleeve, enjoying the feel of the hard muscle tightening as he flicked the reins across the back of Sammy. "Get along there, girl, do your part of the pulling," he urged mildly.

Jenny smiled as she watched the errant mare quicken her step. "Poor dear," she said, "this is beneath their dignity, pulling this creaking wagon with all that canvas popping behind them. They're much more suited to cantering down a country lane with nary a rut, pulling a smart little buggy. But then I suppose you would have fitted me out with oxen like the rest of them had you known at the time that—" Her voice trailed away as she was caught up in the memory of that last fearful day when she had left Ohio, thinking that never again would she see Mark. She shivered even as she dabbed at the moisture on her forehead.

Mark's hand quickly clasped hers. When he looked at her, she saw the dark expression, but his light words bore no relation to that shared memory. "Might yet," he said with a grin, flicking the reins. "Do you hear that, gals? Might trade the two of you for one good ox."

His hand still cuddled hers and they rode in companionable silence. When Jenny finally stirred, she turned to Mark and commented, "They told me it was eight hundred miles to Mis-

56

souri." She was feeling the late afternoon sun press against her like a heavy hand, blotting out all except the weary heat.

Mark shoved his hat back from his eyes and grinned at her. She studied his face, thinking she had never seen him so tanned. There was a band of white across his forehead and below it his face was mahogany brown. Rivulets of moisture drew lines through the dust on his cheeks and dampened his beard. With a sigh, she pushed her heavy hair away from her forehead, rubbing at the sweat, guessing that dust streaked her own face as well.

Jenny tried to stifle the weary yawn rising up within her even as she searched his expression looking again for some indication that he regretted being here on this lonesome road to Missouri. How constantly aware she was of the tiptoe feeling in her heart. Knowing how close she had come to forfeiting forever Mark's presence beside her was a memory that would be with her the rest of her life. She twisted her hands in her lap and felt the talisman snugged securely in the pocket of her dusty frock.

For a moment her lips trembled with a half smile. How much she would give to know just what power had won her husband back when she had given up all hopes of ever seeing him again!

She fingered the talisman again. Either this charmed metal with its secret spirit powers had done the trick, or praying to Luna and God had worked in her favor. For a moment, remembering Mark's new beliefs, she was filled with shame. She moved uneasily on the hard wooden seat of the wagon and wondered at the feeling. Was it because she knew the powers had worked for her against Mark's will?

Mark was speaking and she realized with a start how far afield her thoughts had wandered. "What did you say?" she asked, moving around to look at him.

"It *is* eight hundred miles," he repeated, "and divided into the twelve or fifteen miles we'll make a day, it'll be a miracle if we're there by Independence Day."

"Is it important?" Jenny murmured, thinking now of the isolation this wagon and this dusty road had thrown about their lives. She lifted her head and grinned at him. "At least while you're driving this wagon, Joseph can't be sending you off to kingdom come."

"That's good?"

She searched his eyes for the reason behind the question, even as she nodded. He started to add more and then hesitated. Jenny realized how often nowadays he had been doing that. Impatience boiled up within her, but immediately she trembled, thinking of all the things he might say. It was those very things which had nearly torn them apart—his new beliefs that seemed at odds with everything the church taught. She felt his hand on her arm and covered it with her own.

The next day the wagon train left Ohio behind, and the road turned south. Each day now they watched as the land became more arid. Jenny noticed even the smallest villages were miles apart. Slowly they moved from one watering hole to the next.

Indiana was a short stretch, and across the flat lands, the wagon train sometimes pressed through twenty miles in one day.

Again the way became hot and dusty; tired animals strayed and bawled for water, fretful children quarreled, and the menfolk snapped at each other. When the food supply dwindled, the wagon captains chafed while a day was snatched by the women for laundry and bread-baking.

One evening in June, the wagon train circled late in the evening on the prairie close to the Wabash River.

Their camp was hot and dusty and it didn't help at all, Jenny thought, to hear the distant crash of waterfalls and the shouts of the youths who had taken the cattle to water and then managed to fall in themselves.

Jenny sighed over her supper fire as she moved slowly about preparing a meal. She was recalling the day's travel. Her memory was full of gentle scenes: the clear fresh water of a brook cutting through an orchard, a log cabin with the yard dotted with people waving at the wagon train. She recalled the parents and children—tousle-haired, in stairstep order. Later in the day there had been glimpses of refreshing color on the prairie, masses of flowers growing wild. Jenny yearned after them. She paused, and the memory of it all tilted and tipped, thrusting the components of the day into order and serving up a dream of a home that didn't move every morning. And children.

She sighed and spread a cloth across rough boxes. Mark was watching and she asked, "Do you suppose we'll ever have a family like that?" At his puzzled frown she explained, "Those young'uns who were waving as we passed."

"I expect so." His grin was intimate, and for a moment she forgot their home moved every morning.

After a supper of salty, tough meat and leathery potatoes, Mark disappeared. Jenny spread their blankets under the wagon while she slapped at the buzzing flies and gnats. Thinking longingly of a cool bath, she swished the water around in the bucket. It barely covered the bottom of the pail.

When the embers of the supper fires had cooled and the mosquitoes moved in, Jenny retreated to her bed. She seldom allowed herself the luxury of tears, but tonight they couldn't be ignored. She dabbed at her eyes as she swatted insects and fanned away the heat and smoke.

Jenny heard Mark's step, but before she had time to mop the tears away, he was beside her. "Come," he whispered, pulling at her hand. "Don't make a sound." His hand urged her on as he guided her through the dark, sleeping camp.

When they were through the bushes she whispered, "Mark, they'll think we're Indians and shoot! Besides, you know we're not to leave camp." He tightened his grasp, and she silently followed.

They went up a slope and down a steep bank. In front of them the river shimmered in the moonlight. That dim gurgle of sound she had heard became a roar as they walked upstream toward the falls. Cool spray reached Jenny, and she lifted her face to the moisture. Beyond the mist, the moon was rising over the trees.

"Look," he whispered, pulling her close. "There're deer on the far bank. In a moment you'll see them outlined against the moonlight."

"After that terrible supper you'll *look* at deer instead of shooting?" she hissed.

He turned to answer and instead bent close. His hand touched her cheek. "Tears. Is it so bad? You know we can always—"

Hastily she interrupted, "Mark, it's the heat. I want to bathe."

"Aw!" he exclaimed, "my next surprise. Come." Down the next bend of the river she saw the inlet where the water was calm and shallow. "Perchance the sun has even warmed it," he said with a mock bow. He dug in his pocket and held up a bar of soap.

After the first shock the water was nearly warm. Jenny soaped her hair, then dived and swam the width of the inlet, leaving a trail of suds behind. Mark was beside her. Moonlight gleamed on his wet bare arm. She watched the muscles knot and relax as he floated lazy circles around her.

When he circled her one more time, she touched his wet arm and said, "I've never seen a marble statue, but I've seen pictures. They always look wet and smooth like this. But not warm." He slipped his arm under her shoulders and together they floated, gently rocked by the waves and lulled by river sounds. The moon was misting over with lazy clouds, and above their heads the stars became brilliant. Now center stage, they sparkled; occasionally one shot across the horizon.

Dreamily she said, "Mark, the Saints in Missouri saw a meteor shower. It came at a bad time. A good omen. Maybe tonight's such an omen for us. Maybe—" He bent over her and kissed her gently.

"I don't think we need an omen, do we?"

When morning came and Jenny rolled over in her nest of musty blankets, she couldn't believe the dream of water and star-shot sky, with Mark's wet shoulder against hers. She was ready with a sigh until she saw his smile; then she once more snuggled her face against his shoulder before the day began.

Just as the dusty miles piled up behind the wagon train and became greater than the miles that lay ahead, the sense of excitement began building. The Saints spent more and more of the evenings around the fire.

Some of the men had traveled this route before. Now they were the center of attention. In the evening, after Jenny and the other women washed their supper dishes, they joined the group around the fire, leaning close to watch as the men knelt on the ground and used a stick to draw maps in the soil. Eager questions were fired at them. "Are there mountains ahead?" "Are the Indians ornery in Missouri?" "When do we cross the Mississippi?"

As more miles passed beneath the wagon wheels, the questions changed. Jenny guessed from the anxiety in her own heart that the Saints were wondering as much she did. Finally the question was asked. "What will our new home be like? Will we have all the promises of Zion right off?"

Some of the answers given by the group captains were vague and left an uneasy feeling; she was especially aware of it in Mark's restlessness. Again the fear of losing him crept upon her, as she listened while some of the old-timers compared Jackson County to the new land farther north. She couldn't forget the night beside the fire when Matt Miller talked about Jackson.

The fire had burned down to sputtering coals and the figures about the fire were shadowy outlines against the star-filled sky. Old Matt had been one of the first group to settle in Missouri back in 1832. His voice was dreamy as he described the land. "Gentle acres, they was. Easy to set a plow to, and the seeds sprung up almost before you could get them settled and the soil patted down. Never had to worry about your next meal; the land was teeming with wild turkey, rabbit, deer and sage hen."

A question interrupted his reminiscence. "We've heard how the Missouri settlers mistreated the Saints. Is that a fact?"

He sighed before he answered and he spoke reluctantly. "It's a fact. Seems it hadn't ought to have been. There's room for all who want to work the land. With the Indian problems t'was to their advantage to have a few more around."

"What was the problem?" Jenny recognized Thompson's heavy voice.

Miller replied, "Ya got to understand the old settlers. They's a rough breed, to be sure. But more'n anything, even more'n minding having us around, they objected to some of the lot informing them that the Lord had given the land to the Saints, and that no matter what, they'd get it all in the end." He sighed and passed his hand across his face wearily.

He added, "There's a bunch of us who grew mighty fond of the land. We'd a been glad to keep our mouths shut and work our hands to the bone just to get to stay there." His voice trailed away. When he spoke again his voice was matter-of-fact. "We left gentle, rich acres and growing towns. Our homes and farms we had to give up for unplowed prairie and barren wastes. A mighty price to pay because we believed the revelation and spoke out our belief. Now I hope we keep our mouths shut and live like any other man on this earth." He paused for a moment, and in the silence the last of the fire sputtered and snapped. His voice was filled with sorrow, and Jenny shivered as he said, "If we don't we'll be a running again. Only this time, could be we'll all pay with our lives."

During the following day, Jenny lined up the comments and questions, sorting and discarding the nerve-tender ones and pushing others at Mark. "It's nothing but rumbles; we've been hearing them all winter," she remarked, ignoring Mark's somber expression. "Missouri problems. Back then, back in the beginning, how could Joseph be expected to keep things moving smooth as stirred gravy when he wasn't around to tend to the stirring?"

Mark's smile was tentative as he said, "At least the fellows feel free to chew over the facts."

"That's because Joseph and the twelve aren't around to thunder at their grumbles." She saw his expression and regretted her words. She tried to smooth them over. "No one has a right to dispute when the Prophet has the keys of the kingdom and his word is scripture."

He ducked his head, but not before Jenny saw the white line around his mouth and heard him say, "Jenny, my dear, remember that statement. I'm certain I'll have occasion to remind you of it. But for now, there are problems. All the rumbles I've heard about the difficulties in Jackson County back in the beginning points to a rocky road once we reach Caldwell County."

"You're referring to the treatment the Saints had when they first went into Jackson. Well, that's persecution."

"Can you call it persecution when a fellow balances an apple on his head and dares his buddy to knock it off?"

"Meaning?" Jenny asked.

"For one thing, the articles Phelps published. For another, the Saints going around telling the people of Missouri God has given them the land, and that He'd promised the riches of the Gentiles would be theirs." Jenny opened her mouth to reply and Mark said, "How would you feel if someone told you all your work was for naught, that the Lord was going to pass it all on to someone else?"

"They *pushed* them out of Jackson. Now, up north the land isn't fertile."

"Don't forget what Miller said. Also, consider, they've found a home—and from all reports, they'll be welcome to stay if they try to get along with their neighbors." Mark was silent a moment, then thoughtfully said, "I think I'm going to make it a point to get acquainted with Phelps."

"Why?"

He was frowning slightly as he looked up. "I think I want to find out what makes the man tick."

"Mark," Jenny said slowly, recalling the troubled man she had lived with that first year of their marriage, "I'm thinking you're back to carrying the whole lot on your shoulders again. Some call it trouble-making, and the Prophet doesn't abide that."

His voice was sober as he replied, "Call it as you wish. I'd be less than a—a man if I didn't try to help those around me." Mark flicked the reins along the backs of the horses.

Suddenly Mark lifted his head and grinned. "Hey, you're talking about the *they's*. Do you realize we're going to be some of the *they's*? Think you'll like being a farmer's wife?"

"Mark!" Jenny looked down at his smooth hands. "Have you ever milked a cow in your life?"

"When I was about six."

Jenny laughed. "Finally, there's something I know better'n you. I'll be your teacher. I even know how to clean a pig sty."

But it wasn't the discontented rumbles, or the uneasy questions Jenny was thinking about that first evening they stopped on the border of Missouri. Jenny was remembering that star-studded night and the misty moonlit bath they'd had in the Wabash River in Indiana. What had there been about that time to make her think back wistfully? Was it the isolation of that spot and Mark all to herself? Why did that scene make her think of peace and restoration?

Mark had called it an Ebenezer night and when she tried to get him to explain, he'd grinned and said it was like climbing a hill and passing a post marking the halfway place. Then he added softly, "It means we've come thus far." She searched his face and that light in his eyes reassured even more than the strange words. *Thus far.* She hugged the words to herself and hoped.

It was soon evident that they were inside Missouri's borders. Here there weren't any tidy clusters of homes decorated with borders of flower gardens. Instead, tiny log cabins marked towns where there were nearly as many saloons as homes.

There were other things, too. She saw black men working the fields, while white men bunched around the saloons. She also saw the number of men was far greater than the women and children. While Jenny was still adjusting to this, she became aware that it was commonplace to find in every hamlet curious lines of people gathered to watch their wagons move through.

Sometimes there were friendly waves and children shouting, but often there were hostile, suspicious stares. On one occasion an old man called, "Be ye Mormons?" At Jenny's nod, he called, "Weren't Jackson enough? Bogg is too lily-livered about stopping ya, but we know some who will.

"We ain't forgettin' the past when yer men marched in with arms. 'Tis 'gainst the law. We ain't forgettin' yer men said the Lord gave them this land. Well, we get different information from the Lord."

Jenny murmured, "They aren't very friendly."

Mark replied, "But that woman waved and smiled."

"Then I should make friends of the women?" He nodded, but for a moment she wondered at the shadow in his eyes.

The wagon train pressed deeper into Missouri, heading farther north and west. The terrain was changing nearly daily.

Jenny saw the mountains flattened into prairies of luxuriant grass. While trees clustered the valleys and bordered the creeks and rivers, the dense forests had disappeared.

On the days that it was their turn to ride near the lead of the wagon train, Jenny could watch the deer leaping away in the distance as the wagons approached. The quail and partridges would seek cover in the tall grasses until at last their courage failed. Too often they would rise to confront musket fire, and that night there would be fresh meat for supper.

The night talk around the fire became excited chatter when it was circulated that they were now close to the place where Joseph Smith had settled. Jenny felt contentment in the cozy talk of the women, suddenly happy with life and sure of the future.

While the men talked about this new land they would settle, and about the crops they would plant, the women had their heads together. Jenny listened to the news. Emma Smith had produced another boy child. "My, the Prophet's outfitting his farm proper-like."

A tart tongue added, "Likely those young'uns 'll have life easier than ours."

Once again the women rehashed the old story of the conflict in Jackson. As they weighed the chances of success in this new endeavor, some of the men joined their group. Jenny heard the derision in one voice as the man said, "After being turned out of Jackson County, the big-hearted Missouri legislature thought they were doing us a favor by giving all the Mormons Caldwell County. They don't know it, but Saints will be swarming over the whole state in a year or so." Jenny and Mark's eyes met, and she watched him turn away. For some unknown reason the June night seemed suddenly chilled.

Now, around the fire, the men who knew chortled, "They drew a line, but Joe's already stepped over it. Saints have moved into Daviess and Carroll as well as Ray counties."

The answer given was smug, and Jenny mentally squirmed over it, even as she acknowledged the truth of it. The woman sitting beside her said, " 'Tis true. The Lord's promised the land to us. Zion it will be, and already we're knowing that it's going to have to be taken, most likely by the sword, since they're resisting. 'Twill be a difficult time for us, but the promise of the lands and houses being ours as well as the gold and silver, well, that helps."

Jenny felt Mark stirring restlessly, but wisely she chose to hold her tongue.

CHAPTER 6

Jenny had been asleep when the stealthy rustle reached through her dreams. With eyes wide, she listened. In the silence of the camp, she was aware of the freshening air. The last of the smoke was gone and the circle of wagons was dark. She guessed it was very late. Again the rustle came. Slowly she reached for Mark. At the quick pressure of his hand she allowed herself a sigh of relief.

As Mark left her side she heard a clink of metal and a muffled curse. There was Mark's low voice and an answering voice. It must be just one of the men. After listening a moment longer, Jenny snuggled into the blankets. Her eyelids had begun to droop when she realized the tenor of voices had changed, and another voice was added.

For a moment more she strained to hear the muffled words. Finally she slipped out of the blankets and crouched behind the wagon wheel. Although she couldn't understand the words, she recognized that voice.

Crawling out from under the wagon she moved toward the men and whispered, "Oliver Cowdery, whatever are you doing here?"

Mark turned to pull her close, saying, "Be quiet and just listen. These men have come from Far West."

"Far West? That's in Caldwell County where we're headed, isn't it? What do they want?"

"Food for their families and anything else we can spare. They are destitute."

"There's bread and cold beans, dried meat and apples. We

still have flour and—" Mark's words began to sink. She turned to Cowdery. "Destitute! Whatever has happened?"

Now she became conscious of other dark shadows in the background.

Cowdery sighed deeply and wiped a hand slowly across his face. Impatiently Mark said, "Jenny, don't we have extra quilts and dishes?"

"Quilts! It's nearly July. Dishes . . ." Mark's hand urged her toward the wagon and the men followed.

Inside the wagon Jenny tumbled through bundles, her mind in as much confusion as the jumble before her. The men pressed into the wagon. "Four of you," she said in surprise. Slowly she reached for plates and forks and found an extra skillet. Her mind was busy bringing up facts about the men while their haunted, lined faces were giving out information that bewildered her. She paused to peer at the men. Surely she was mistaken—they couldn't be fleeing Zion!

There was Oliver Cowdery, schoolteacher and newspaper editor, but most importantly, one of the witnesses to the *Book of Mormon*. What could have forced him to leave? And Johnson. She knew nothing about him. Could he possibly be the brother of the Nancy Miranda whose name had been linked with Joseph's? They said the man Eli had led a mob against the Prophet. Jenny bit her lip. What trouble was being raised against the Prophet now? The man beside him, David Whitmer, was also a witness to the *Book of Mormon*. His brother John was the fourth member of the group. At their father's home Joseph had completed the translation of the golden plates. She ventured a peek at the stony faces, and her questions grew.

As she pulled out the flour and bacon, she cast a bewildered glance at Mark.

"They haven't had anything to eat since early morning," Mark said. "They've obtained wagons, but not much else. Whitmer says that now the word's passed, some are afraid to be seen talking with them, let alone give help. That's why they've come at night."

"Like common criminals," Cowdery said bitterly. "Rigdon's been after my neck since I came to Missouri. Just once too often

I aired my feelings. Said I blamed him for the troubles the Saints are in. He'll never forgive us for being disheartened when the bank failed in Kirtland."

One of the Whitmers said, "I can see him gloating now that we've been reduced to running like rats, and begging like the scum of the earth instead of Israel's chosen."

Jenny studied the lined faces as the men talked. She was conscious of the germ of uneasiness growing inside. When she turned, Mark's serious face multiplied the feeling.

Mark gathered up the quilts and food. "You've told me enough to convince me the whole lot of us need to hear your story first thing in the morning. For now, let's take these things to your families and have you settled for the night."

As the group filed silently out of sight, Jenny was remembering the last time she had seen Cowdery. He, David Whitmer, and Martin Harris had been watching the black-robed girl as she had whirled on the streets and promised to read their futures. For a time the three men had been leaders in the group that followed the seeress with her black stone—the dissenters, as they'd been called.

Everyone knew how Joseph Smith had shaken them loose from their folly. Shortly after the Prophet returned to Kirtland, he had sent Whitmer and Cowdery to Missouri; Martin Harris had left the church completely.

When Mark came back to the wagon and crawled into bed, he murmured, "They've told me little. I know only that they've been run out of Zion on threat of their lives. I could see they were exhausted. I've promised to listen to their story tomorrow."

For a long time after Mark's even breathing told her he was asleep, Jenny lay wide-eyed staring into the darkness, wondering what portent was being heralded. Certainly evil was stalking into her life again. She sensed that when the men had talked.

Tossing and turning on her hard pallet, Jenny became convinced that the hints of happiness she had felt for the past few weeks were again being threatened. She tightened her hands around the talisman and vowed to renew her search for power and success. Success? She rolled onto her elbow and looked down at Mark. She thought of those empty days just before she had left Kirtland. Never again would she risk losing him.

Jenny tightened her grasp on the talisman and silently her lips moved through the incantations, invoking peace, happiness, and safety. Now she was holding her breath, willing stillness, waiting for intimations of peace; but in the quietness, a new vision pressed itself across her mind. There was Jenny on a seesaw, rising high only to plunge earthward. But even as she swooped down, she knew she could scoot to the middle and ride both sides. With a pleased grin, she turned on her side and snuggled against Mark. Little did it matter that both sides of the seesaw were books, one green and the other gold; she would use them both.

The next morning the four men and their families trailed into the wagon train's enclosure. Silent, questioning faces were turned toward them. Jenny was well aware of the tension moving through the group. The very air vibrated with it.

Early this morning, before breakfast, Mark had met with the men in command of the wagon train. She had watched that silent group as they had been called into council. She watched the hunched figures around the fire and listened to the low murmur of conversation. She saw the worried frown, the glances toward the strangers' wagons, and she felt her own skin prickle with an unidentified apprehension. She knew others were feeling it, too. She saw it in the worried faces of the women as they tried to busy themselves around camp.

As Jenny went about her tasks, from the camp next to them, Libby Taylor straightened her back and groaned, "Why do we have to get mixed up with dissenters before we've even a chance to settle in this new land?" The woman who answered her in a murmur looked in Jenny's direction. Libby said loudly, "I don't care if she does. I intend to stay in the good graces of the presidency." Jenny paused, towel in hand, thinking back to those statements Matt had made. It was while she still agonized over his concern that this same woman had skimmed over it all with her words, saying, *"The Lord promised the land to us. Zion it will be—most likely by the sword."* This same woman's husband had said, *"They drew a line, but Joe's already stepped over it."*

Still staring at the woman, Jenny wrapped the towel around her shoulders and murmured, "Dear Lord, what are we getting ourselves into?" Immediately the incongruity of her statement swept over her. Jenny sighed as she turned back to the pan of dishes.

By midmorning the wagon train was still circled beside the trail. The group around the men had been growing since breakfast time. The men's story had been repeated, analyzed, and passed around the group. Jenny watched as they shifted uneasily from one foot to another, while the women stood apart in a miserable group.

She watched Mark's face. That furrowed brow made her uneasy. It held the expression she had seen often during the first winter of their marriage. Mark was being pulled asunder by things he didn't understand.

Now Mark's voice rose, "What started this? Was it talk over the Fannie Alger affair?"

Jenny looked at him in surprise. Mark wasn't prone to listen to gossip, and since the incident Nettie had reported to her had happened while Mark was in England, she supposed he knew nothing of the affair. While the excited babble surrounded her, Jenny was studying Mark's face, surprised by the play of expression, as his frown gave way to distaste, then anger.

The man spoke slowly, "I suppose it was partly to blame. You don't question Joseph and stay in his good graces."

Jenny couldn't keep the hard note out of her voice as she walked up to the group and addressed Johnson. "You were making terrible accusations against the Prophet right there in the temple. Everyone knows that."

Ignoring her, Cowdery said, "What really caused the problem was buying land here in Missouri and not deeding it to the church."

"The United Order," a knowing voice added. "Just like we had in Kirtland, only out here it seems the only takers were those who didn't have anything to consecrate to the church."

Another rough voice on the fringe of the group broke in. "I say, leave these men to their own devices. I'm feeling we're picking up a quarrel we've no need to. All who's for heading for

Far West today, fall in behind me."

Jenny watched the string of men and women snaking along after the man; bemused, she recalled his name was Daniels.

Abruptly Jenny realized she was still standing beside the fire, clinging to Mark's arm. The midnight thieves, Oliver Cowdery, Lyman Johnson, David Whitmer, and John Whitmer, were standing there, too. But there were others.

Mark was saying, "You realize what you're doing? You're saying you believe these men and that you want to help their families. That could put you in bad with Joseph and Ridgon right off. Are you willing to stick your neck out like that?" In a moment he broke the silence, saying slowly, "Your reputation will tarnish before you even settle in Zion. Do you want to run the risk of being labeled as dissenters?"

Matt spoke up. "You know, I left Missouri just long enough to fetch my young'uns from Kirtland. I believe in the land. Maybe I don't believe enough in Joseph right now, but I like it here enough to fight for what I want."

"And what's that?" Mark asked slowly.

"A home in Missouri, freedom. Joe's gotta let us have more head room. He's gotta give us a chance to act like men, with minds to think and choose. Some of us are gettin' tired of being treated like bad little boys, havin' our hands smacked for havin' our say."

There was an uneasy ripple through the crowd, but Jenny's quick glance around the circle told her many were approving of Matt's words.

She had just a quick glance Mark's direction, noting the relief on his face, when Silas Jenson quickly added, "But there's other reasons. The Whitmers have been good friends of ours since the church began. Take year before last. My wife nearly died birthin' and Missus Whitmer was right there long as we needed her. It pains me to think of what she's feelin' right now."

From the back of the circle a thoughtful voice added, "I can't believe Joseph's meanin' those things he said. Sure I believe Cowdery's telling the truth when he repeated the story, but I'd like to hear some more."

"Everybody knows Rigdon's a rant and raver. Everybody

takes him with a grain of salt." There was a wave of nervous laughter.

Jenny said, "I've just finished the dishes. I didn't hear the men talk, neither did Clara or Betsy. Seems like, if we're to be following the menfolk into who knows what, then maybe we should be hearing their story."

"We don't have time. Let's get these wagons on the road."

There was a snort behind Jenny and she turned. Bella Partridge folded her arms across her ample body and stretched to her full height. She was nearly as tall as the tallest man in the group. The silence lasted another second and Jenny saw Bella's chin jut out while the flesh under her chin quivered. Words were unnecessary. Her husband sighed, "Might as well tell the whole story over again, or we ain't goin' no place."

The day was heating up rapidly. Mark led the way to a shady grove. As they settled in the shade of the trees, Jenny noticed most of the group were middle-aged and somber.

Cowdery spoke first. "I'm convinced Joseph is a prophet holding the keys of the kingdom. You know I'm wanting to obey the Lord and make it in the hereafter, or I'd not be out here in Missouri, following the Prophet."

David Whitmer was speaking now. "It goes against the grain to give up on a project. But a man's got to have some say about his life."

Cowdery continued, "Rigdon particularly is wanting us outta the state. He's made up his mind and won't rest until he's driven us out. Me particularly. I've made no bones about my feelings. Rigdon's the troublemaker. He's responsible for the Danites. They are his baby. Missourians are a tough lot, I grant, but Rigdon made up his mind he'll be tougher."

John Whitmer added, "They'd been putting the screws into me to give over all my property to the church. Rigdon was the one who started the tide of feeling against me. He did it with his preaching when he gave out that salt sermon on last June 17. Since then feelings were running high."

" 'Ye are the salt of the earth,' " Cowdery quoted bitterly, "and if the salt's lost its savor, it's to be trodden underfoot. The Saints were duty-bound to trample underfoot those who wouldn't go along with all the church taught."

Whitmer continued, "Corrill came to me secret-like, saying it was Rigdon's signal to the Danites to get me. He advised I hightail right then. I didn't want to give up everything I'd worked for because of that feeling, so I went to Joe."

Mark interrupted, "Did Joe sanction Rigdon's sermon?"

"He didn't come right out and say so, but he did say that the Lord revealed to him it was Peter who done in Judas." There was silence and Jenny pondered Joseph's statement.

The mild voice from the back of the crowd spoke again, "I ain't heard more'n whispers about the Danites. Some of you fellas explain."

David Whitmer faced the man and spoke tersely, "You're not the only one. Information is thin, but the bald facts are it's a band of cutthroats pledged to enforce the laws."

"What laws?"

"Anything the Prophet says is to be. Don't bother quoting me; it won't do no good. They're denying the bunch even exist. But they do, and you don't have to be too smart to know one of their first jobs is to get rid of dissenters."

Whitmer was speaking again. "We had enough trouble with money in Kirtland. The United Order didn't work there, and it failed out here. But they're getting set to try it again. You mark my words. Getting my hunk of land is the first step."

From out of the crowd a man spoke, and his voice reflected his abiding doubt. "They call you dissenters, saying you're fighting against council. We'll never get anywhere 'til men pull together."

"Depends on which direction you're pullin'." John Whitmer was sober. "There's other things; you haven't heard the end of our story yet."

When he paused, Jenny asked, "What brought on the salt sermon?" The men turned to look at Jenny.

Cowdery replied, "Well, it started up when Corrill and Marsh objected to the decision council reached on our case. Corrill reported back that I was faulted for objecting to the way things were running. In truth, it was the Danites and Avard with his cutthroat tactics I was against. But council decided we four best be done in."

"Corrill and Marsh," John Whitmer took up the story, "objected and then argued the matter needed to be brought before the whole body of Saints."

"So," Cowdery continued, "the sermon. Rigdon took it from the Bible, in Matthew about the salt having lost its savor; therefore it was good for nothing but to be cast out. He laid it out that the duty of the Saints is to take anybody that loses his faith and trample him under their feet. He went on to say there was a group of men in the bunch who had dissented from the church and were a doin' all in their power to destroy the presidency, laying plans to take their lives. He laid out accusations of counterfeiting, lying, cheating, and anything else you could name. He said it was the duty of the Saints to trample them into the ground, and he would construct a gallows in the middle of Far West to hang them."

Jenny shivered and rubbed her chilly arms; she looked at the faces around her, seeing the disbelief and shock she was feeling. The memory of Rigdon's scathing address to the people in the Kirtland temple flashed before her. She was seeing his pale face contorted with rage.

John Whitmer's words were nearly lost to her. "That's when the Prophet said what he did about the Lord telling him Peter did old Judas in. So then I tried to right things by going to Joseph and asking what I should do, and he said it would help if I were to give my property into the church—that way there would be good feelings about me, and the men would have confidence in me again."

" 'Twere only a couple of days until we got the letter." David Whitmer said, pausing to look around the circle of faces. "It was signed by eighty-three of the men of the church. It was in Rigdon's fine words, though. He was saying all kinds of dirt, and addin' that the citizens of Caldwell County had borne the abuse long enough; then he gave us three days to pack up our families to get out of the state."

"We had too much invested to walk out on it all," Cowdery said, glowering. "Land, cattle, furniture. So we headed for Lib-

erty over in Clay County to hire us a Gentile lawyer. We knew
a Mormon one daren't listen to us. When we headed back we
met the womenfolk riding down the trail to meet us. Mind you,
they had been sent out of their homes with only a team and a
little bedding and their clothes. It was the Danites that did it.
They surrounded the place, ordered them to leave, and threatened to kill any one of the bunch who would dare return."

It took Mark and the fragment of the wagon train two days
to escort the dissenters to the Missouri state line. There they
were stocked with food and fresh teams. Jenny saw Mark pressing money into David Whitmer's hand.

When the fragment of the wagon train turned again, pointing their teams toward Far West, Mark was the chosen leader.
His first task was to open the crude map and outline the route.
"We've worked farther north, see. The rest of our train is still
pressing west along the southern route. I suggest we cut straight
across on this trail." He traced his finger along the map. "We
are small and can move faster; if we are fortunate, perhaps we'll
arrive at the same time the other bunch does."

Jenny saw the level glances the men exchanged; she also
saw the puckered frowns and worried eyes of the women.

She didn't need to question further. Mark knew how important it was to be in Far West when the other group arrived.
How well aware she was of all those wagging tongues primed
and ready to challenge Mark's humanitarian actions! Without
a doubt, his help to those four families would be taken to mean
he supported the dissenters. But then, didn't he? She studied
his serene face and decided that, right or wrong, Mark would
help those people.

Back in the wagon, Jenny moved closer to Mark and touched
the coarse texture of his shirt sleeve. Beneath the fabric she
could feel hard muscle flexing with each movement of his arm.
She looked at his sunburned face, noting that the deep color
intensified the curious blue-green of his eyes. "Do you know
you have a million more freckles?" she asked.

He looked at her and the wary expression in his eyes disappeared. "And do you know that your curious owl eyes are
twice as big today, and that they are very wise?"

"Because you are being the Mark I expected you to be?" She closed her eyes for a moment, and from far out of the past rose a vision of the long-ago Mark, somehow glowing and set apart, with a quality of life she didn't understand.

CHAPTER 7

During the remainder of their trip across Missouri, Jenny was torn by the need to see Joseph. Torn because in her innermost heart, she sensed a hint of disloyalty in her decision. But try as she might, she couldn't identify the reason. Joseph needed to know the fears, even the gossip about the Danites. He also needed to be warned against Rigdon. What could be wrong about her decision to search him out at first opportunity? Jenny glanced at Mark and couldn't help feeling a touch of guilt.

True to Mark's prediction, the smaller train of wagons had moved quickly through Missouri, bending north and west through the prairie land.

When the news was passed through the line of wagons, Jenny leaned over the wagon seat to survey her new home. "So this is Far West," she said slowly as their wagon creaked down the main street until they reached the town square.

Mark stopped in front of a building—log, like the cabins, she noted, comparing the scattering of dwellings fanning out from the square. But most certainly, with that size, it was more than a house.

The last of the wagons pulled into the square and Jenny waited for the dust to settle before turning to study this place they were to call home—Zion. She thought of the awe that word had built in her and, with a sinking heart, compared the emotion with reality.

It was only another frontier town, just like all the other Missouri towns they had passed through. There were no neat door yards with tumbling flowers and shady trees, no houses of milled lumber or quarried stone. Crude log shelters, tiny and raw, were the only buildings.

Then she began to notice other things. The streets were wide. Half of their little wagon train could travel abreast down this avenue, half of the twelve wagons.

Remembering, Jenny looked around for the rest of the original wagon train. "Mark, have we arrived first?"

"I doubt it," he said casually as he knotted the reins to the seat. "They've probably been sent on to settle another area. It's not likely everyone would find enough land right around here."

As he jumped to the ground, the door of the crude log building opened. The man in the doorway was a stranger, a curious one. "Welcome to Far West. The Prophet is out of town right now. He's left instructions to head your bunch up Grand River way. Gallatin is Gentile, but beyond, up off Honey Creek, there's good land and a townsite picked." Jenny's heart sank. Joseph wasn't here.

The men from Mark's wagon train had gathered around him. The man looked pleased. Jenny saw him take a deep breath as he shifted his hat to the back of his head and say, "Now, folks, you're going to like it up there. The Prophet has bought a big parcel of land, and he's prepared to give you a good price on a nice little farm. Right now he has his agent up there to take your money or your notes and lead you on to your own lot. I predict that within the week, you'll all be settled on your own section."

The mingled voices and the man's instructions blocked out Mark's question. Jenny watched him lean back against the wagon wheel until he could gain an audience.

While they waited, Jenny got out of the wagon and joined the women forming a circle in the middle of the wide road.

"And to think we left Ohio for this!" The woman dabbed at her eyes as she peered around.

Jenny said, "But it's new. Far West has only been here for a year. Look at all they've done. It's a shock to me too, if I just look at the raw dirt and log huts. But look yonder. From here you can see the plowed fields. That building—it's surely a schoolhouse. That house over there in the middle of the big plot has a window with a curtain. There's corn nearly ready for eating." Even as she spoke, she wondered why she must defend Joseph's Zion.

"I hear there's Indians and snakes. Rattlers. They're poisonous. I had a cousin, came out here in '34. Died from snake bite."

"They're shippin' us on. I heard the fella say up north to Daviess County. The town—I've never heard such a name; he's calling it Adam-ondi-Ahman. All I want is a spot where I can put my feet up and call home."

The group of men broke up, all heading for their wagons.

Jenny joined Mark on the crude porch of the log building. She was breathing deeply of the air, noting the smells around her. The building still oozed resinous sap, and its pungent odor was only a backdrop for the sweet freshness of the towering evergreens, beginning just now to move with the evening breezes. Supper fires threw their own homey scent into the air. Again Jenny sniffed deeply and the fearful knot in her stomach loosened. Surely in such a place there could be only peace.

Then she thought of the people they had met fleeing for their lives. Again she studied Far West. This time she was convinced: Cowdery and his bunch were lying.

Behind her Mark was speaking to the man on the porch. "Where do I find David Whitmer's house?"

The man paused for a moment. Now his eyes grew cold as he studied Mark's face and said slowly. "Whitmer isn't around here no more. How's come you want him?"

"I don't. I have agreed to buy his house." Jenny caught her breath and Mark gave her a sharp glance as he waited for the man's answer.

"Sorry, but it isn't his to sell. Rigdon's living there now. Take it up with him." He started to turn away, but then he paused. "If you want to be happy in Far West, you best forget you even know that bunch of dissenters. They've caused enough trouble around here. The first presidency has suffered enough grief at their hands, and they're not making any bones about the purge. The purge will continue as long as we get men who can do nothing except buck the presidency."

"The purge?"

"The salt that has lost its savor is fit only to be trampled. Or hung."

Mark and Jenny slowly eased back into the line of wagons already heading out of Far West, cutting north toward the Grand River.

Jenny tried to keep her troubled thoughts to herself and concentrate on the changing scenery, but over and over the words moved through her thoughts. *Purge. If the salt has lost its savor. . . .*

They were on the prairie again, and the view before her caught her attention. In this place the tall grasses were filled with color. Like a giant carpet, the wild flowers had painted a design that changed with every fancy of the wind. First blue, then sunrise rose pushed through, and finally golden blossoms of varying intensity became evident.

Startled wildlife fled the area, protesting with honks and crashing hoofbeats. Mark pointed his whip at the awkward rush of a wild turkey.

True to the man's word, in less than a week, Mark and Jenny were settling on their own acreage.

On the northern bank of Grand River, close to the little town with the strange name, Mark and Jenny found the section allotted to them. No matter that Joseph didn't appear and give them a choice. Like the others, they took their place in line and waited to be led to their homes.

They pulled their wagon into the clearing facing the river, and that first morning Jenny stood looking over her domain. She was still deeply conscious of the little stone cottage they had left behind, but now she was being caught up in the poetry of this place.

From undulating grasses to dark-hued trees, from rolling prairie to rearing stony cliffs, there was a theme that wrapped itself around Jenny leaving her wide-eyed and on emotional tiptoe.

As she faced the west, behind her the water of Grand River crashed and roared, while before her the dark trees whispered in the gentle breeze. Even now, in the beginning days, she felt she knew it all as a soul-deep experience.

"Oh, Mark," she whispered, "may we stay forever?"

When he turned she saw first his puzzled expression and then as he looked across the water, the deepening quiet began moving into his eyes. Looking out over the tumbling river he said softly, "It seems like heaven; but, my dear, we will be hard-pressed to make it so."

As if loathe to move away from the spot, for the two weeks which followed, Mark and Jenny stirred about their acres, learning it all, loving each tree and bush.

One day, watching Mark in his beginning efforts to clear land for a cabin, Jenny giggled, and when he looked at her, she said, "I was thinking, we're making a nest as if we're reluctant to move a twig out of its precious spot."

Mark wiped perspiration out of his eyes and nodded. His only answer was a kiss pressed quickly against her cheek as he reached for the axe.

While Mark continued to cut trees and tried to hide the crime, Jenny stacked river stones into a beehive of an oven. She reordered her wagon into a home while Mark removed its wheels and fashioned them and part of the box into a reasonable buggy.

And then it was Independence Day. From the first day of their arrival in Far West, they had been regaled with the glory of the celebration planned for Far West.

Jenny and Mark took a holiday from their house building, and early the morning of July Fourth, they joined the crowd moving toward Far West.

"Mrs. Cartwright, how festive you look!" Mark grinned down at her as he guided the crude buggy on its maiden voyage. "You look fresh out of *Harper's Bazaar*. No one will guess you've bathed in river water, with a laundry tub for a bathtub."

"And despite your calluses, you look more the fine gentleman than a bumbling farmer."

"I'm not even a bumbling farmer yet. And I won't be that for long if I can help it."

"You think there will be a place for you with Joseph?"

He shrugged and eased the buggy onto the main road heading toward Far West. They were silent until the road smoothed and then Jenny asked, "Have you heard about the program for the day?"

"Only hints. I know the ground-breaking for the temple is to take place. I know there will be speeches and food and quite a little horsing around. I'd almost guarantee you that Joseph will start a wrestling match and that someone will grease the new flagpole and wager against anyone climbing it."

Jenny patted the bundle covered with a tablecloth. "I hope this cake is good. I've never before baked a cake in a stone oven."

"I doubt you are alone in that. At least you have the sugar and flour—some don't have that."

"Seems strange to see stores so empty of food—and everything else except shovels and scythes, harnesses and ammunition. Joseph must plan for us to kill our daily bread." She leaned forward to look at Mark's face. "Mark, are things bad for people?"

"Of course, but then what would you expect? Many have expended themselves completely in order to make this journey."

They had nearly reached the outskirts of Far West when Jenny realized the line of buggies and wagons in front of them had slowed. "What is the problem?" she asked, stretching to see ahead.

"People," Mark replied. "In this one spot there're more people than we've seen in a long time."

"All Saints?" Mark didn't answer; he was leaning over the edge of the buggy to talk to the man who had run forward.

"You people Saints?" At Mark's nod, the man continued, "Joseph's having us all in the parade. Join the group ahead and go to the edge of town. We're marching to the temple site for the laying of the cornerstone. There's a pack of Gentiles here, and he's set on giving them an eye- and earful. Let no man doubt the strength of the Saints after today."

When Mark and Jenny joined the crowd, Jenny began eagerly scanning the group, looking for Kirtland friends.

Then she saw the trio of dark-coated men and unexpectedly her heart quickened its beat. While she was seeking out Joseph's face, she frowned, dismayed by the unexpected response of her errant heart. But her attention was quickly captured as Joseph turned his face toward her.

She studied the tall figure and bright hair. Beside him stood his brother Hyrum, and Sidney Rigdon. As she watched, a group of men stepped in front of the trio. She looked them over and asked, "Who are those men standing just in front of the first presidency? Those ragged-looking fellows with the guns?"

"I don't know," Mark murmured.

"Them's the infantry," the old fellow beside Mark said proudly. "Gideon's band, the Danites, whatever you want to call them. They look right ready to defend the Prophet, don't they?"

Mark's answer was drowned by the shouts of the horsemen cantering toward them. The old man added, "The cavalry's to bring up the end, so's we best be getting in line or they'll go off and leave us."

As they marched through the streets, Jenny was deeply aware of the line of men standing at the edge of the road. She knew they were not Saints. They not only looked rough, she decided, observing their scowling frowns; they also didn't look as if they had come to enjoy the celebration. She noted several kept their hands fastened firmly around the guns they carried. Jenny's uneasiness grew as they continued down the street.

Only a few of these Gentiles were women. She spotted them dotting the crowd. As she studied them, Jenny realized they varied from the weatherbeaten ones wearing homespun and bewildered faces, to hard-faced women, corseted and wearing flamboyant hats decorated with plumes.

Jenny was so caught staring at these women that she stubbed her toe on a rock. Mark grasped her arm and with a grin asked, "Haven't you ever seen a fancy lady before?"

They had reached the end of the parade route and people clumped together. Jenny had only begun to recognize some of her Kirtland friends when the mass of people parted and Jenny saw they stood on the rim of a large hole.

She arched her eyebrows and Mark whispered, "The excavation for the temple."

When the silence became oppressive, a solemn-faced Rigdon took his place and spread his crackling papers. "Better, far better," he cried, lifting his face toward the sky, "to sleep with the dead than to be oppressed among the living."

The shock of his words swept through the crowd. Jenny felt it and was caught by the expression and murmurs of those around her. Soon she realized that after his glorious beginning, she had nearly lost the thread of the speech until she heard, "Our cheeks have been given to the smiters—time after time, again and again. I advise you, this we will do no more. Let there be a mob come upon us to disturb us again and I advise you"— he paused and leaned forward to fasten the crowd with an unwavering stare—"that mob we will follow until the last drop of their blood is shed. It will be a war of extermination. We will carry the war to them, one and all. One or the other of us will cease to exist. We will, remember, my men, not be the aggressors, but we'll stand for our own kind until death." His voice was hoarse and cracking as he concluded, "On this day we proclaim ourselves free—our determination will never, no, never be broken."

The crowd cheered and shouted, "Hosanna, hosanna to God and to the Lamb!" Jenny stood transfixed, watching as the Gentiles, hands on guns, melted away in the crowd and disappeared. For a moment, as she shivered and hugged her arms, Mark looked at her. She saw the darkness in his eyes and turned away.

But the shouting crowd had set the holiday mood. Joseph built upon it with his address, although secretly Jenny thought only his presence was necessary to bring his people to a state of adoring frenzy.

Nevertheless, there were his words, giving out the revelation in slow majestic tones that seemed to roll over the people, building in volume. He stood, hands clasped behind his black-clad figure, his head thrown back, saying, "My beloved Saints, I want you to hear from the Lord just how precious in His sight are the events transpiring here today. First off, He has instructed me of a name change. Henceforth the church is to be known as the Church of Jesus Christ of the Latter-Day Saints. His word to me is that the city of Far West is holy and consecrated land. It shall be called most holy. The very ground whereon it stands is holy. Next, He commands that we build a house to Him. Today we laid the cornerstone. In one year from last April 26, He commands that we commence building. From that time until it is finished, the work must continue. The counsel of men has been thwarted, but now is the appointed time. Saints from all over the world are commanded to assist in the building."

He paused and looked over the crowd. "Our Lord instructs us in the manner in which He will allow His house to be built. This most holy place will be acceptable to Him only if we carefully follow His instructions in the building of it. He has laid careful plans for the financing of our building."

When the last speech was ended, the crowd broke, separated, and regrouped. For many of the new settlers, this was the first occasion for visiting. As they moved through the crowd, Jenny and Mark were seeing many of their Kirtland friends for the first time since the wagon train had divided. At the time, a hint of coolness in the reunion was overlooked in the excitement of being together again. Only in looking back was Jenny able to identify it.

Just as Mark had promised, there were all the foolish, lighthearted displays of valor. It was very late before Mark and Jenny started their return trip the thirteen miles home, and then Jenny mulled over the slight.

Mark answered her question with a short comment. "Could be, not that they were shunning, but that there's a fear abroad of being labeled dissenter. You've heard the talk. There's fierce and abiding loyalty demanded here. Jenny, already I detect a touch of cynicism in the Prophet." Slowly Mark added, "He's no longer the jolly Prophet I first met. I would say he's felt badly used and will try his best to avoid being seen as soft."

"Soft?" she repeated.

"The opposite of hard as nails," he said in a teasing voice. In the twilight he looked at her thoughtfully and in a gentle voice he added, "Perhaps it's just that Joseph has lost some of the stars in his eyes. Might be that now he sees himself and others in a more realistic way."

Three days later a storm tore through Far West. Some said the Lord was hurling his thunderbolts at the city. Saints shivered in their cabins, wondering at the fury of the Lord's actions.

And when the storm was over, the liberty pole in the center of Far West's town square was shattered on the ground. Some whispered it was an evil omen and they couldn't help thinking it was signaling the end of freedom in Missouri.

In Adam-ondi-Ahman there was a rumor abroad. Mark reported it to Jenny. "They're saying Joseph is getting ready to reveal revelations from the Lord regarding the new United Order. You know Cowdery and Whitmer predicted this. They're giving out hints that indicate there's a significant benefit for us all."

Jenny looked up at him and said, "You're not believing that, are you?"

"No, like the dissenters, I believe every man should hold his own land. Besides, I believe Joseph and Rigdon are assuming too much control. If this keeps up, we'll all be wooden puppets."

Far West had scarcely time enough to settle into the post-Independence Day routine when Joseph announced the new order.

On July 8, he called together the church members. Standing before the assembled people, he read the revelation, calling upon the Saints to deed their property to the church. As she listened, Jenny was thinking of all the land just purchased by the Kirtland wagon train.

From behind her came a mutter, "This is a fine time to pull that. The bunch from Kirtland's just sunk a big bundle into land over at Adam-ondi-Ahman. The Saints pay Missouri for land and then turn around and give it to the Prophet."

Jenny moved her shoulders restlessly and tried to ignore the man behind her. She glanced around the vast group, trying to pick out her friends in that sea of faces. Where were Sally and Andy? She hadn't seen them on Independence Day. What had happened to those disgruntled foes of Cowdery, Johnson, and the Whitmers? What about old Mrs. Applewaite? Joseph surely wouldn't be asking for the property of the old and poor!

Now the Prophet was explaining that in return for their deed of property, each Saint would receive a deed for an everlasting inheritance. "The real property," Joseph called it. The surplus property—which was the Saints' donation to the church—was to remain in the hands of the bishop, to be used in building the temple and for supporting the church presidency, as well as laying the foundation of Zion.

In front of Jenny a man in a tattered shirt snorted and said, "And then on top of that there's the tithing we'll be having to pay on the everlasting inheritance. I can't give my family a decent life now, and look at the Prophet in his pretty black coat. He's never had it so good. I remember when he was a barefoot boy like my young'uns. Propheting is good business."

There was a low voice coming from behind Jenny. "Hansen, watch your complaints; even the ground has ears." The complainer drifted away as Rigdon stood to speak.

Jenny was watching Hansen as he limped away, but she turned back as Sidney Rigdon's voice rose. "I prophesy, just as surely as I stand here, those who fail to heed the warnings from the Lord will lose their property to Gentile thieves and robbers. I can assure you"—his voice dropped and he leaned across the podium—"sooner or later, those who refuse to comply will be surrendered to the brothers of Gideon."

From behind Jenny came the hiss, "The Danites."

Later, when the vote was taken, the Saints had voted unanimously to consecrate their property to the church.

On the way home, Jenny broke the silence. "Mark, what do you know about these Danites, or brothers of Gideon?"

Quietly, he replied, "I don't know, Jenny. But I intend to investigate the matter."

Thinking of the dissenters, Jenny whispered, "Mark, be careful." For a moment, as she continued to watch him, Jenny thought again of her resolve to see Joseph. With a sigh she turned away, wondering why she felt as if she were being pulled in two.

"What?" She questioned, realizing she hadn't been listening to Mark.

He was shaking his head, and then with a frown he added, "I will be careful, Jenny, my girl."

And then in another moment, she added with a sigh, "At least you voted to consecrate your property to the church."

He chuckled, "I haven't given a bride price yet—I think it

will be worth it. Besides, right now, they aren't getting much. I've done little to improve the place except to pull out a few trees to clear a place for our cabin."

"It will be wonderful to have a cozy home before winter. That storm two weeks ago was an awful warning of what the winter will hold. Right now I just wish Tom would get here with the furniture. I'm worried about him."

"I think Tom can take care of himself. It isn't the first trip he's made out here." Mark was quiet for a moment and then slowly, thoughtfully, he said, "So the Prophet plans to acquire all land in a twelve-mile radius around each stake of Zion. That's our property, in the name of the church."

CHAPTER 8

When Tom pulled the heavily loaded wagon into Far West, the place seemed little like the sleepy western town he had left at spring planting time.

Tom had been in on the birth-pains of this village just one year ago when Jackson County Mormons had moved into the area. From a clearing marked with tiny, crude cabins, Far West had grown into a presentable town with sturdy cabins and acres of tilled land. Even the first season crops had been good.

Although it wasn't until this spring that Joseph Smith had finally moved to Far West from Kirtland, Ohio, he had been responsible for the planning of the town. Wisely, Tom admitted with pride, Joseph had laid out the town with large lots and wide streets.

Tom knew that initially the area had been settled with fifteen hundred citizens. Since the exodus from Kirtland, Ohio, had begun, he had lost all count of the emigrants who had moved into Caldwell County and subsequently settled in the surrounding counties.

Looking around, Tom decided any man would find Far West a town to be proud of. Tom knew the Saints' industry had aroused the envy of Gentile neighbors. Besides the one large building serving multiple purposes and the scattering of little log huts, stocked with a goodly supply of every commodity necessary on the frontier, the Saints had also built a schoolhouse. Just this spring the basement of the temple had been excavated shortly before Joseph had moved his family to Far West.

Now Tom guided his team toward the town square, sawed

on the reins, and scratched his head. The once-towering liberty pole in the center of the square was a splintery stub the size of a fence post. "Me thinks," he said slowly, "that the town of Far West has had some interesting life lately."

He headed for the long, low-slung log building which housed post office, saloon, and general store.

When he settled himself at the bar and ordered bacon and eggs, he said, "So, Mike, what's been happening in Caldwell County since I left? Specifically, who tore the flagpole down?"

Mike shrugged. "They're saying the Almighty. But 'twas lightning."

When Mike went back to polishing glasses, Tom concluded his question had been answered and went on to the next. "Wagon train from Kirtland arrive?"

Mike nodded. "While back Joseph completed dickering for land over Adam-ondi-Ahman way. He sent them up that way to buy their lots. Some of the die-hards in the bunch objected to being pointed in the direction Joe wanted them to go. Seems they wanted to settle closer to Far West."

"Spring Hill area, huh?"

"Don't let Joe hear you call it that. He's trying hard to get the Jackson crowd to calling it by its new name, seein' the place has something to do with Adam building that altar up the hill aways." His voice was dry.

"How do the Gentiles feel?"

"Excepting me?"

"I keep forgetting you're a Gentile—fact, I think you'd make a pretty good Mormon. Wanna join?"

Mike chuckled and shook his head. "More interesting just to watch. Them others? Mad. More mad because it was Joe sayin' that's where old Adam came out of the Garden of Eden and built an altar to worship Jehovah; he advised us 'tis prophesied through Joseph that Adam, the ancient of days, will return there to visit his people, sittin' on a fiery throne of flame, like is predicted by Daniel."

Mike snorted softly. "Old Handley, he's a Gentile, he's been tellin' me that Ancient of Days means God, and ole Adam sure ain't God." He shrugged, and his eyes were carefully examining

Tom. "Where you been, watcha been doin'?"

Tom had just started on his plate of eggs when the door behind him creaked open. Mike's face brightened. "Joe!"

Tom stood and pumped the large hand of the Prophet. "Hey, Joe, it's good to see you!"

Joseph slid onto the stool beside Tom and accepted the glass Mike shoved toward him. "So, you've been gone a long time. How's things in Kirtland?"

"Ghost town."

"I can't feel sorry; they've brought the troubles upon themselves. Now I know how deep a man's loyalty goes—just as deep as his pocket. Satan buffeted me sorely there with the money problems, but now that's all behind me—why did it take you so long to get back?"

Tom waved toward the town square. "I brought back a load of furniture for my brother-in-law. Also, I tried to sell their house while I was there. There's just no buyers."

"I gave specific instructions concerning that." Joseph's voice was sharp. "The Lord said just leave the places if they couldn't be sold. I know it seems hard to us, but if that's His will—" He shrugged. In another moment he asked, "Mark, huh? He and his wife moved out this way? I didn't know they were here. I'll have to see them."

"Mark going to be working for you again?"

There was a long pause, then Joe slowly said, "He's a lawyer, isn't he? I'm thinking myself that Rigdon and I should be studying law. Sure's anything, we're going to need all the law knowledge we can get. We've been thrown a few loops already. We need to be on our toes."

Tom finished his egg. "Where you livin'?"

Joe looked as if he'd just come back into the room; he slowly focused on Tom and said, "Living? With the George Harris family, just a couple of miles outta town. Emma's just produced another son for me. Things are going well, and I plan on building my own place pretty soon."

"Harris," Tom said slowly. "Is his wife that pretty gal who used to be married to the anti-mason fella who got murdered? Think Morgan was his name."

"That's the one."

"She's a right pretty gal." Tom stood up and reached for coins. "This is quite an interesting place. Looks like the biggest building in Far West now, since that section was added on."

"It is. Come look around." Tom followed Joseph to the other end of the long dark building. Rows of shelves and piles of barrels formed narrow aisles which, Tom saw with surprise, unexpectedly opened into a wide space in front of a second stone fireplace. There was a table littered with papers and books. An easy chair was drawn close to the fireplace.

Tom said, "I'm guessing I've just discovered your hideout."

"And it will be until there's time to build a proper office building."

They walked back to the bar and Joseph pointed to the line of pigeon holes. " 'Tis a post office too." He turned to Tom. "What's your plan now?"

"Find Mark and get rid of my load. Then look for a way to occupy my time."

"I've got you tagged."

"What d' ya mean?"

Joe jerked his head toward the door and with a shrug toward Mike, Tom followed him out the door.

Behind him he heard Mike say, "Looks like Joe's tagged another one for his Danite group."

Jenny stood in the clearing and looked around. Although it was only the second week in August, on their bluff overlooking the Grand River she sensed a touch of autumn coolness in the air.

Behind her the neat little cabin was rising in the clearing Mark had hacked out of the woods. He had hired two men to help him with the construction. Just today the three of them finished lifting the last log into place. Jenny was hoping that by tomorrow they would be ready to use the pile of shingles Mark had been cutting and stacking to dry.

She raised her hands to her mouth and called, "Mark! Men! Come to dinner!" She knew she needn't call a second time. With a smile she turned back to her stone oven and checked the bread browning within.

"Miz Cartwright, that bread sure smells good."

It was John, the youngest member of the building team. Jenny had known his family in Kirtland; in fact, his mother had been Jenny's greatest nursing failure. She still winced thinking about Annie. With a sigh, Jenny turned away from the thoughts and went to lift the pot of meat and vegetables from the fire.

Mark was beside her now, carrying the heavy pot to the crude table. When he brought the jug of milk from the stream cutting through their property he said, "Jenny, you won't even have a chance to get your nose nipped by frost before you move into your new castle. By the way, you can start chinking anytime now."

Jenny wrinkled her nose in pretended disdain. "I'd thought myself too old to play in the mud."

Homer cleared his throat. The older man was graying and bent, but after watching him wrestle the heavy logs, Jenny realized he was still powerful. His words were so few that when he spoke everyone took notice. Today he said, "I hear the election in Gallatin didn't go well."

"That's the county seat of Daviess County," John informed Jenny.

She passed him the bread and replied, "I know. We've been there. Not much of a town for a county seat. Ten houses, and three of them saloons. I couldn't even buy a hank of thread there."

Mark's words were overlapping hers, and she heard the tension in them. "What do you mean, Homer?"

"The Saints round about decided to vote. First time in five years, since that time in Jackson County. They weren't supposed to."

"One of the stipulations?"

He nodded and continued. "Now Joseph Smith's moved out here from Ohio, things are different."

"How's that?"

With his head to one side, he paused to think. Casting a

quick, almost apologetic glance at Mark he said, "I don't rightly know. Don't want to pin any blame on the presidency, but we were all treadin' lightly.

"Seems in general, since this place was to be Zion, we needed to be making the best of the situation. People movin' from Jackson to Caldwell County had one desire—that was to make a go of clearing their land and buildin' up their places. They were tryin' hard to get along with everyone."

He paused for a moment while he used bread to sop up the last of his gravy. "It's like peace fled since he came. Take the Danites. None of us gave a thought to such a thing—an army to scourge those who disagreed, sending them fleein' for their lives?"

Mark was leaning forward now. "What about Jared Carter?"

The man's expression was wary but he answered Mark, "Started out to be the big shot in the Danite group. See, you have to understand the oaths they take."

John's eyes were focused on Homer as he slowly said, "But the Lord's raised up a prophet. 'Tis only right we give him the best."

Homer's eyes were steely as he leaned across the table and demanded, "Boy, did you join up?"

John shook his head. "My pa wouldn't let me. But one of my friends who joined says with all the fussin' and rumbling goin' on, soon all the fellas will be *required*."

Homer's eyes were still holding John's as he said, "The oaths instruct that a man not question nothin', not even the orders given, whether they agree or not. No one is to speak evil of the presidency, every fella's to be completely subject to their control. The secrets of the bunch are not to be let out on pain of death."

When the silence became uneasy Mark prompted, "Carter?"

"He complained to Joseph about something Rigdon said." Homer paused for a moment before he added, "He was dumped as leader. According to Danite principles he should have been killed. Peck told me himself that Carter deserved death according to the oaths. Joe admitted he should have cut his throat but didn't do it. They had a trial in front of the Danites, and Huntington said at the trial he came within a hair of losing his head."

The memory of that conversation was still with Jenny that next week when Tom came.

"How did you find us?" Jenny cried. "I'd nearly given up on you."

"Joe gave me a clue. It'd help if you were a little more friendly with the neighbors. Nobody in Adam-ondi-Ahman had heard about you."

"But they are mostly Gentile."

"Not now. There's several families from Kirtland livin' just a couple of miles away. The Hansens, and the Lewis family."

Jenny could see Tom was thin, and he looked strained and tired. Jenny led him into her house and seated him at the table. "You can live with us. There's not much room, but you could sleep in the loft."

He was shaking his head as he helped himself to the bread Jenny placed in front of him. "Too far for me to be travelin' back and forth."

"What are you doing?"

"Shoeing a few horses, pounding some nails, and plowing a few acres."

"You bought land?"

"Naw, just helping my friends."

"It doesn't sound like much."

He finished eating his slice of bread and drained the cup of milk. "You got yourselves a cow?"

"Yes, chickens too." There was laughter in her voice. "Oh, Tom, you should have seen Mark struggling to be a farmer. He didn't know how to milk a cow. He's just not cut out for the plowing and such."

"I 'spect Joe'll be tappin' him on the shoulder. Way things are goin' around here, there'll be clashes, and Joe needs all the legal help he can get."

Jenny stopped to look at Tom, her eyes searching for clues in his face as she said, "It seems all we've been hearing the past few weeks is fearful rumbles about trouble between the Saints and the Gentiles. What is causing this? All the Saints I know want nothing but peace and a chance to have a decent life." She paused, but when he didn't answer, she asked, "How do you know Joe needs legal help?"

He didn't pretend innocence. "I've joined the Danites." When he saw that she understood, he added, "We're keepin' busy, such as the Gallatin affair."

"Old Homer Thompson mentioned Gallatin when he was over helping Mark build the cabin. The conversation got sidetracked and I didn't realize until later that he'd never finished his story. What happened when the Mormons tried to vote?"

Tom leaned back and whistled softly. "You *are* isolated up here." He got to his feet and paced to the fireplace and back. "In Gallatin not too much happened. Oh, there were a few heads cracked and then the Saints were allowed to vote. It was the stories that circulated afterward that did the damage. It's like there's a bunch of soreheads out there just waitin' to swing their fists."

"Mormons, too?"

"Yes, I believe so." He was quiet for a moment. Jenny watched him chew at his lip, but she couldn't guess the reason behind it. "Though there were only a few heads that got knocked and a few insults spilled, rumor was there were men killed. I talked to John Lee later while he was busy tryin' to calm Joe down before he did more damage."

"More damage," Jenny said in a low voice. "What did he do?"

"Joe was told that Justice of the Peace, Adam Black, was gettin' together the Gentiles to chase the Mormons out of Adamondi-Ahman."

"But that's us!" Jenny's hand clenched over her mouth.

Tom continued. "Result was, Joe took his army and headed for Gallatin. The beggars took to the woods like scared chickens. But Joe couldn't be content to let sleepin' dogs lie, and he strong-armed his way into Black's cabin."

He paused before saying soberly, "This took place after he went to Adam-ondi-Ahman and found out the rumors were false." Tom took up his pacing again.

Finally he said, "Shoulda had sense to head for home. Anyhow, he forced Black to sign a paper sayin' there would be peace. As soon as he was out the door, things started rollin'. Old Black went a stompin' out of there and got up a warrant for Joseph's arrest."

"I—" Jenny paused listening. "That must be Mark. He's been into town." She moved to the door just as Mark appeared in the doorway. "What's wrong?" Jenny whispered.

Mark was still frowning as he lifted his face and looked around the room. "Tom, I'd heard that you were back in the state." He threw a quick glance at Jenny and answered, "I've just come from the miller's. Things are bad. Joseph was arrested for strong-arming Justice Black the other day. There was a trial but he got off with only a fine. They could have done much worse. It was brought out that the Saints were crossing county lines with arms. That's a pretty serious offense in Missouri."

Tom responded, "Yes, we were there, tucked just over the county line to make sure no one tried to do in our Prophet."

Jenny moved impatiently, "Oh, Tom! No one's going to kill the Prophet. Don't be so morbid."

Mark's steady eyes moved from one to the other. Finally he spoke. "Perhaps not do him in, but he's causing trouble for the rest of us. There's not a miller in this end of the state who'll grind a sack of wheat for us."

After Tom had left, Jenny faced Mark and said, "I didn't realize we were so cut off from all that's been going on. It's my fault. I like being up here alone, feeling like I was part of the whole universe, and that only we existed in this whole world—" Jenny paused, realizing Mark was looking at her with a strange expression.

In a moment he said, "It's my fault. Partly it's because there's not a newspaper in the area. But I don't intend to be left in the dust again. First thing, lady, we're going into Far West and see Joseph or someone who'll tell us what's going on."

"Tom told me Joseph and Sidney Rigdon are intending to study law. They've talked to Doniphan and believe that with hard work they'll be able to—to accomplish this within a year. He also said Joseph indicated he'd probably be seeing you, because he thought they'd be needing all the legal help they could get."

It was a long time before Mark's resolution to see Joseph was carried out. But late that same night Tom again paid them a visit.

He faced the groggy couple and said, "If I'd been a Missourian intending to take your life or steal your goods, you'd be easy prey. Get out, Mark and Jenny. Do you understand? The Gentiles are heading this way. Soon DeWitt and Adam-ondi-Ahman will be under attack."

While Jenny shivered in her shawl, Mark passed his hands over his face and sighed. Going to the fireplace, he pushed at the slumbering log and then turned. Slowly Mark said, "Tom, this is unbelievable. Things just don't happen like this. Under attack? Surely you're overrating a hot-headed fisticuffs."

Tom was shaking his head. Jenny could see her brother was trying to remain calm, and that was even more frightening. Tom said, "It's all because a bunch of hot-headed Missourians want the Saints to get out of their precious state and leave them alone. It started years ago with them fearin' that Mormons would work to free all the slaves in the state; from then it snowballed into fearin' we'd shove the Missourians out. All we want is peace and quiet."

"All?" Mark asked softly. "What about Zion? What about the Saints making no bones about saying the lands and riches of the Gentiles had been given to them by the Lord?"

Tom was quiet for a moment. Now calm, he answered thoughtfully, "It's the truth. We are the people of God and the place is ours. But I guess you're right. Comin' in here and—" He sighed deeply and said, "We've got ourselves into a fix. I'm supposin' we'll end up fightin' ourselves outta it."

While they watched him, Tom paced nervously back and forth. Now his voice rose again. "These madmen will not be satisfied until every home is burned and every Mormon driven into the wilderness." He whirled on Mark. "It's the Gentiles turned against us, just like it was in Jackson County." He paused to take a deep, ragged breath and then in a low voice said, "Mark, take her and go. Guard my sister. She's all I've got."

CHAPTER 9

Jenny stood in her doorway and breathed deeply of the crisp morning air. In the distance she could hear the crash of Grand River. Its turbulence was intimidating, but on the bluff high above the river, surrounded by the pine forest, Jenny felt safe.

Mark had chosen to build the cabin on a slight rise, where the morning sun drenched the logs with warmth and the one large window with light. This morning she felt the warmth of the sun on her face as she tilted her head to see the birds. They were disrupting the quiet of the forest, filling the air with their feisty complaints. Now she saw that the squirrels were causing the upset. She chuckled as a jay swooped down on his adversary.

Behind Jenny the pine fire was crackling in the fireplace and the kettle began to steam. With contented eyes, she turned to look around the room. "Not a bad job of chinking for a beginner," she murmured, but she was measuring the effect of bright quilts and shiny china against the rough bark of the walls.

The aroma of fresh wood still lingered about the cabin. Often at the most unexpected times, Jenny found herself touching fresh pitch, but it was a minor inconvenience.

She was happily aware of harmony in the mix of her belongings, Mark's saddle and rifle, and the polished rocking chair. She heaved a contented sigh. It was good to be in Zion and settled in her own home. " 'Tis a spot of heaven on earth."

Mark pushed through the open door with an armload of milled lumber. "Oh, there you are," Jenny said turning with a smile. "I heard the axe. You've been out there for ages. What is that?"

He was leaning the planks against the wall beside the window. "I'm building shutters." He began making marks on the log walls.

Jenny watched another moment and then said, "I'd rather have them outside. They are terribly heavy, but hang them on the casing. It seems more fitting. Also, could we paint them blue?"

When Mark turned, she saw him take a deep patient breath before he said, "Jenny, these shutters aren't for beauty. They are to—to keep people out."

"Mark!"

He rushed on before she could say more. "I was in Adam-ondi-Ahman yesterday long enough to hear some things that kept me awake most of the night. Jenny, there's going to be trouble very soon. I don't understand it all, but I'm making this place just as safe as possible. That window is big enough to let an army through. These shutters will at least slow them down."

Jenny blinked at Mark's serious face, and all the silly, light-hearted words that had tumbled to her lips were forgotten.

She watched the distant expression steal over his eyes. It was a look most apt to leave Jenny feeling left out, separated by unseen barriers. She whispered, "What is it, Mark? What are you thinking?"

He looked at her in surprise, and as she watched the change in his eyes, she realized he didn't recognize these times when his spirit fled away to an unknown place she couldn't follow. She touched his arm, feeling the familiar warmth, very conscious of knowing the man but not the soul of him.

She saw the caution, the hesitation, and then he said softly, "You really want to know? Jenny, can you—" He paused and walked a step away. When he turned to face her, his eyes were bright with an expression she couldn't understand. Mute, she waited.

"I was just thinking about homes, shelter. I suppose, back in the beginning, man's initial need for shelter was *against* wild animals and *for* his family. Here I'm getting ready to put up shutters, not to keep out the wild animals, but my fellowman. Jenny, that ought not to be. Anywhere. But it seems to me that in the Lord's Zion, it hadn't ought to be at all. Aren't you a mite disappointed in Zion?"

Jenny reluctantly said, "Well, yes. But Mark, didn't we have false hopes?"

"What was your hope?"

She spoke slowly, trying to pull deeply buried disappointments out to study them. "First, I suppose, since it's the Lord's place, and we are *commanded* to build it up, and we've all the revelations saying the land is ours and the wealth is ours, well—" She met his eyes and took a deep breath. "Oh, Mark, nothing is going right! It's scary! Since we've been here, there's more grumbling and fears than I've ever heard before in my life."

She stared at him silently, wanting to point at the fearful times in Kirtland just before Joseph had left. But Mark didn't know about those times. Surely it wouldn't do to mention it now. Also, it wasn't possible to tell him about the dreadful need for power, because he wouldn't approve of her power source.

Now she spoke quickly, wanting only to divert Mark's questions away from herself. "But you were thinking. What is it?"

"I was comparing all this with what I've been learning about God." Jenny moved impatiently and Mark spoke quickly, his voice sharp, "You've asked, and I think you need to hear me out. Jenny, I've been reading about a God of love, about a Savior named Jesus Christ who says if you love Me, prove it by your love for others. Where's Joseph's love? Why are the old-timers in the state—those Joseph sent out here in the early thirties to settle in Jackson County—saying that things were calming down and getting peaceful until Joseph came? Why were these same people content with life until he came? Jenny, I'm comparing my Bible with Joseph's golden one, and I don't like the difference. I fail to see where his gold book and his revelations have produced a holy people." He turned to pace the floor and his voice was low. "Jenny, these people around us matter. It isn't right to take their land and goods, to consign them to hell just because they disagree with us. Even Jesus Christ didn't force people to accept Him, and He was God, with the holy mission of dying for our sins."

Jenny heard Mark's words, but more than the words, she felt the impact of his expression: the sudden heavy lines twisting his face, the shadows in his eyes, the imploring hands that he lifted before shaking his head helplessly; Jenny saw clearly for one moment a strange darkness surrounding them.

But his words were lost as she shivered and turned away. Briefly she felt as if a curtain had been lifted, and she didn't like what she had seen. He whispered, "Jenny, forgive me. It's a load you aren't able to bear. The dear Lord himself wants me to restrain my hand." She looked and he was holding out his arms. Because there was no place to flee, she ran into them. And in another moment she lifted her face. "Mark," she whispered urgently, "please don't repeat this—I don't want you to be labeled a dissenter. That's what you are when you talk like Joseph isn't really a prophet from the Lord."

After breakfast, when the dishes had been washed and Mark was busy fastening heavy hinges to the wall, Jenny took her place beside him and reached for the screws. Trying desperately to forget his fearful words, with her voice low, she said, "Don't you think you'd better tell me all you've heard?"

When he turned to study her face, he said slowly, "I've been trying to think of some way to get out of the state without causing alarm among our neighbors or outrage in Joseph's camp."

"Mark, we've been here only two and a half months!" Even as she spoke, she was hastily pushing Mark's words and the black picture out of her mind. "How silly to give up before we've even tried to make a success of settling Zion. I know neither one of us is the adventuresome type, but, after all, the Prophet has said God commanded we settle and build up Zion." Her voice was dreamy as she continued, "This is God's kingdom; we will have power—"

"Jenny, every once in a while you mention having power. I am growing curious; just what do you mean?"

Jenny opened her eyes wide and looked at the frown on Mark's face. For a moment she felt trapped. "Oh," she said quickly, "it's not *political*, it's spiritual. Mark," she added brightly, "at times I feel we're miles apart spiritually."

"Yes," he said slowly, "I feel the same way." He turned back to his work.

Jenny watched for a time before saying, "Besides, I love it here in our cozy cabin, away from the push of people. I like having you all to myself. I like nature and the quiet. It makes me come alive."

He turned to pinch her cheek, "You really are part owl, aren't you?"

"If you weren't fearful for me, you'd stay, wouldn't you?"

Without answering her question, he said, "There were a bunch of strangers in town yesterday. Men I didn't recognize. From the expressions on their faces, I don't think they were interested in making my acquaintance."

When she remained silent, he added, "There are other things—rumbles, discontentment. You know the agreement between the Saints and the state of Missouri, set up to settle the Jackson problem. The stipulation was that the Mormons were to move to Caldwell County. Now Joseph's strong-armed himself into this place, Daviess County. The old settlers around here are angry because of the large number of Saints emigrating into the area. I can't say I blame them. The Gallatin situation, with the Missourians fighting our men when they came to vote, shows how fearful they are of the type of control Joseph has placed on the people."

"They'll just have to learn to like it," Jenny said impatiently. "I'm convinced, Mark, that Joseph is obeying the Lord." She lifted her chin, and when he said nothing, she continued, "It's His will that Joseph be leader in temporal as well as kingdom affairs."

"But in truth it's going against the constitutional right of man to think and act for himself. That was the whole problem at Gallatin. The Missourians knew the Saints weren't voting any conscience except Joseph's."

"Mark, that is a harsh statement. You best make certain that the walls haven't ears to carry the news back to Joseph."

"And that, my dear wife, is precisely what I mean." Mark turned away, shoulders hunched.

Jenny stated, "You might as well say it. Agree or disagree,

it's better'n stewing over it. It didn't take your conversation with Tom to tell me we don't see eye to eye."

"Jenny, let's leave. I feel the Lord urging this on me."

She looked at him curiously for a moment before asking, "How can you say God is putting this on you when you know Joseph'll object?" Mark's long look was thoughtful. Jenny watched as he pressed his lips tightly together.

He turned back to the shutters and she watched him work silently. When he finally turned with an exasperated sigh, she had guessed the problem. "They are too heavy for those hinges, aren't they?"

"Looks like I need to make another trip into Adam-ondi-Ahman for hinges."

"Oh, Mark, take me with you." She saw his eyebrows raise at the unusual request. "I need thread, besides—"

"I was going to ride Sammy. I suppose we could take the wagon."

"I don't mind riding Patches," Jenny protested.

The memory of the look Mark gave her stayed with Jenny as they rode into the small village. He hadn't questioned her, and Jenny couldn't explain the need to push herself back into life and discover for herself just what was happening. It wasn't that she doubted the stories she had been hearing, she insisted to herself as she hurried the mare along.

"Adam-ondi-Ahman," she murmured to herself as they entered town, "the place where Adam settled after being expelled from the garden." It *was* different. From a pleasant village with Gentiles and Saints on nodding acquaintance, it had become a city of strangers.

She noticed them immediately: the hard-faced men carrying guns. She also noticed the absence of women. Without the usual cluster of wives visiting in the door yards, the neighborly feeling was missing. Now she realized no children played in the streets.

Mark dismounted in front of the general store, and Jenny slipped from her horse, handing the reins to him. "Mark," she whispered, "Where are the families?"

"I don't know," he murmured. "It wasn't like this last week.

Get your thread and stick close to me. I don't like the feel of this."

Inside the store the proprietor, Ned Wilson, greeted them with a level stare. He filled Jenny's order and when he turned to the back of the store after the hinges, Mark followed.

"What's going on?" Mark was speaking softly as he glanced Jenny's direction.

"Not much." He hedged and then glanced at Mark with a worried frown. "You folks would be wise to stay on your own acres." Wilson murmured, glancing around. "The rumors are flying and I don't know which one to believe. God knows that most of us just want things to settle down. If you Mormons would just quit scratching the dust, it could happen. Right now everything you do gets the dander up.

"There's fellas moving in from all over the state. Rumor has it they're tired of waiting for the state militia to settle the scrappin'; and they're scared that if they don't take things into their own hands, you Mormons will run them outta the state before the year's out."

Jenny waited beside the long counter heaped with a jumble of tools, nails, and kitchen utensils. She noticed that the hooks which had held hams were empty, as was the flour bin and the barrel which had brimmed with dried beans just a month ago.

Just as she glanced at Mark and Ned Wilson, wondering whether she dared join them, a wagon creaked to a halt in front of the store. She moved to the open door as Moses Thornton stepped through. She smiled, and as she moved toward the man, a former neighbor from Kirtland, there was a rustle and a sharp voice behind her.

Jenny turned as the woman swished through the store from the living quarters in the rear. She was wiping her hands as she took her place behind the counter and leaned toward Moses. "Just don't you bother coming in here with your sad stories. We don't want the likes of you around. You and the missus will just have to do your buying where you're more welcome."

Moses' voice matched hers in hardness. "Look, ma'am, my money's just as good as the next fella's even if he happens to be Gentile." Jenny cringed at the contempt in his voice and turned away.

"The likes of you can't understand, can you?" There was scorn in her voice. "It isn't the money; though the chances of its being counterfeit is bigger'n I want to take. The reason you Mormons can't get a body willin' to sell to you is because there's a move to starve you outta the state. Now, what do you think of that?"

Jenny watched Moses as he straightened and threw back his head. His lips curled as he said, "Ma'am I think you're wastin' your time. Through the Prophet, Joseph Smith, the land and all the riches of the Gentiles have been promised to us. There's not one thing you can do to prevent the hand of the Lord, nor thwart His purposes."

Ned was standing beside his wife now. Jenny turned from listening to Moses, as Ned's hand on his wife's shoulder squeezed her into silence. His voice was heavy and loud. "The truth is, Thornton, there's no goods to be had—food or materials."

He paused, "Truth is, you Saints have descended like a horde of grasshoppers and just about cleaned us outta everything."

Out in the dusty road beside the wagon, Moses said, "There's news that the governor has begun to sit up and take notice of our cries for mercy."

Mark took a deep breath and Jenny knew he was getting ready to say hard things. She watched with interest as Mark carefully untied Sammy's reins and just as carefully turned to the man. "Thornton, you weren't in the state when the Jackson County problems took place. Governor Dunklin was negotiating a settlement which would have benefited the Saints. Joseph's marching on Missouri with an army ruined all hopes for a peaceful settlement. Things aren't much better now.

"Through a grudging concession to the constitutional freedoms of every man, Governor Boggs is trying to be fair, even giving us an opportunity to settle the differences neighbor-like. I'd say we're seeing the hands of the clock of Missouri's patience just about to midnight."

Moses didn't reply, but Jenny couldn't help her outburst. "Mr. Thornton, can't you see? You're saying the same things those people did—that God's on our side, not theirs. We know it's so, but doesn't faith mean we keep our mouths shut and wait for the Lord to *dump* the riches into our laps?"

During the week that followed, Jenny and Mark continued to work around their acreage, improving and preparing for winter. They didn't talk much about the things heavy on their minds. But as Jenny watched Mark fasten the last hinge to the shutters, she wondered if by *not* talking they were willing the problems to disappear.

Mark was still working on the corral the day Jenny found her hands idle for the first time in weeks. After washing the dishes that noontime, she said to Mark, "I'm going to walk over the hill and visit the Durfees. I've promised nosey old Mrs. Durfee I would, and though I don't like spending a beautiful day with her, I'll keep my promises."

Mark's eyes were twinkling, " 'Tis a lesson, young lady. Don't make promises you'll regret." Now the laughter faded from his eyes. "Jen, I worry. Don't stay into the dusk."

"I won't, my husband," she murmured, standing on tiptoe to press her lips to his cheek.

The way to the Durfee farm was a short walk downstream. Jenny chose to walk the river path instead of using the road. Avoiding the tangle of trees and bushes, Jenny climbed the high riverbank and was rewarded with a new view.

At Durfees', the older woman shoved the only chair close to the table before sitting down on the crude bench. Jenny threw aside her shawl and said, "The walk was wonderful—so warm I didn't need my shawl. Have you taken the river path? I could see for miles. Who owns the little ferry I saw chugging across the river?"

"Lyman Wight. Take it you've been fording the river?" Jenny nodded and the woman continued. "He's Joseph's right-hand man when it comes to running the battle."

"You think we'll be fighting?" Jenny asked slowly.

"If Wight has his say." The woman's answer was smug and her expression complacent. "Right now Joseph's got him moving his men into Adam-ondi-Ahman just as fast as the Gentiles can gather here."

Jenny shivered. "I'm beginning to wonder if we're safe."

The woman shrugged. "We are. But I'm hearing things are getting worse in town every day. The women and children daren't move outta their cabins, and food's mighty short."

"Where's Joseph?"

The woman's glance was sharp. She studied Jenny's face for a moment before answering slowly. "Most likely he's either still in Far West or moving this way. Could be he's at the Ferry conferring with Wight. Why do you ask?"

Jenny's thoughts were on all the things churning around inside of her, all the things she needed desperately to say to Joseph now before it was too late. Abruptly she came back to the present. "I—I just need to talk to him."

"You and fifty other young ladies," the woman said dryly. "Seems you could wait until the bad times are over and things are settling down for Zion."

Later, as Jenny walked homeward, she thought about the things Mrs. Durfee had intimated. "Me and fifty others!" she snorted. The classification rankled.

Jenny thought back on her unique relationship with the Prophet, and then she smiled. What a long time it had been since she had locked horns with the man! She chuckled, suddenly wistfully aware of the lack in her life.

It was Joseph the man she was missing. She thought back on all those scenes with him—the verbal sparring, the times when she had bested him when he'd tried to pressure her into line with the rest of the females in his camp. She snorted, "Relief Society, my eye! Namby-pamby women trotting along to obey the Prophet."

And there was that unique request Joseph had made of her: to be his friend, to report the pulsebeat of the people. Again she was filled with the need to see Joseph. He must know of every rumble among the Saints. These poor people had placed him on such a high pedestal that they dare not approach him even with information that might save Zion!

Now Jenny stood on the riverbank, looking downstream to the cluster of log cabins and the little ferry boat moving slowly across the Grand River.

"Joseph, I must see you," she murmured; and as the gentle

breeze rippled across her hair, rumpling its smoothness like a careless hand, she shivered. Rubbing her arms, she contemplated the fear rising up, tightening her throat and speeding her pulse. "I didn't know he still had the power to frighten me. Obey the Prophet or be damned! Joseph, it's been such a long time since I've seen you, touched your hand. Now, I must rid myself of this fear and this nameless something, or I will be a slave again, trembling with fear lest I fail to keep the word of the Prophet." Her hand tightened on the talisman pinned to her pocket. "Adela, how desperately I need you now!"

Jenny turned away from the river and slowly walked homeward. She was studying the ground, even now searching for the fresh herbs Adela would demand before a suitable charm could be concocted.

She had forgotten the dangers, forgotten everything except the need to see Adela. When she heard the snap of dry branches and lifted her head in time to see the flash of red, there was only one thought in mind, and she ran forward.

"Adela!" The woman turned to face her as Jenny plunged through the forest. Now panting, Jenny stopped abruptly and walked slowly toward the stranger. The woman was dressed in red, a vivid slash of crimson satin, stretched tightly over every curve of her ample body, revealing so much bosom that Jenny blinked in surprise. Even as she spoke she was guessing the woman was one of the fancy ladies. "Oh, I'm sorry. I thought I'd recognized my friend."

The woman smiled cheerfully, "Well, you didn't. Since you frightened off my friend, you might as well tell me about her. She's around here? What's her last name? Sounds like she should be a friend of mine with a name like Adela."

"I—I don't know her last name. At least I'm not certain. It could be Martindale."

The woman frowned and settled down on a fallen log. "Don't think I recognize Martindale. What's she look like?"

"Well, she's dark and slender, about as tall as you are." The woman was frowning and Jenny realized her description said nothing. "I've mostly seen her in red chiffon, all floaty. You'd see her in the woods looking for moss and herbs. Sometimes she gathers swamp water in a jug that's shaped like—"

The woman was shaking her head while an amused smile lighted her eyes. "Baby!" She exclaimed. "Babe in the woods. You look at the wrong bunch of ladies. What you're running after is a witch." Now her glance was shrewd. "You're a Saint, aren't you? Things are getting pretty bad when the Saints have to consult the witches." Before Jenny could think of an answer, the woman continued. "I can't claim to be the best Christian in the world, but I know enough about religion to see through this business of Joe's. He's gotta good thing going and you're all just tagging along behind."

Jenny's voice was level, flat, as she said, "We happen to have enough faith to believe he's a prophet sent from God. God's revelations to him are guiding us all."

"Like the revelation that God's given Missouri to him for Zion, and that the riches of the Gentiles are for the Saints?" She waited a moment, before softly adding, "Then if it doesn't happen, who you going to believe?"

Jenny was still readying an answer when the woman spoke again. Now her voice was thoughtful, not jeering, and when Jenny looked into her face, she saw a flash of pity in the woman's eyes as she said, "You know, the whole of Missouri was watchin' last summer. It was reported back to us, the things that fella Rigdon had to say back in June when he was rilin' at the fellas. I think their names were Cowdery and Whitmer." Jenny nodded, and the woman continued. " 'Twas strong language he used." Now there was a sneer in her voice as she said, "Talking like 'twas best to kill your people 'cause they don't agree with ya."

At Jenny's gasp of dismay, the woman bobbed her head and continued, "Now you and me know that's just what he was meanin' when he preached that sermon about salt losin' its savor and 'twas fit only to be trampled underfoot. He was making it clear the Mormons had a duty to trample these men under their feet." She paused to snort. "We knew he meant kill, 'specially when he said he'd be willin' to erect gallows in the middle of Far West and hang them himself."

Jenny searched for words to defend even as the churning

inside was turning her sick from the ugly words. Hotly she burst out, "You're blaming the whole of the people because of the wild words of that man. Don't believe his words were the words of the Prophet. We're not proud of the bad feeling Rigdon stirred up that day."

"No?" the woman questioned softly. "Then why didn't your prophet smack him down? Seems I recall him comin' back with one of those glorious revelations sayin' the Apostle Peter had informed Joseph that Judas hadn't hung himself. It was instead Peter, himself, that hung him."

She started to turn away then faced Jenny again. "Little girl, there's goin' to be trouble. Take yourself outta Zion before the state crumbles in on your head. And don't go outta here saying it's persecution like they did down south. There's as much ugly goin' on in Zion's camp as there is in ours." She paused again. "Now take a message to your prophet. Tell him Frances said forget it. Forget the whole shenanigans and high-tail outta here before the militia stitches his hide to the liberty pole God broke in two, just trying to tell him something." Again she paused before adding, "See, we believe in God, too. And I'm thinking we're just as holy."

CHAPTER 10

Jenny wandered aimlessly toward home. She was no longer conscious of the autumn glory and the desires which had spurred her out into the day. She was recalling the woman, Frances. Everything about her, from the red satin dress straining over her bulk to the dirty creases on her fat neck, was sending a message, and Jenny didn't like the message.

That woman seemed to know too much about the Saints, and the advice she had asked be passed on to Joseph had left an implication as gritty as sand in the teeth.

Jenny hurried her feet along the path, but she was remembering the expression in the woman's eyes. She *pitied* Jenny!

As she entered the silent, empty cabin, Jenny was uneasily aware of the woman's words. They were lying against her heart like a lump of ice.

Jenny restlessly paced the floor of her home. The fire was only a glow of embers, and Mark seemed to have vanished. She cocked her head, listening for the sound of the axe, the thud of the hammer. There was only silence, and in the silence Jenny became uneasy.

Once again she paced the room, chafing at the echo of the woman's words. Still wondering and now worrying, Jenny began searching the cabin, fretting over Mark's absence. His coat was missing but his hat was beside the rocking chair, as was the harness he had been mending. His gun was in the corner, but there was something missing. Jenny frowned, carefully studying the room.

Her gaze traveled over the table with its lamp centered on

the circle of embroidered linen. His Bible had lain there this morning; it was gone now.

Puzzled, Jenny slowly pulled the shawl across her shoulders. Had Mark been troubled this morning? She couldn't recall. With a nagging sense of need, Jenny left the cabin and began to wander across their land, first to the far edge of the clearing, past the makeshift corral.

The sense of need had become worry. She paused and listened. There was only the high swish of wind in the trees and the distant crash of Grand River. With a shiver she turned and ran back across the clearing, past the cabin.

On the edge of the heavily timbered area, she paused to glance behind herself, shivering at the strange sensation of being both repelled and attracted by the dark woods.

As she fought her way through the tangle of brush, the setting sun cast its last glow and allowed the gray of twilight to dominate. The shadows were deepening and Jenny fought back a sob. She turned to go back, and the naked branch of a sapling clung to her shawl.

Her trembling fingers were snatching at the soft wool when she heard the sound. Motionless she listened, unable to identify what she was hearing.

Frantically Jenny tugged at the captive shawl as she turned away from the tree. Then she saw the figure. Most surely that sprawled man was Mark, face down, with arms outstretched! As she watched, she saw him moving in agony. All of her fears became real; that was her Mark down the hill, and he had to be badly injured! She was powerless to move, caught in despair that overwhelmed and paralyzed her.

Now her trembling fingers tugged weakly at the imprisoned shawl. As she watched she saw Mark rise to a kneeling position. His shoulders shook as he bent over something in his hands.

Now Jenny's grip on the shawl loosened and her fear turned to astonishment. Never had she seen her husband like this. She clung to the tree for support as she looked down the glade and listened as Mark lifted his hands; he was holding his Bible! She heard him shout, "My God, I praise You, I adore You. Maker of heaven and earth, Redeemer of all the universe, how glorious You are, how worthy of praise!"

Jenny's dismay turned to relief. With a final tug at her shawl, she started toward Mark, and then without understanding why, she stopped.

Now Mark was on his feet. With agitated steps he paced the glade. When he paused, she watched him lift the book. She could hear low murmurs as if he were reading aloud and she strained to hear. But the words became unimportant as she saw him turn, clasp the open book to his chest and lift his face. Were those tears on his face—surely the twilight was deceiving!

For a long time, Jenny continued to watch, twisted by an emotion she didn't understand. Was it envy informing her that she was seeing more joy, love, and happiness on that face than she had ever seen in their most intimate, loving moments? She had moved to leave when she heard him pray, and again she was powerless to leave the spot while she listened.

His voice had changed, becoming vibrant and deeper. "Father, God of truth! How conscious I am of Your own dear self. How firmly do I feel Your hand, constraining me, reminding me of Your love. I know You are all-powerful. You have reminded me that You hold my most dear treasure in Your hand and that You have heard my prayer." There was silence for a moment and Jenny watched his shoulders once more transmitting agony.

Could she believe that her strong husband wept? Still she waited and Mark was speaking again. "I know Your power, Your promises," he was saying in a broken, humble voice. "You have never failed to keep one promise. I trust Your love as I have never trusted before."

Jenny's hand crept to her throat. Suddenly she turned and crashed through the bushes, running away from Mark. When she stood in her cabin, panting and trembling, she pressed her hand against her pounding heart and closed her eyes. Strangely the scene in the forest had left her feeling as if she were teetering on a high, crumbling shelf of rock. Slowly she crossed the room and reached behind the chest, fumbling until her hand touched the green book.

Changes were taking place in Daviess County. Jenny mentioned it to Mark. "Suddenly we are having a horde of visitors. Why? These are the folks we traveled with from Kirtland. For a time they were shunning us; I'm guessing it was because we helped the dissenters. Now they're acting like they can't get enough of us."

Mark leaned on the hoe and pinched her cheek. "Hey," he said gently. She bit her catty tongue and Mark nodded at the pile of firewood. "Probably, like us, people have been too busy fixing up before the winter cold sets in."

She wandered off the subject, saying with a tired sigh, "There's still much to be done. Passing down the road, we've seen people still living in wagons or poor bark shanties. There are garden plots to clear and trees to cut. Even with us—we've got to get that corral built."

"Haven't you heard misery likes company?" Mark grinned in answer to her original question while he turned back to his task of hoisting sacks of grain to the rafters in the lean-to.

"Do you really think you'll keep the squirrels and mice out of those sacks?" Jenny asked, although her thoughts were elsewhere. His smile reminded her of the Mark she spied upon in the forest. She sighed and turned her attention back to him.

"I'd better get this grain milled soon or you'll be reduced to scraping corn and baking it with pumpkin like they're doing down the valley," he said, heaving the last sack overhead.

She watched the muscles ripple across his shoulders and compared their power with that moment of weakness she had glimpsed in the forest. Weakness? Somehow that word didn't describe the scene she had happened upon, no matter that tears had been raining down his cheeks.

Later that evening Jenny thought of Mark's statement as she pulled the loaf of bread out of the oven and thumped its crusty top. It sounded hollow and she nodded with satisfaction as she put it on the table to cool. The aroma filled the cabin.

"Mark, the little stone oven you built in the corner of the fireplace does a good job. This bread's nigh perfect."

"Smells wonderful," he responded. He concentrated on his task of splicing the leather harness together. "By the way, I'm thinking the Andersens and the Guffries will be here this evening. Might be they'll bring a few others."

"What's the problem now?"

"Do or don't do, stay or go," he said wearily. Jenny turned away with a sigh.

One thing she knew, there wouldn't be bread by morning. Thinking of the shrinking mound of flour in the tin, she tried to set her mind in a charitable mood.

Jenny had barely time to cover the bread and set it aside before she heard the knock. Mark's glance at her was full of concern as he stood to open the door to his neighbors.

Jenny was right about the bread, but she didn't realize how fast it would disappear, or how hungry these people would be.

While the men huddled over the table, the women gathered by the fire and folded idle hands over the piles of mending they had carried with them.

Dora slanted a worried glance at the men and said, "I wish things would settle. Little Ruth Campbell is about to deliver, and she doesn't look able."

After the silence had stretched again, Lila straightened and said. "Late last night my Tyler heard a ruckus out yonder. He sneaked out there and found a fella settin' a fire in the hay. Tyler fired a load of buckshot at him."

There was more silence and Maudy gave a belated nervous laugh and said, "I just wish they'd do something. This waiting, for who knows what, is killin' me."

Now the women were listening to the low murmur of voices from the men. They were seeing the worried expressions and hearing the occasional angry outburst.

Dora whispered, "You know, the Prophet's said if we're living right, there's to be no harm done us, but I still worry." She had opened her mouth to add more when the low murmuring of the men caught their attention.

They had been sitting with their heads together around the table. Abruptly Tyler pushed back his stool and jumped to his feet. "I don't care what you're sayin', I intend stickin' with him. Seems if we're bent on believing he has the keys of the kingdom, then there's no other choice but this."

"Right or wrong? How about the way he goes at it?" Mark's

voice was low; only Jenny caught the sharp edge of controlled anger in it.

"I'm with Tyler," Guffrie said slowly. "I'm in too far to back out. Maybe I just don't have the sense to figure out for myself whether I oughta run."

"Yes," Mark spoke heavily, "when you don't have a better reason, it's hard to choose."

When they moved to the door to leave, Mark and Jenny stood together watching them. The circle of lamplight highlighted the women's faces. Their eyes were darkening pools, shadowing away the fears.

In the morning Jenny stirred cornmeal into the boiling water and addressed Mark. "Missus Hardy said Tyler found a fella trying to fire their hay."

"They're also stealing horses and cattle," Mark said slowly. He was thinking of the other things he had heard. When he turned to face her, Mark found he was being forced into saying some things he had been keeping from her.

He took a deep breath, waiting for the guidance of the Holy Spirit. He was still fearful of probing the tender spots in their relationship which he had created with his criticism of Joseph Smith.

"This is getting to be more than just persecution." He paced the room as he spoke, "The Saints are in on it, too; and, on their part, it's a good case of retaliation."

She faced him squarely. From the expression in her eyes, he guessed that she was struggling to accept a new way of looking at the situation.

For a moment he felt like applauding her, but he must push one step more. She was well aware of all that was happening, that he knew, but he must go over the events again. "In the first place, this is an ongoing fight. It started way back when Joseph sent his men into Missouri in 1831, with the prophecy that the Lord had ordained Missouri to be the new Zion. This land, he told them, was to be the site of the New Jerusalem, coming down out of heaven. The people under Joseph were to claim the state and build up Zion, an acceptable land getting ready for the Lord to return. How do you think that set with the people?

Especially when the Saints made no bones about fighting to gain their objective if necessary?"

She was still thinking as she said, "I can see them not being pleased, maybe angry, but—"

"Remember these were and are still rough frontiersmen. You saw the people on Independence Day."

Jenny nodded hesitantly. "The women were either fancy ladies or they were as tough as the men." She frowned, remembering that woman and feeling uneasy about her. It was starting to look as if she couldn't delay seeking out Joseph. There was that message.

Mark continued, "Things were starting to settle down a mite. The Saints from Jackson moved to Caldwell, just like the state legislature told them to. You recall I told you what some of the old settlers told me? They were talking about how it was until Joseph came to town last spring. The word was *peaceful.*

"This one fella told me the Jacksonites have one desire and that is to build a place up, get in a crop and live at peace with their neighbors. Sounds good as far as it goes, but peace is out of the question. Why? Now along with the information that hordes of Mormons are moving into the area, the Gentiles hear Joseph is building up an army with the intent to take the state, the country, and eventually the whole world."

He heard her protest. For a moment Mark paused to study Jenny's face. There was bewilderment and disbelief on it. He took a deep breath, conscious of the sure feeling that now was the time to face his wife with the facts she had chosen to ignore.

"Jenny," he pleaded, "right now I'm not asking you to judge his merits; instead, just try to put yourself in the Missourians' shoes. Their state isn't taking the action they feel is needed so the men are scared. They've resorted to mobbing, trying to make things miserable for the Saints, hoping they will leave on their own. Of course it isn't working, not under Joseph's hand. These people dare not leave under threat of being labeled *dissenter.* But in addition, some of the Saints are thieving and burning right back. For every bad tale you hear about the Missourians, there's another one about the Saints."

"Mark, I don't believe that. They say—" she paused and

lifted her chin. It was at that moment Mark realized the change in Jenny.

His despair overrode his good sense and he whispered, "Jenny, what is happening to you? From the very beginning I saw what a wonderful mind you had. I watched you because I knew you were special, and I fell in love with that special person. You're closing your mind! Don't let others do your thinking for you—not now, not after all these hard years of scrapping for room to stand tall."

She was caught, and her eyes widened. She was wondering as she looked into his face. Was it possible Mark was seeing something she didn't? For a moment she toyed with the idea that at times she did feel as if her thoughts were only echoes of some other voice.

In another moment she shook her head. Whispering, she said, "Mark, you're wrong. My ability to think, to grasp what is right, that's just the very thing that's bringing me along the way to be a strong person." He pulled her close. For a moment, just before Mark bent to press his face against hers, she saw the shock in his eyes and the white line his lips had become.

CHAPTER 11

Late that same afternoon Mark thought about Tom again. That bleak conversation with Jenny had pushed the incident from his mind, and now he knew he couldn't discuss his unexpected meeting with Tom.

In Adam-ondi-Ahman, Tom and some of his fellow Danites had been assigned the task of building a fort in the middle of town.

What a shock, walking into the town square and finding the crude fortification! The silent streets, the sullen expressions on the faces of his Gentile neighbors hurrying about their business had alerted him to change, but when he heard the pounding of hammers, his heart sank.

When he confronted his brother-in-law, Tom's crooked grin hadn't cancelled the dark, hard look in his eyes. Tersely he said, "We're building Joseph a fort. Under siege, we are. Gentiles are banding together, moving this way. Like locusts, they're comin'. Like tender grass, we're moving. Joseph says head for Far West or Adam-ondi-Ahman."

His eyes followed the movement of the Gentile crossing the road, hurrying toward his horse. "We'll run 'em out. Next year this time there'll be only Saints about. The Lord's goin' to fight our battles for us."

Today Mark paced his lean-to, cracking his knuckles and reviewing Tom's statements. That expression in his brother-in-law's eyes! The angry frown that had underlined the words made it impossible to dismiss the unbelievable statements. But he was wondering what was twisting his brother-in-law's placid disposition.

Tom was talking as if the Danites were the Lord's avenging instrument, a sword to be lifted against the Missourians.

But it was the anger in Tom which had bothered Mark the most. Mark had been about to point out that the Danites' being in town would make it impossible to live in peace with these Missourians. He was about to point out that Gentiles owned as much of the town as the Saints did, when Tom's tight-lipped statement had cut off the conversation. Tom snapped, "Remember Rigdon's speech. Your concern comes too late." Mark knew Tom was referring to the Independence Day speech when Rigdon had thrown down the gauntlet.

Mark watched Jenny walk slowly down the path toward the tumble of wildflowers still vibrant with color. She bent to bury her face in the blossoms and his heart constricted with fear. "Dear Jesus," he murmured in agony, "help me. I'll never forgive myself if I stay here one moment past the time it takes Jenny to get her eyes open to the truth. I know it could mean the difference between life and death. My Lord," he pleaded, "I can't lose her now!"

In the following week, Mark and Jenny watched events pile up and then tumble like a rock slide, growing, crashing, sweeping up everything in its path.

The bands of desperados continued to plunder; the Saints daily reported new losses.

After visiting the nearest neighbors, Jenny brought the latest stories to Mark. "The Andersens are saying the mobs are concentrating on DeWitt and Adam-ondi-Ahman because they've made up their minds to rid the county of Mormons. There're only two Mormon families in DeWitt, the poor souls. If nothing else, they'll die of fright."

And still he was silent. But it was a troubled silence as he recalled Tom's angry face and the sound of hammers in the streets of Adam-ondi-Ahman.

In the middle of September, on the day Mark returned home with news of Joseph's petition for redress, Jenny had noticed the touch of autumn. Distant hills, rolling up and away from

Grand River, were touched with a new glow of color. She also saw the grasses in the valley turning golden.

While Mark sat at the table and hungrily spooned up the wild plum preserves, Jenny ladled out bowls of barley soup. Mark commented, "The honey with plums gives a good flavor. I like it better than sugar."

He finished the soup, and Jenny said, "I can tell by your face that there's something brewing."

Startled he looked up. "Oh, I was pondering it all, trying to understand." He was silent while Jenny waited. Finally, "I've just heard Joseph has petitioned the judge of Ray County. I suppose he just didn't know what else to do. It's on behalf of those of us in Daviess County who are being threatened with expulsion."

"Are *we* being threatened with expulsion?" Jenny asked slowly. Then she added, "Is that what they call the mob action against us?" She waited, then asked, "There's more?"

He nodded soberly, speaking reluctantly, "Word's run ahead of them. General Lucas has dispatched Generals Atchison and Doniphan to settle our differences. They are headed this way with five hundred men under them. Quite a bunch to keep peace in a county this size."

"What does Joseph's petition ask?"

"He's complained about the treatment the Saints are receiving at the hands of the Missourians. About the fights, the looting, the harassment."

"When will these men arrive," Jenny whispered, "and, Mark, what shall we do?"

"I don't know." When he threw her a worried glance, her hand crept to her throat. "Don't start worrying yet. We're far enough from town; probably won't even know they're there. Besides, these men represent the state. They're coming to settle the differences, not start a war." He grinned at her.

He was picking at a piece of cornbread when Jenny stated, "Mark, you're not saying, but you're thinking the Saints are making a mistake."

"Yes," he said slowly, "it's just a feeling, but seems Joe would be smart to do his best to keep the peace by cooperating instead of pushing his luck. I can't help thinking the old settlers in the county are seeing it in the same light as a youngster running to his pa to complain because he's being mistreated, when in truth his teasing caused the problem in the beginning."

Jenny lifted her head. "I hear a horse." They both went to the window. As the horseman turned off the road, Jenny exclaimed, "It's Tom!"

And when he was standing in their cabin, holding out his bowl for soup, he said, with a grin, "Mind if I call this home for a spell?"

"What's that to mean?" Jenny asked, searching his face.

"I've just come from Far West. Seems Joe's sent a petition askin' for help to—"

"So we've heard," Mark interrupted.

Tom sat down at the table and added, "Well, then you know that Doniphan stopped in Far West with orders for that place."

"What were they?"

He piled plum preserves on his cornbread before looking up with a pleased grin. "To disband all parties found under arms. And he found a heap of us, even caught us totin' our guns around. We were ordered to clear out of there and head for our homes."

"Like little boys with their hands slapped."

"Aw, Sis. You've never seen a bunch of fellas so glad to go. We're hopin' this means the end of havin' to snatch up a gun and run when there's orders."

Mark was studying Tom with keen eyes. Slowly he said, "That surprises me. From all I've heard about the Danites, I had it figured you were all spoiling for a fight. I thought you were reconciled to having to take Zion by force, and the sooner the better."

"Mark, you have it wrong. Given our druthers, you'd find most of us a peaceful bunch. Oh, sure, there's a few hotheads in the group. But we fight because our salvation's at stake."

"Obey the Prophet or be damned," Mark said slowly, and Tom nodded.

Jenny sighed deeply. "I'm glad to have you. Seems we need all the kin we can get. Even Mark's worried about affairs around here."

"Well, they're not good," Tom continued soberly. "The bunch of Danites holed up here'bouts, they tell me, has been livin' on cattle, hogs and honey. They're callin' it bear, buffalo, and sweet oil. But they're not foolin' a soul. There's bound to be more'n a few heads cracked when the old settlers get fed up with havin' their stock feedin' the bunch fightin' them." Jenny saw the look the two men exchanged, and shivered; she dared not question further.

Tom stayed on with Mark and Jenny. In reflecting on the whole uneasy situation, Jenny decided that had Tom taken up whittling or fishing—anything except running about the country, she would have been able to dismiss the strange visit as loneliness.

Her worst fears were confirmed late one evening when Tom came home long after supper was cleared away, when the evening mists were creeping down the crimson hillsides.

He dug into her stew of venison and dumplings made of corn as if only it stood between him and starvation.

Sensing his troubled spirit, Mark and Jenny waited until he had finished eating. He drank the last of the milk and said, "I've been over Far West way. I'm mighty uneasy about how things are goin' to set. Joseph's got his ire up and it's bound to cause trouble."

"Haven't the troops Joe stationed in Daviess returned to Far West?"

Tom nodded. "It's DeWitt now. The old settlers have been tryin' their hardest to get those two Mormon families out of there. Finally they drew up a resolution statin' they couldn't live with Mormons. We found out it was decided they would use force to get rid of them. But before they could get goin' on it, Joseph moved a big bunch of Canadians into the area. He was mighty set on keepin' a foothold in DeWitt, since it's a good river port."

Mark got to his feet and paced the room. "Tom," he said thoughtfully, "Doniphan's been trying to negotiate a settlement in Adam-ondi-Ahman. Things were starting to look pretty good for us." Jenny listened to the growing excitement in his voice and looked at him in astonishment. She was beginning to understand his frequent and unexplained trips into town as he talked.

He was saying, "The way things were going, the Missourians were ready to sell out to us. I was ready to plunk down money myself. How's this new event going to set?"

"Not good," Tom said slowly. "That's why I've come back."

"I don't understand," Jenny said dully, her heart sinking in response to the anger and discouragement on Mark's face.

Tom continued and his voice was level, emotionless. "I'm a Danite. Joe's ordered us to DeWitt as soon as we can get there. I'm not here for arms, like Joseph's thinkin'; I'm here, Mark, to beg you to get my sister out of Missouri. Even if you have to leave without a thing and on horseback, just go!"

"What about you?" Jenny whispered.

Tom's face twisted in a half grin. "Accordin' to the promises Joe's given us, there's nothin' that can touch the Lord's anointed. He's promised God will send angels to do the fightin' for us."

Tom gathered up heavy clothing and took the gun Mark pressed upon him. Your life may depend on it," Mark added; "besides, I'll have yours."

"Just don't go to DeWitt. The Missouri mobs are gatherin' as fast as they can."

"Whatever for?" Jenny cried. "Surely a few families of Saints couldn't have brought that on."

"I forgot to tell you the Canadians have a breastwork of wagons stationed down the middle of town. That doesn't sound like innocent settlers bent on plantin' wheat."

It was dawn when Tom rode his horse into DeWitt. From the bluff overlooking the town he saw the peaceful river port, gently touched by the light of the rising sun. But he also noticed only a few trails of smoke rising from the chimneys of the log cabins clustered along the wharf.

Until his gaze moved to the center of the community, he had nearly convinced himself that this *was* a peaceful little river town. Then he saw, stretching down the middle of town, a barricade of wagons. Beyond the breastwork, he saw the Mormon camp and caught his breath in surprise. This was no mild response to the burning of one Mormon house and a few stray gunshots—this was a major offensive. In the pale light of dawn, the positioned Mormon troops were spread, as far as he could see, the length and breadth of the open space.

Carefully Tom made his way down into town and into Israel's camp. He found Joseph and his men ensconced with the Canadians behind the breastwork of wagons. Joseph's usually smiling face was creased into a worried frown.

He greeted Tom. "We didn't have any trouble marching into town, but I'm afraid we're in trouble now." Bewildered, Tom looked around. He could hear children's voices overlapping the voices of women, but the area around the fires was empty.

Joseph was pacing rapidly back and forth. "The settlers from Canada have suffered severely at the hands of the mob. Now the mob won't give us freedom to leave. What a trick! They let us in while they were pulling reinforcements from every county in the area. They'll all be down our necks—but we'll fool them. We've only to sit it out."

"Not fight!" Joe and Tom turned. Lyman Wight had been listening; his face was red with anger. "We've the Lord to fight our battles; march on!"

But in the end, Joe's will prevailed. An express was dispatched to the governor, but this time there was nothing of encouragement in the answer.

Joseph wadded the paper and threw it to the ground. Tersely he said, "The governor informs us that since we got ourselves into this fix, we should get ourselves out."

Tom slowly turned. Just beyond the fringe of town, away from the threat of the Canadians' guns, he could see the cluster of Gentiles with rifles raised. "Is that a cannon?" Tom asked. Joseph nodded briefly; then the Prophet slumped wearily.

Tom squatted in front of Joseph and said softly, "Joe, these people are in a bad way. The mob's been goin' through the bunch beating them. I guess they were in the wrong, out tryin' to find something to eat."

"I know," Joseph said slowly. He got to his feet. "For the sake of these people, I guess I have to admit we're licked for now. Get me a flag of truce."

Wight's face contorted with rage. "You are a fool! Not only

are you backing down on the promises of God, but think of the message the Gentiles will get! I promised the Danites would take these people. You'll make a fool outta me."

Tom faced Wight and stated, "I can't believe you have a better plan."

Wight spun on his heel and flung his arm toward DeWitt. "See this little town? They'll boast they sent us crawling out of here on our bellies."

Joseph was still impassive, but he was watching as Wight whirled toward him. Tom cringed as Wight yelled, "You're embracing defeat like a friend!"

But Joseph shook his head. Under a flag of truce, the starving, beaten settlers were led to Far West.

A short time later, Tom was there when Joseph received the dispatch from Adam-ondi-Ahman.

When the ragged man with the message stood before Joseph, his voice was dull and discouragement bowed his shoulders. "They're saying up yonder—the Gentiles are—that if Carroll County can turn out the Saints, then Daviess County can too.

"General Doniphan's sent word negotiations have broken down and the settlers aren't going to sell out to the Saints. Sir, we've lost more'n DeWitt." He started to turn away, then added, "They're saying a mob of eight hundred's moving toward Adam-ondi-Ahman."

CHAPTER 12

Jenny stood in the one room of her home, bewildered. All of it was unbelievable: one moment the little cabin had seemed a bit of heaven, her place forever; now it was being wrenched out of her life.

"Mark, we've been here such a short time. It seems we've just settled in and now you're saying we must go."

"Little owl-eyes, don't look so sober. This isn't the end of the world, and we will be back. If you like your little cabin that much, we'll return to stay forever." Mark's finger flicked the tears off Jenny's cheeks before he bent to kiss her.

"Oh, Mark," she wrapped her arms around him and held him. "It's just that I can't understand all this. Why is it necessary we leave now?"

"Because I trust your brother, even the things he doesn't say. Now stop your fretting. We'll be back soon. Pretend that all along we've planned this trip to visit my mother. We'll have to do a little night travel to avoid causing offense to some of—of the militia." He held her away to see her face.

"Mark—" she studied his face and he tried to snuggle her against his shoulder again, lest she see the fear. She resisted him, and he faced the intensity of those gray eyes. Her next question surprised him. "Does it trouble you that because of me you must go, and that you aren't able to fight with the other men?"

Carefully he asked, "Why the questions?" She shook her head without answering, and he pushed her head under his chin and considered the question. "First of all, I'm not sold on fight-

129

ing as a way to settle differences. Second, I think Joseph's in the wrong. Third, I'm a follower of Jesus Christ, and He says love your enemies, pray for them, and turn the other cheek." She fought away from his restraining arms. He was aware of resistance throughout her whole body. Again her eyes reminded him of an owl, a creature of the dark, with thought and feeling hidden away.

He sighed and said, "I'm not convinced we'll make it through with this buggy, but pack as much as you can in the way of food and clothing. Wrap the luggage in quilts. I intend to grease those wheels until they are completely soundless." He saw her shiver as she turned away.

With a heavy heart, Mark went out to the lean-to and gathered up his tools. He again felt that nudge reminding him time was fleeting. If only they had left a week ago when Tom had urged them to action!

Dawn was just a smudge of color in the sky when Mark bundled Jenny into the crude buggy and turned his team down the trail toward Adam-ondi-Ahman.

As they rode through the town, Jenny gasped with dismay. "Mark, it's been such a short time since we were here, but look at the difference! Look at the trash lying about. It troubles me. And there's scarcely a sign of a breakfast fire."

Mark had been aware of the forboding air of the town, but he said nothing as he studied the area, looking for signs of change. Someone was sweeping the steps of the general store—that was very ordinary. He recognized the owner, Wilson, a long-time resident, and a Gentile.

As they passed, the man paused and leaned on his broom. "Good morning, Wilson," Mark called. The man turned and headed back into his store.

Jenny was shivering. "Don't worry," Mark said, "Silence doesn't mean anything. Mormon sympathizers aren't popular."

They continued on down the road toward Far West. The buggy wheels were nearly soundless, and the pleasant clop-clop of the mare's hooves sounded reassuring, normal.

It was nearly noon when they met the horsemen. Mark recognized several of them. Lyman Wight was leading the group, and Mark recalled hearing that the man owned the ferry on Grand River, just a short distance downstream. "Hello," Mark called as they reined in their horses.

Wight asked. "You've come from Adam-ondi-Ahman?" Mark nodded and Wight said, "Then you've probably seen the bunch with the cannon."

Mark felt Jenny's grasp tighten. "I haven't seen any group of men, let alone a group with a cannon. When we left town this morning the place seemed peaceful. Not many residents though—there was hardly a breakfast fire in the village."

The men rode on. Mark and Jenny continued south over the prairie, mulling over the terse statements the men had made. "So the Danites are going to rescue Daviess County from the DeWitt mob, which is moving this way pulling a cannon."

"Do you believe them?"

"I believe they *think* they'll find a cannon and a skirmish." Jenny relaxed and smiled for the first time in two days. Mark leaned over to kiss her. "That's my girl. Now let's just concentrate on getting back to Ohio."

"Is there any way possible to avoid Far West?" Jenny asked.

"Not that I know of, but if there's anyone I dare ask, I will. Right now it would be nice to run into Tom."

Her face brightened, "Oh, would that be possible?"

He chuckled, heartened by her mood swing. "In this state anything is possible." Then he added slowly, "Particularly if they're calling out the Danites to go to Adam-ondi-Ahman."

Within an hour they again heard the sound of approaching horsemen. Mark frowned. "Jenny, I don't like this. These horses are coming too fast to be pulling a cannon; it's more like they're intent on catching up with the others."

"Let's get off the road!" Jenny exclaimed. But Mark was shaking his head, and she realized it was too late. Across the prairie a cloud of dust was moving toward them. In all that expanse there was not one tree to shield them from sight.

For a moment it seemed the troops would pass them by; but at the last moment there was a shout and the horses veered toward them. The man in front wore the fraying clothing of a farmer, but he carried himself like a general.

Jenny watched him leave his men behind and canter forward. "Why, you're Mark Cartwright!" the man exclaimed. "You don't know me, but I heard about you, back Kirtland way. Name's Lewis."

His expression was quizzical as he continued, "We've reason to believe a mob of Gentiles from DeWitt is headed up toward Daviess County, towing a cannon. They're intending to run the Saints out of Daviess. Have you seen or heard of them?"

Mark shook his head, "No, but just over an hour ago we met Wight and your men heading toward Grand River." His voice became thoughtful as he said, "This is starting to look pretty serious."

Nodding, the man squinted down at Mark. "You best believe it. I suppose the word's been spread and you're headed for Far West."

Jenny chimed in, "Actually, we're hoping to avoid Far West. Is there another road?"

He was grinning at Mark. "Missus have the last word? Ma'am, orders is orders. Don't try to talk him out of it. Don't you worry your pretty little head. There's plenty of company for you ladyfolks while the men are away."

There was a horse pressing through the troops behind Mark and Jenny, and then a familiar whinny. "Mark! Jenny!" Tom's face peering around the buggy was filled with dismay. "You should have stayed at home," he said carefully. "It isn't safe with those cutthroats on the loose."

Jenny opened her mouth to question, but Mark's hand squeezed hers tightly in an unmistakable message. Hastily he said, "Tom, I'm glad to see you. What's going on in Far West?"

"You mean Lewis here didn't tell you? The Prophet's called for all the men to assemble there." His voice was level and deliberate as he informed them. "We understand nearly all the men in Caldwell County are heading there right now. They are called under arms."

Even Jenny caught the message. She shivered, saying with a glance at Lewis, "Then I guess that's where we'll be going."

Lewis gave Jenny a pitying look. Turning to Mark he said, "I see you aren't fitted out for livin' in your rig. Better head for my house. Tell the missus I sent you. We've a good-sized loft and are expectin' to have it full by morning. Joseph's going to have to build a hotel if he intends to keep up this kinda thing."

In the morning, after the two of them had spent a restless night tossing on a straw pallet spread in the Lewis cabin, Mark faced Jenny and whispered, "I've every intention of getting out of this if it is possible. I can't believe Joseph will demand I fight. He knows how I feel about the whole affair. I'll let him know our plans are to return to Ohio right now."

Jenny's face brightened, but he saw her bite her lip. "Mark, you have more confidence than I do. I hope you are right."

"I want you to stay here until you find out just what is going to happen. Last night I found Andy Morgan. He's as reluctant to join this army as I am. He did say that Sally is alone and would welcome you. I've written the directions to their section; it isn't difficult to find. If I must leave, go to Sally and stay there until this mess is over." She stared up at him. His voice was flat and his eyes shadowed.

Then she understood. Mark had no hopes of leaving. She clenched her hands behind her back; he mustn't see them trembling.

Later that morning when the two of them joined the crowd of men and women pressing toward the town square, Mark looked at the sky and murmured, "That sky is promising nothing good. If it were December instead of the fifteenth of October, I'd expect snow." Jenny shivered in her shawl and decided that even snow couldn't make her feel worse. Mark left her with the group of men and women standing on the gentle slope facing the town square. She looked around at the somber faces and reminded herself that these women were feeling the same misery she was experiencing. There were some she recognized from Kirtland days, but they seemed as disinclined to talk as she.

Down below, in the crowd of men, there were a few excited voices; but for the most part only uneasy silence held the group as they waited for the Prophet to appear.

When the women began to stir restlessly, Jenny stood on tiptoe, guessing there was something of interest happening on the square. Far down the street she spotted a group of men coming. It was easy to guess who the dark-coated figure was. Dressed in somber black, Joseph towered above the men around him.

The pulse of the crowd quickened. By the time Joseph stood before them in the town square, the murmur of excitement had changed to a rumble, then a roar of welcome.

His voice was quiet and controlled as he began to speak. Wearily he began cataloging the events and listing the offenses of the Missourians against the Saints. To all the people listening to him it was a familiar tale, and they shifted restlessly.

Now his voice rose as he said, "We have heard from Governor Boggs in answer to our demand for relief." His voice rose, "We innocent people have suffered at the hands of the citizens of this state. Misunderstood and abused until our souls are sick within us, we have petitioned only for peace and fairness at the hands of our enemies."

His hand trembled as he lifted a paper above his head. "And what is our answer from the governor?" He paused, and silence gripped the group. Sardonically he said, "Our governor has advised us to fight our own battles." Leaning forward, he stated, "And that, my brethren, is just what we intend to do."

Amid the uproar, he continued, "We have tried to keep the law long enough. What has it gained us? It has been administered against us, never for us."

Over the cries of assent, Joseph raised his arm and with a shout said, "Hereafter, I do not intend to keep the law. We shall take affairs into our own hands and manage without Boggs or his laws."

When the roar of the crowd again subsided, he continued, "In DeWitt we yielded to the mob. Now they are heading for the homes of our people in Daviess County. I have determined that we shall not give another foot to them. No matter how many shall come against us, ten or a thousand of them, God will send His angels to our deliverance. We will be the victors, whether we fight one or a thousand of them."

Joseph started to move away, then with a grin he turned back. "There are those wondering how we shall supply the needs of our troops. Some will say I have told you to steal, but I have not. That isn't necessary when you can get plenty without. In closing I will tell you about a Dutchman and his field of potatoes. A colonel with his men was quartered nearby, and going to the old man, he offered to buy the field of potatoes. The old Dutchman refused to sell. When the colonel returned to his regiment with the tale of woe, he stated, 'Now remember, don't *let* a man of you *be caught* stealing potatoes.' " Joseph paused and then added, "In the morning there wasn't a potato in the patch." There was a moment of silence and then a few chuckled. The relief from tension was contagious and the rumble of laughter grew.

Joseph was still standing and waiting. From Jenny's position she could see the change taking place on his face. The half-smile slid away, and as the excited babble increased, rage contorted his face. Leaning forward, he cried, "If only they would leave us alone! Then we could preach the gospel in peace. But if there's an attempt to molest us, we shall establish our religion by the sword."

Sidney Rigdon stepped to the front and said, "We have a group of *'Oh, don't'* men in our midst. They are those who decry the order to support our right, saying, 'You are breaking the law, you will bring ruin to the society.'

"While others are fighting, these men are bringing division and disturbances to our midst. We must have unity. I say that blood must first run in the streets of Far West before we are worthy men to venture forth to fight the enemy. Is it fair for these *Oh, don't* men to stay behind while their brothers risk their lives? Should these men attempt to leave the county, their lives shall be forfeited and their property confiscated. I say these men should be rounded up, pitched on their horses with bayonets and placed in front as you go to battle." As Rigdon moved away, the crowd erupted in a frenzy of shouting.

From where Jenny stood the next words were only cacophony, but as she watched, men separated into groups and moved among the assembly. She saw men singled out, and led off one by one. Frowning, Jenny tried to find meaning in the actions. When two men surrounded Mark and led him away, she clenched one fist against her mouth, the other against her pounding heart.

The meaning was clear. Mark had been labeled an *Oh don't* man.

After the men had been lined up and marched away, the women began to move. Just as Jenny was doing, they staggered like sleep-walkers. There was an occasional sob as they picked their way over the rutted streets of Far West and headed for the warmth of the general store. But Jenny lingered behind. That dark-cloaked figure was still in the town square, talking to the cluster of excited men pressing close. She waited until he broke free and headed down the street.

The sound of her feet pounding on the road made him turn. Staring up into his cold face, she could only stutter, "J—Joe, I—I must see you."

For a moment his face cleared, he nearly smiled. "Little Missus Cartwright," he drawled. "If you've come to plead for your husband, don't. We need every man we can get. Jenny, my beautiful dear, neither tears nor promises will get your heart's desire. This is war."

He turned and moved away while Jenny stood stricken and trembling, first with anger and then with fear. When she had recovered, he had rounded the corner and disappeared.

She whirled around. A young man standing just behind her was watching with a sympathetic smile. "Begging your pardon, but please don't trouble the Prophet. Seems he's wearied by all the women who think they have a special place—"

"No, no!" Jenny cried impatiently. "I need to see Joseph. I have information he needs to hear."

The man's expression was totally disbelieving, and she snapped, "Where's the Prophet's home?"

He spoke slowly, still looking at her with doubting eyes, "He lives with the George Harris family. If you look yonder, right through those trees, you can see the chimney. But don't expect to be seein' him right away. He doesn't have the time to spare." Jenny turned away. For a few minutes longer she lingered in the square, wondering what to do.

It was growing colder, and she rubbed her numb hands. Finally, with a sigh of frustration, she turned to follow the women to the store.

Until evening, the group of chilled, pinched-face women lingered on in Far West. Huddled around the fire in the general store, they waited, only to hear that the men had been divided into companies. Jenny watched their misery as they paced before the fire. Later they heard the first company of horsemen had started on their way to Adam-ondi-Ahman.

It was Tuesday afternoon before Jenny gave up hope of seeing Mark sprinting across the town square toward the Lewis cabin, saying he had been released.

Mrs. Lewis, sitting before the fire, knitting and keeping tabs on the affairs of Far West, said, " 'Tis life, my dear. Go about your business just like the rest of us. You heard the Prophet. There's no doubt about it; our men will be the victors, and soon this land of Zion will be free from the taint of the cursed ones."

Jenny's hands were trembling and tears burned her eyelids as she unfolded the paper and read directions to Sally's farm. At the end of the paper, Mark had written, *I love you; remember, I'll be back—we've promised.*

She closed her eyes, thinking back that long-ago time when he had pressed his lips against her hair. He had thought she didn't hear the whispered, *In sickness or in health*, but she did, and her heart had added, *'Til death, I promise you.*

Jenny picked up the bag which had been packed for Ohio and went to the stable to find the awkward buggy Mark had designed from scraps of their wagon.

It was dusk by the time Jenny followed the lamplight to Sally's door. And Sally, with Tamara beside her, stood wide-eyed and pale, waiting to welcome her.

CHAPTER 13

That first day at Sally's home, Jenny voiced her fears. She was drying the dishes as Sally washed. Slowly turning the cup in her hand, she said, "Sally, do you *really* believe Joseph's prophecy?" She glanced at Sally's face and protested, "Don't look at me like that. I'm not a tattletale. I'm scared, and I just wish you'd make me feel better about all this."

"You're just missing Mark," Sally protested, but her eyes were on the dish she was holding, and Jenny was caught by the feebleness of her reply. Her heart sank. Sally was knowing the fears, too.

Later beside the fire, with Sally cuddling Tamara on her lap, Jenny faced the pair. She pushed aside her uneasiness for a moment, thinking instead how much a miniature of her mother little Tamara was. As Jenny reached out to touch the child's cheek, Sally glanced down at her daughter and said, "Too bad you haven't produced a young'un; that'd help the time pass for you." She sighed. "Jenny, I know it's bad. I hate it all just as much as you, but dwelling on it and chewing over all the things we shouldn't even been thinking about—well, that doesn't help at all. Can't you leave the fussin' to the menfolk? It'll all work out."

Tamara held up her arms and Jenny took the child. "Sally, I know just what you'll be saying next. You're going to start chiding me because my faith is feeble and you'll tell me again that to question is to doubt, and that doubt is sin. Somehow I can't just accept anything in life without giving it a few questions. Why did God make me this way if asking questions is wrong?"

"Tell me what sense it makes to question?"

"Well, for one thing, I suppose it gives a person a good desire to change what ought to be changed."

Sally picked up her mending and asked, "Just what would you change in this affair if you could?"

Jenny looked around the little cabin. There were things from their past which had been disturbing her for some time. She had been recalling Kirtland. Closing her eyes she could see the Morgan home with its spacious rooms and big windows. She pictured the flower garden, the white picket fence, and the flock of chickens picking at sunflower seeds.

"Sally, don't you pine for that lovely house in Kirtland?"

Sally sighed and nodded, "And the furniture we couldn't bring with us." She stopped abruptly and Jenny saw her press her lips tightly together before she continued. "Jenny, we can't be fussing over *things*. Every one of us is called upon to make sacrifices for Zion."

"I don't know why I'm thinking like this right now," Jenny said slowly. "Maybe it is not having Mark around. Up Adam-ondi-Ahman way I could see the poor lot we had, but somehow it seemed to be just a passing thing; I expected it to be better tomorrow. Now—maybe it is just missing Mark."

Sally shook her head over her sewing. Her voice sounded wistful as she said, "No, it isn't just that. Seems you can take anything if you believe in it. I guess what you're trying to tell me is that maybe you no longer believe?" She lifted her head and searched Jenny's face. "Doesn't it make you feel terrible to *not* believe?"

Jenny stared thoughtfully at Sally, seeing the worried frown on her face, the anxious lines that had replaced the smiles. Sally didn't seem to know how she had changed. Finally Jenny said, "Sally, you wanted to know what I'd change. It's the help-less feeling."

"Helpless? Jenny, we're to be praying, trusting the Prophet to bring the word of the Lord to us. We're to believe everything will work out just the way Joseph prophesied it would."

"And if it doesn't?" For a moment fear spread across Sally's face and then she straightened on her stool and opened her mouth to speak. Hastily Jenny said, "See, deep down you're scared to death it won't. Well, that's where we're different. You'll sit and shake in your shoes. I intend to get out and make certain it does happen."

Jenny began to grin. She could see from the sparkle of hope in Sally's eyes that she had her attention. "And," she leaned forward, "one of these days, I'm going to say, 'Joseph, remember the hard times in Missouri's beginning days, back before we really became Zion with all these riches? Remember when we lived in log cabins instead of these white mansions? Remember when it looked like we were losing? Well, Joseph, that's when I—'"

Jenny stopped abruptly. It was as if she had suddenly dropped back into Sally's presence, and here was this weak, timid woman waiting for her to change the world.

Sally was holding her breath, waiting. Now Jenny didn't dare say those final things. Sally's little-girl eyes gazed at her with eyes so much like Tamara's. She wouldn't understand. For a moment Jenny felt as if she were Sally's mother. Her heart swelled with love for the timid little one, and then she knew, for one brief moment, the surge of power.

But even now it seemed life was falling back into a pattern of failure. She was very aware of a spirit of powerlessness and fear twisting around her, like the fear mirrored in Sally's eyes and echoed in Tamara's whimpers.

For a moment she teetered, powerless to help either herself or her friend, and then she remembered her resolve. She must see Joseph, now. She must tell him about all that was going amiss in his church. But would he listen to her?

Just two days ago he had brushed off her words as of no account. She puzzled over that; what had happened to the Joseph she had known in Kirtland, the man who had seemed eager to keep his finger upon the pulse of the church?

Then she realized the connections. She needed power at her disposal before she could be successful with Joseph. Jenny looked down at her hands lying limp and useless in her lap.

Was it all a dream, a useless, futile dream, or was there really power out there for the having? She waited, checking the response of her own spirit. There was that time, just before coming to Missouri, when she had *known* the only hope for power was through Joseph's church, through obedience to the Prophet.

For the rest of the day the two women tried to skirt the fearful things they had conjured and content themselves about the fire. But in the night, when chatter was done, Jenny's mind was filled with that painful picture of Mark, seeing him again as he was surrounded and marched out of her life.

During the dark lonesome hours, Jenny did a great deal of thinking, and she came to a single conclusion. She knew, with a deep-down spirit conviction, that Joseph was doomed to failure unless much more power were brought to bear upon the forces fighting him.

Now Jenny moaned softly as she twisted her face into the pillow. What careless folly! During the rush of the day, just before leaving their cabin at Adam-ondi-Ahman, Jenny had forgotten to pin the talisman into the folds of her fresh dress. It was still pinned to her work frock, left hanging behind the door of the cabin. And the green book. At the last moment she dared not hide it in the buggy lest Mark stumble across it. She whispered into the pillow, "No matter what the cost, I must go after the talisman and the book!"

The next day, as soon as she dared, Jenny was into the forest, searching the undergrowth for the power-filled mushrooms and herbs to round out her dwindling supply. The memory of the charms and chants in the green book were as fresh and alive in her thoughts as they had been the last time she had used them.

Unfortunately, there were many sections of the book she had never had the occasion to use. She thought of the book secreted back at the little cabin perched above the rapids of Grand River. How desperately she needed that book! And Adela. How badly she needed that woman's wisdom and counsel now, before it was too late!

With renewed passion, Jenny fought desperately for spirit

power and the strength to know the secret vibrations of the other world. The following day she spent hours in the forest, while a listless Sally rocked beside the hearth and played with her child.

When Jenny returned to Sally's cabin, there was a strange discontent wrapping itself around her heart. Coming out of her meditations in the forest, she felt as if she were trading reality for a misty world without substance.

But that night, when the faint glow of the fire touched the shadowy room, Jenny felt herself alive to the spirit influence. She beamed her prayers toward the full moon and directed her spirit energy toward pleasing those fearful spirit entities.

Just two days after the men marched out of Far West, heading toward Adam-ondi-Ahman, an unseasonable snowstorm paralyzed Missouri for a brief time.

Jenny watched the snow from Sally's window and fretted about Mark, but at the same time she was taking credit for the storm. The influences from the spirit world knew better than she just what power must be used.

Heartened by victory, she redoubled her efforts, now adding incantations that left her shivery with the sense of power flowing through the universe. Meanwhile, Jenny watched Sally's fears and doubts grow day by day. But Jenny observed her friend's anxieties with an oblique sense of detachment, aware of her own power growing.

On the day that the snow melted back enough to reveal the crushed grasses and brown-earth path, Jenny rode Patches into Far West. Her plans were vague, but she knew she must try to find Joseph, even if it entailed walking up to the Harrises' front door and facing Emma Smith with her demands.

As she rode slowly through the deserted streets, she felt the air of desolation, even abandonment, and she shivered in response. In front of the sprawling log building, Jenny slid from the horse and tethered her beside the only other horse. She measured the gelding with a critical eye. Black, several hands taller than her mare, with a deep, powerful chest. As she headed for the door, she smiled to herself. That could be Joseph's horse. Just possibly she would have him to herself!

Inside, the man behind the high counter was polishing glasses. "Hello, Mike," she said, pulling the mittens from her hands.

"Miz Cartwright." His genial face crumpled into a frown. "No matter what you're a wantin', we probably don't have it."

She cocked her head and nodded with a pleased smile. "Yes you do. I hear Joseph's voice, and it's him I want."

Mike's eyebrows arched in surprise, "Well—"

Another voice roared through Joseph's murmured words; both Jenny and Mike faced the jumble of shelves and boxes that shielded the far end of the building. Jenny didn't recognize the voice, but she forgot that as she listened.

"I tell you, there's no other way. We will prevail. We will win! The Lord himself has given us this plan; you've said so yourself. The law of consecration will not support the building of the temple. These people are too poor. We must convince them that this new plan will work. Think of it—everyone divided into four companies, everyone placing their property under his company for the good of all. Everyone with a task to do, and we'll all prosper."

The roar subsided to a low rumble and Jenny looked at Mike. "Who is that?"

He cast her a pitying glance. "You best get acquainted. That fella is a big shot who's gonna get bigger. That's Avard, the wheel that runs the Danites."

"Avard!" She'd only time for a gasp of surprise when the man thumped his way into the room. He elbowed past her and slapped the bar.

"Mike, a stiff one." Now he turned with a sardonic grin, and she guessed he had been fully aware of her presence when he pushed into the room. "Well, well. A camp follower?"

"I'll thank you, sir, to watch your manners. I am a wife."

He slapped his knee and howled with laughter. "Aw, got your temper up, didn't I? Now you see me, what do you want?"

"Want? Nothing, I—" Stepping closer she peered up at him, "So you're the famous Avard who runs the Danites. I've heard about you. Why must you have such a fearful, secret army? Isn't it more proper to be all out in the open? I mean, if you're in the right and there's to be a fight, why the *secret?*"

"Well, now," he scratched his head and then grinned. "I guess 'cause the fellas like it."

"That's no reason. I've heard the menfolk are frightened, scared to step a toe over the line. They're talking about you having absolute control of the men. Why, I've heard that even Joseph Smith doesn't know what you're doing behind all that secrecy—"

"I've heard," he mimicked, with a snort of a laugh. "That ain't so. Joe knows what's goin' on. When we organized, he came before us to bless us. The presidency gave us to realize we're here to do a marvelous work on this earth. It's promised to us that we'll have glorious military victory, and it will be by the power of God. The revelation said that one of us will put a thousand to flight; besides that, we'll be assisted by angels in the work of the Lord as we go out to battle."

"You think you will?" Jenny's voice was only a whisper. She was thinking of Mark and Tom.

His glance was shrewd. "He prophesied that the time has come for us to take up arms in our defense. Joseph even promised that if trusting in him fails, we can use his head for a football." He was studying her face with eyes so sharp that Jenny steeled herself to endure the scrutiny.

Slowly he spoke, "You know what the worst thing on this earth is for a Saint?" She shook her head and he added, "To disbelieve or go against the Prophet and his men."

In a moment she recovered enough to say, "I heard you talking about the companies of workers."

He nodded, his gaze was still piercing as he said, "All persons who attempt to cheat by deception, holding back some of their property from the church, will meet the same fate as Ananias and Sapphira did. Peter killed them."

He turned back to the bar and lifted the glass. But Jenny was caught motionless. When he faced her again, she was still waiting. "There'll be a fight, lady, whether you and the *Oh, don'ts* want it or not. I do, and we'll see the matter out; there's no other way." He finished his drink; without another word, he headed out the door.

Jenny heard his shout and the sharp whinny of his horse before she recalled the reason she was here. She turned to Mike. "Joseph. I must see him."

Mike was still polishing glasses. His look was level as he said, "Went out the back way 'bout five minutes ago. He's headed home and walkin'. I suppose you could catch him."

By the time Jenny was back on her mare and headed for the edge of town, she could see the dark figure cutting away from the road and moving into the trees. She was certain it was Joseph. That fellow had pointed out the George Harris home just beyond those trees.

As Jenny guided the mare away from the road and into the trees, she lost sight of Joseph. "Oh dear," she murmured, "one second and he's disappeared. I was certain he was moving that direction, and now—" Jenny blinked.

The path in front of her had been empty, but now there was a figure moving toward her. She had guessed it was a woman wearing a dark cloak, and now she saw a flash of red with every step the woman took. Red. Surely not.

Jenny leaned over the horse's neck and peered through the shadows. Was her silly heart playing tricks again. Had her deep need conjured an apparition? "Adela," she whispered. Her heart was pounding in confirmation of what she was seeing.

At the moment Jenny straightened and screamed, "Adela!" she brought the reins down across Patches' flanks. The horse lunged and reared. Jenny fought for control as they plunged through the bushes.

When Jenny had calmed the horse, she slipped from Patches' back, still trembling.

Joseph came loping through the bushes. "Jenny Cartwright, is that really you?" He reached for her with a pleased grin, then exclaimed, "What happened?"

"Nothing, really. This mare took off like a scared rabbit when I yelled."

"That was you? Who were you calling?"

"The woman. Did you see her?" Jenny ran past him to the path and stopped. "That's strange. She's completely disappeared. I would have expected that—" She shrugged and turned back to Joseph. "But it's you I've come to see."

He was frowning, looking around uneasily. When he turned back she saw he was puzzled, lost in thought. She studied his uneasy grin, saw how hard he tried to concentrate on her words, and, surprisingly, a crushing disappointment settled over her.

"Joseph, remember a long time ago in Kirtland, you said you needed me." She saw the astonishment flare in his eyes and paused only to wonder as she continued. "You said you needed a friend, to—to let you know what was going on. Do you still need me? I've been hearing so much—she faltered when she saw the thundercloud expression.

"Of course," he said hastily. "What is it?"

"The people. Please give them a chance. They grumble and argue, but they daren't tell you what they are thinking. Joseph, it hadn't ought to be." For a moment she was lost in reflection, and then recovering, she added, "Even I miss the old Joseph. You were so much fun, and they adored you."

His eyes softened for a moment and then with a sigh, he said, "Those were the old days, Jenny. How I wish I could have held them forever in that way. But no! It is not that I wished differently; it was them."

His eyes were blazing and he grasped the hand she held outstretched. "Jenny, I've found how deep their devotion goes. It's only as deep as their pockets. If I am a cynic, it is because I have discovered I can trust no man. They want to own me, shape me to their image. I will be owned by none. I am the Lord's anointed. I hold the keys of the kingdom. If I must control these people with an iron hand in order to bring them into the kingdom of heaven, then I will do so."

"Love?"

It was a question, and he stared into her eyes as he slowly asked, "What do you mean?"

"Mark says God is love. He thinks it is possible for people to be controlled by love." Joseph's mouth was twisting in amusement, and hastily Jenny continued, "I don't agree. I think it's power." She recalled the woman. "That's why I was so excited when I saw her. Do you still have the talisman and the seer stone? Do you still believe—"

Now Joseph threw his head back and laughed heartily, "Jenny, my dear! Do you mean to tell me that you haven't outgrown those childish ways? How have you escaped the pious clutches of your husband's holy fervor?" Now he leaned close and whispered, "Don't be foolish, my dear! Of course I don't believe the old witching tales. I am Prophet, Seer, and Revelator. I am the anointed. What I say is the word of God to my people. Don't forget that. When I say jump, my people must jump. When I say a thing will happen, it will happen."

"Like the riches of the Gentiles will be ours?" She was staring into his face. Without wavering, his eyes met hers. Slowly, she whispered, "Joseph, I wish with all my heart that I could believe as surely as you do. Then maybe it wouldn't make any difference whether I ever saw Adela again, whether I got back my talisman and the book."

He blinked. "What's happened?"

"Nothing. Silly-like, I left them in Adam-ondi-Ahman."

And then in another moment he said thoughtfully, "So the people aren't happy. What do they want from me?"

"They want you to stay your hand. They want to live in peace with these people in this state. It can't happen as long as you insist on crushing everyone around you, Saints included."

"Jenny, my dear." His voice was sorrowful. "It is for their own good. Have you not heard enough of the revelations to know that when the people disobey, God will punish them? It is my unhappy lot to be standing between the two as prophet. I get blamed for all the Lord does to His people." He paused before adding, "Now go. When the questioners come to you, tell them that when they quit sinning, they will experience all the fullness of the blessings of the Lord. If they refuse to consecrate their property and do the work of the Lord, well, they'll suffer for their sins." His shiver was tiny and controlled, but Jenny turned away with a new seed of despair in her heart.

Joseph lifted Jenny to her horse. Once again he was distant, cold. She rode away with a heavy heart. Back on the road to Far West, she allowed the mare to amble along while she thought about the things Joseph had said.

She was deeply conscious of sin and failure. As she headed

up the road to Morgans' little cabin, she murmured, "I went expecting to improve the Saints' lot, and I've come back crushed to the ground by all our faults. No wonder the Lord can't bless us. I'm guessing I'd do well to quit blaming Joseph for something he can't help and go to work on changing things."

She rode silently for a time and then with a grin, she straightened and lifted her face. "Seems it really is hopeless, Joseph. You told me not to be childish, but you don't know what you're talking about. No sense advertising to you, but I intend to get that book and the talisman. But I don't expect you to thank me for saving your neck!"

Joseph watched until Jenny was out of sight and then he turned. "All right, Lucinda, come out of those bushes. I know you are there."

She raised her arms and Joseph caught her close. "But you are a witch, of the very best kind. Miss me?" He bent to kiss her before she could answer.

Lucinda leaned back to study his face, saying, "For a moment I thought I had competition." His grin wasn't reassuring. As she snuggled close, she stifled a sigh.

CHAPTER 14

As Mark left Far West with the newly formed militia, now called the Armies of Israel, he soon discovered that he was part of the derided group. Rigdon had referred to them as the *Oh, don't* men. Right now they were called the "bayonet outfit" by the old timers. As nearly as he could determine, the name either had reference to the position of the men in battle line— right out front—or because it took the urging of a bayonet to get them on the horses.

His chagrin over the stigma was short-lived when he met his illustrious companions. "John Corrill, Phelps, Cleminson, and Reed Peck!" he exclaimed when the men were forced into line in front of the foot soldiers as they prepared to march to Adam-ondi-Ahman.

The first day their march extended into the cool autumn dusk. The troops passed up the road he and Jenny had traveled just a few days previously. Toward evening Mark and his companions talked in low voices while the remainder of the army abandoned caution and sang one song after another.

The morning of the second day of march, the troops began seeing caravans of people heading down the valley toward them. Mark pointed them out to Corrill and asked, "What do you make of that?"

He didn't get an answer until the group had passed, and then Corrill's answer confirmed his guess. "From the looks of those poor beggars, I'm guessin' we've routed the rest of the Gentiles out of Daviess County. I recognize some faces. They don't impress me as goin' on a pleasure trip."

The troops watched the exodus of the Gentiles as they passed with wagons piled high with furniture and stuffed with people. The oxen were having a hard time of it and the wagons moved slowly. Mark saw the pinched-faced women staring stoically ahead, while solemn children watched wide-eyed.

"It's enough to make you feel like a perfect rotter," Peck muttered.

"Can't say I'm too proud of myself running a neighbor outta his home," Corrill added.

When the exhausted men reached Adam-ondi-Ahman late Tuesday evening, Mark discovered the character of the small town had undergone a radical change. True, he and Jenny had sensed abandonment as they had ridden through, but now the Gentile settlers seemed to have vanished. As Mark studied the half-finished fortress in the middle of town, he recalled his conversation with Tom, and how, at the time, the bunker had seemed like a feeble joke. But clearly the Danites were in control now.

Mark turned in that night, crowded between the other dissenters and placed under guard. Corrill murmured, "One advantage to being labeled an *Oh, don't* man is that we get to sleep inside the stable on the hay instead of outside with the tough ones, and, man, is it getting cold out there!"

By the morning it was snowing heavily. The men clustered around the campfires and shifted from one soggy foot to another. A chosen group was sent out to hunt dinner. Seeing Tom in the group, Mark hailed him and was surprised to see his curt salute as he turned away.

All that day, as the snow continued to pile high in Adam-ondi-Ahman, the men huddled around the fire. Mark's thoughts were gloomy as he recalled Jenny's white face and terror-filled eyes. When he caught Phelps' eye and the man gave him a twisted grin, he decided his thoughts weren't much different than the ones others were having.

Moving closer to Mark, Phelps murmured, "I'm not liking it either. My family isn't faring better; fact is," he gave a twisted grin, "I'm out of favor, too. Guess I did too much thinking out loud." After a moment he added, "I'm not a man to be out totin' a gun, but when pushed in the corner, I guess I fight."

As the morning wore on, the small talk around the fire dwindled to discontented murmuring, given with eyes slanted toward the known Danites in the group.

The men's restlessness carried them back and forth between the livery stable, the stockade, and the fire. Mark was eyeing Phelps as he moved back into the circle of the fire about noontime. He pulled a log close to Mark's and grunted, "Some status, from newspaper editor to Joseph's flunky. Still, I guess that means living your religion, and I'm not too much different than the others. You're an attorney, aren't you?" Mark nodded.

While Phelps stared into the fire, he spoke slowly, as if thinking aloud, "I still believe in Joseph. There's too many indications that his revelations are truth."

"What are you referring to?"

He looked up. "I was thinking about all the Indians being moved this way by Andy Jackson." He chuckled and shook his head, "He'd a pushed them into the Atlantic rather than serve the Lord's and Joseph's purposes by gathering Israel so close to Zion." He paused and then added, "I predicted then that the second coming was less than nine years away."

"The deadline is close," Mark observed, studying the man. Phelps shrugged, and Mark asked, "What did you do to rate the title of an *Oh, don't* man?"

"Just what any decent newspaper man would do. I was sticking up for the rights of those unjustly persecuted."

"You mean you think the dissenters were persecuted?"

"Isn't that right? They spoke out against oppression and lost position, favor, property, and were forced to run for their lives. It was fortunate that they survived the interview with the Danites," he murmured, glancing quickly around.

Mark looked too, and then said, "That's plenty. I did less and got myself in hot water."

"Yes, I know. You helped them out of the state and then flapped your big mouth over Whitmer's house when you knew Rigdon had confiscated it for himself."

"And Joseph sanctioned all this by his silence." Phelp's eyebrows raised, but he nodded. Deliberately pushing now, Mark added, "And no law, nothing, is superior to the word of the Lord given through the Prophet."

"When you say it like that, the whole thing sounds ridiculous."

"Phelps, you're a thinking man. You can't continue to follow a man so obviously wrong in his dealings with his fellowman."

The man looked at Mark for a long time, studying his face thoughtfully. Finally he sighed and shifted his weight on the log. "You're overlooking the most important thing. I believe he has the keys to the kingdom, that he has given us the sacred word of God."

"What about all those things that happened back in the early days before he had a following? What about the South Bainbridge days, the money digging and witching? Surely a thinking man wouldn't accept without questioning."

"You're right," Phelps said. "I did question. It was an advantage to do my questioning *first* instead of as an afterthought."

"You did?" Mark knew his surprise and disappointment was showing, but he must ask. "How did that happen?"

"Just after the founding of the church I heard about Joseph and his men and decided to inquire.

"And you were satisfied?"

He moved restlessly and looked away from Mark. For a moment he was silent, and Mark saw the uncertainty on his face. When he squared his shoulders and looked at Mark, he grinned. "I guess we all have our moments of doubt—but to doubt is wrong. I was curious and looking. At the time, I'd been involved with my soapbox, Masonry. When I found out how dead set Joseph was against the secret societies, and how he'd had revelations showing God commanding against them, well, that just sealed my determination to be a part of the group."

Mark moved restlessly. Then Phelps was speaking again. "From the beginning, Joseph's spirit was consistent with what we see now—a man of God."

"Tell me more."

"You know the rest of the story. About the finding of the gold plates."

"Phelps, can you believe his holy calling on the basis of this?"

"I told you, I'd worked my way through belief and disbelief. It was hard; the story was incredulous. But just like the others, I had to ask for a sign from God, and He gave me a burning in the bosom in confirmation." He was silent a moment and then added, "Besides, there's something about the man. Sometimes I get angry at him, but I can't help it; I've got to believe his calling. There is a divine cord about me which will not let me go."

Mark found he couldn't control the ridiculous question: "Are you afraid?"

Phelps looked up in surprise. "Of course! Mark, don't you realize eternal salvation for you will depend on whether Joseph *approves*? I've heard him myself, saying that he will stand at the entrance of heaven and turn back those who haven't won his approval."

They were still standing in front of the fire, silent with their own thoughts, when they heard the clatter of hooves on the river road. The men around the fire turned to watch. It was a lone horseman, and Phelps muttered. "The Ram of the mountain. It's Colonel Wight—wonder what his problem is?"

Mark watched the man dismount. He was wearing only a light jacket with his hairy chest open to the snow. His long, heavy hair was tied back with a soiled red kerchief.

Wight impatiently flipped the bearskin covering his saddle, and strode to the fire waving a cutless. Watching him swish the short curved blade as he impatiently kicked a log into the fire, Mark murmured, "The name fits."

One of the Danites who had just approached the fire slanted a glance at Mark and Phelps. "Second to Avard, he's a man the Gentiles fear. There's trouble on the Millport road. I heard them talking last night. We all just might be called out there yet unless the rest of the army in Far West is moved this way."

"What's the problem?" Mark asked, turning from the fire to meet the man's frown.

"Yesterday Wight was addressing the men in camp. I was there and, I'll tell you, it was a speech to put fire in the veins of a dead man. He was in the midst of telling us how the Lord had made us invincible and that there's not an army around who can defeat us when this fella up and cut out of there, riding like his life was on the line. And it would have been if we'd known who he was.

"Information leaking back later let us know it was a dispatch from the other side. He'd been sent from the Missouri militia, mind you, to advise that their group was mutinous and that they were joining the DeWitt mob.

"Later we heard more from one of the spies. He told us this fella, the one we saw bust and run, carried back the report that Wight had fifteen thousand men under him and would be in their camp in two hours. Intelligence said they broke camp and left, but Joseph's sweating it out, getting ready to send more men this way."

It was late in the afternoon before the men took up the thread of conversation again. Mark heard Pratt reviewing the Lord's plan for Missouri, but he paid little attention until the man sat up and declared, "There's coming a day when the Lord will give these people a chance to accept the *Book of Mormon*. If they refuse to hearken to it, the remnant of Jacob, that's the Indians, will go through here and tear these people to pieces."

"Do you really reckon it will happen, Pratt?" came a wistful voice from the far side of the fire.

Pratt got to his feet and paced back and forth. His hands were linked behind his back. Mark was thinking that Pratt was a fellow who would catch anyone's attention. When Pratt answered, his sonorous voice made the hair on Mark's neck prickle. "I prophesy," he said, "that there will not be an unbelieving Gentile on this continent in fifty years' time. Furthermore, if they aren't to a great extent scourged and overthrown in five or ten years from now—this year of 1838—then I say the *Book of Mormon* will have proved itself to be false. I intend to write this prophecy for posterity. I may not be suited to fighting, but I have the ability to prophesy."

Late that evening the hunters returned. Mark was still mulling over Pratt's statement when he heard the questions shouted to the men. "Same old fare," they called back. "Bear, buffalo, and sweet oil."

Phelps rubbed his cold chin and said, "That means we dine

on Gentile cows, pigs, and honey. I just hope this doesn't mean someone's going hungry."

Cleminson answered, "I was on one of these thieving missions when the fellows helped themselves. Some old lady was left to watch her only cow being led away to feed Mormon bellies. I tell you, I felt like a rotter."

Phelps said in a soft voice, "Better keep your thoughts to yourself if you don't want to join the group tomorrow night."

The men were eating the roasted beef, cooked over the open fire, when a lone man rode into their encampment. "Lee, come have something to eat," Pratt called, waving his chunk of beef. "You have news?"

He nodded. After taking the stick impaled with chunks of roasted meat, he said, "I'm here to round up volunteers to ride out with us in the morning."

Mark studied his furrowed brow as Franklin asked, "What's the mission?"

"Joseph, Wight, and Patten have cooked up a plan. You'll hear about it tomorrow." He looked around the group and said, "Just give me some men. About forty will do."

CHAPTER 15

After being housebound by the snow, Jenny's restless spirit couldn't get enough of roaming. The snow, still piled under the trees, and the paths, a soggy mat of torn branches and snow-packed grass, didn't stop her. However, she did spend one day dragging her skirts through the soggy mess and dampening her boots almost beyond saving before resorting to Patches.

One day she was thinking, as she rode into Far West, that she would much rather crash through the deserted woods than ride the trails around town, but riding was better than nothing—and there were advantages.

She had just let her restless horse shy away from Anna Briton. She chalked up the first advantage with a sly grin. A horse made it possible to escape busybody neighbors whose total enjoyment was checking out how others were living their religion.

Jenny dug her heels into the horse's ribs and refused to rescue her hair when the wind caught it and flung it over her shoulders.

She was riding helter-skelter through Far West when the difference in the town caught her attention. More than just a sprinkling of frightened women were on the street, there were men as well—tattered, dirty, but jubilant. And the men and women who surrounded them were either frowning and backing away or pressing forward with eager hands and welcoming cries.

Jenny watched the milling crowd, realizing now that the focus of their attention wasn't the returning warriors home from battle. Instead, all eyes were on the loaded wagons in the town square.

Slipping from her horse, she joined the group, where Mrs. Lewis greeted her with a smile. Jenny returned her greeting and turned to watch the eager hands pulling furniture—feather beds, a churn, even a mirror—from the wagon.

When Mrs. Lewis stopped beside her, Jenny asked, "What is this?"

The man tossing down bundles of clothing answered, " 'Tis the riches of the Gentiles. Come get your share." He tossed an embroidered shawl to her, and Jenny held it away to study it.

It was of soft creamy wool, gently scented with lavendar. She could see it was old; the folds were yellow with age. Closing her eyes, she could nearly see the woman who had cherished the shawl. "Her mother," she murmured. "I'm sure it was her mother's shawl, and she's grieving the loss!"

"What did you say?" Mrs. Lewis was looking into her face.

"I shall keep it," Jenny declared. "And when this nightmare is over, I shall return it to its owner. It belonged to her dead mother. We've no right to take it."

The man on the wagon roared, " 'Tis the Gentiles. They'll be consigned to hell and there's no need for shawls there!" The laughter spilled around Jenny, and she backed away, still clutching the shawl.

Mrs. Lewis was chiding gently, "Child, are you disputing the word of the Lord through Joseph? You know the revelation. You know that now is the time for the riches of the Gentiles to become our inheritance. Come, don't sound like a dissenter." Her fingers were grasping the shawl, prying it out of Jenny's hands. She added, "If you've no need for it, I can use a new one. I wonder if the yellow streaks will come out."

After watching the Saints rummage through the wagons and cart off their choices, Jenny shook her head and turned her horse away. "Atta girl." She heard the soft comment and glanced up. Jake was grinning at her. Then she noticed others leaving the town square empty-handed.

Guiding Patches away from the main streets, Jenny worked her way slowly toward the fringes of town. She was passing the cluster of log cabins, noticing, with a sharp stab of surprise, the number which had been deserted.

She was uneasy, still pondering that discovery as she rode past the schoolhouse. A group of men stood close to the steps, one of them Sidney Rigdon. With a casual glance, Jenny had started on when the sharp voices caught her attention.

She pulled on the reins and turned Patches. Rigdon was standing on the steps, looking out over the men. His face was contorted with rage as he waved his arm and shouted, "The last Saint has fled Far West! So you don't like the directions of the Lord? We'll see to it that you do! The next to leave will be chased, brought back—dead or alive. I bring before you a resolution: if a man attempts to pack his belongings, take his family, and leave, I propose that the man who sees this happening shall, without revealing his intentions to any other, kill the fleeing Saint and hide his body in the bushes." He paused and in the silence added, "Yesterday about this time, one man from Far West slipped his wind and was dragged into the bushes to die. Now, I warn you, any man lisping a word of this shall have the same happen to him."

That evening as Jenny sat beside the fire, poking at the tumble of yarn in her lap, she thought about the afternoon scene around the wagon. The memory had become doubly troubling since she had heard Rigdon's tirade.

Under the ripple of conversation Sally was releasing, Jenny was thinking. It hurt to imagine these people deprived of their possessions, but that wasn't the reason she was hearing warning bells in her soul. It was something deeper.

With a sigh, Jenny straightened on her stool and said, "Sally, I've got to go back to Adam-ondi-Ahman." As she described the afternoon's events, she saw Sally's expression change from placid content to shock and disbelief.

"Jenny, how ridiculous! You risk your life to go fuss at Joseph. I'm certain he knows how Rigdon feels. I don't understand it all, but where'd we be if every man fled Far West? As for being in danger, they're not. They are doing just what the Lord's commanded them to do. How could He fail to keep them safe? Besides, they'd never listen to a woman."

There was an urgency, an underlying current of fear in Sally's voice. Jenny searched her friend's face and could see the dark circles under her eyes, the weary lines on her face. Without a doubt Sally needed her, but Jenny's need to get the talisman and the green book was growing deeper every day. This afternoon's ride had confirmed the uneasy impression that something very wrong was happening in Zion. She needed all the power she could possibly conjure if she were to help these people.

As she studied Sally's face, Jenny had the distinct impression that she alone sensed disaster moving close.

Jenny dropped to her knees beside Sally and clasped her hands. Even now she guessed that Sally would let her go, but she couldn't endure leaving her without hope.

"Sally, listen to me. It isn't just what happened this afternoon. There's something else. When I went into Far West that first time, I met that horrible Samson Avard."

"The leader of the Danites?" Sally whispered. Jenny could see she had her attention. She nodded. Sally was still speaking softly, as if she expected the walls to hear. "He's terrible. I've heard whispers about how he's deceiving Joseph and how he's so cruel."

"That's why I must go. Surely Joseph doesn't know of his influence with the men and the terrible things he's planning. Sally, do you see? I *must* go."

She watched the woman's countenance fall and lunged for the nearest word. "Faith. Sally, you must have faith. You're going to be ill if you continue in this hopeless way." *Faith*. The word mocked Jenny, and she nearly thought she could hear the spirit's laughter.

"You heard Joseph and Rigdon and the others. They've promised that the Lord will fight for the men and that not a hair on their heads will be lost. Don't you believe it?" Sally studied her face without answering, but now there was a spark of a question in her dull eyes.

"Faith is just believing when your good sense tells you it's all wrong," Sally finally whispered.

Tamara was holding up her arms and Jenny lifted the child.

She buried her face in the toddler's hair and hoped Sally wouldn't ask her for her own definition. How could she convince Sally of the faith she had professed? Faith was having a green book with instructions for living. Faith was having charms and the sure knowledge of power.

Jenny's lips twisted as she imagined this woman, a devout follower of the Prophet, being exposed to Jenny's beliefs. She closed her eyes and imagined the horrified expression on Sally's face were she to know how she really believed. But still, faith was faith. "God of nature, God of all," Jenny murmured, "bring me power to help this woman."

"Jenny, I—I," Sally stopped with a gulp. "I'm so fearful. It isn't just about Andy. That's part, but not all. I—I keep thinking that if I don't do something soon—" She was silent for a long minute and Jenny, busy with her own thoughts, wondered how she could give Sally hope without shattering her tenuous faith in the Prophet.

"Jenny," it was a timid attempt, and Jenny raised her head. "I—it's been so long since we've seen each other to really talk and now I feel so—so bound up that I dare not say a thing."

"Sally, I'm sorry. I didn't mean to make you feel that way."

"Oh no," Sally said quickly. "It isn't that, it's just that I've been entrusted with secret things—responsibilities. I dare not say more. It's just that I feel the weight of it all so deeply." She dropped her face into her hands, and Jenny saw her press her lips with a gesture of despair.

When Sally lifted her face she said, "The Prophet says we must obey if we are to have the assurance that the Lord will take care of us. Jenny, it's a fearful responsibility."

Slowly Jenny said, "You're talking as if having faith is similar to lifting a sack of potatoes. Hard." She looked curiously at her and thought of her own faith. And when she had examined it, she decided Sally's definition just might fit.

Early the following morning Jenny rode through the woods. She headed north, away from Log Creek where Sally and Andy Morgan had built their cabin close to Haun's Mill. As she approached Far West, she walked the horse deeper into the woods, making it appear as if she were out for a leisurely ride. She was also thinking it might be a good idea to have an excuse ready to offer since she would be traveling into forbidden territory.

As she rode, Jenny was still thinking about Sally. Momentarily she frowned, wondering at the depths of the woman's agony. Finally Jenny's lips twisted in amusement. To think she had once thought herself shackled to Joseph's church, fearful and duty-bound to obey. Now Sally's face served as a tonic, freeing her of the past.

She chuckled as she rode on, secure with her decision to win power, all the power the church boasted, plus more. "I've come full circle," she reminded herself in a pleased whisper. "All I need now is Pa's green book."

North of Far West, Jenny turned back to the road and whipped her horse on toward Gallatin. Effortlessly, the horse flew with the wind, carrying Jenny's light body.

At Gallatin she again left the road and cut around town at an easy walk. This was Gentile territory, and it was wise to avoid strangers these days. She began to relax, to enjoy the day and the ride.

She was on the far side of town, beyond the store and stables, when she met the man. The trail was dim and shadowed, and she was picking her way carefully when she heard his horse. Her heart began to pound, pressed by all those fearful stories.

Raising her whip, she waited for him to approach. He dismounted. Jenny jerked the reins and the man leaped for them. "Take it easy, ma'am, I mean no harm. Gentile or Saint, it isn't safe for pretty young women to be out."

She thought he looked familiar. "Saint, and I've business in Adam-ondi-Ahman."

"Aren't you Mark Cartwright's wife? I'm John Lee. The missus and I met you at the last meeting. If you're headin' for home, I say don't. Go back the way you've come."

"But why?"

He turned to point toward the north. "See that and that? Them ain't supper fires. The Gentiles are burnin' and the Mormons are burnin'. Both are snitchin' everything they can and burnin' what they can't."

"Mr. Lee, that's terrible! Burning! If we treat them that way, we'll never learn to live with these people. What will happen if this keeps up?"

He shrugged his shoulders. "Joe says this is civil war, and by the rules each of us is justified in spoilin' the enemy."

"Mark would call that wrong—lawlessness. Where does it end when we're all doing that?"

"I'd guess it ends when there's nobody left to fight." It was a light answer, but peering up at him in the dusk, Jenny saw his brow was furrowed and his eyes unhappy. Thoughtfully he said, "I'm seein' men becomin' perfect demons as they spoil and waste each other. Seems to be the natural inclination of men to steal and plunder. But the thing that surprises me most is that these men got religion in the only true church left in the world. I'd expect there's somethin' wrong when religion's not got the power to subdue the animal passion in man."

"Animal?" she asked thoughtfully.

He nodded. "That's what they're like. The church takes its restrictions off, and they're animals. Seems the ideal would be you wouldn't have to pressure a man with fear of death to get him to act right."

"But how do you learn what's right? Don't people have different ideas of right?"

He scratched his head and looked thoughtfully at Jenny. "Seems strange to be philosophizin' beside the road with a pretty lady—but, no." Jenny's horse snorted and pawed restlessly. "Seems there's some kinda standard built into a person. But I'm thinkin' some squash it down, 'til you'd never know the man had a right idea." Lee straightened and sighed. "But now. You can't ride on to Adam-ondi-Ahman today. These men are roamin' the countryside, doin' all the damage they can. Go back."

"I must go on," Jenny insisted; "besides, it's as dangerous to go back."

He thought a moment and then admitted, "That's true." In another moment, he added, "I have a friend up the way here. Name's McBrier. An old gentleman who's been mighty good to me regardless of being Gentile. I'll point you in the way. You go stay with McBrier until you don't see smoke comin' up around the place; then you high-tail for home, get your business done, and then get back to Far West."

"How long will that be?"

"Day or so. Right now things are bad. While back, they pulled the state militia out here." He shook his head. "The Saints sent them on back, saying they could handle the situation. Don't know why they did it, seein's Joseph called for help in the first place. So the fellas mobbing on both sides are gettin' mighty brave about doing anything they want.

"In a day or so the squabbling will be coolin'." While his restless horse pawed and snorted, Lee said, "Come along, I'll point you in the right direction." And Jenny knew it was useless to argue.

When Lee stopped at the end of the lane leading to the low log house, it was dusk. There was a faint glow of light coming from the windows. Jenny thanked the man and slowly rode toward the light. The house was pleasant, she could see that. She could also see the corrals and barn, the cows and horses, and she could hear the contented barnyard sounds. For the first time since Mark had left, the tightness around Jenny's heart eased.

The gray-haired woman who opened the door at Jenny's knock stood staring in shock. Then reaching out she pulled Jenny through the door. "My dear!" she exclaimed. "Whatever are you doing out alone?"

"Well, I thought I was safe," Jenny explained, "until I met Mr. John Lee. He scolded me and brought me up here. Said I should stay until the fighting is over."

As Mrs. McBrier bustled out to call her husband, Jenny unwound her shawl and looked around the large room. As she had ridden onto the farm, she had noticed the mellow look as if it had been here a long time. Inside there was a settled, homey look. Heavy timbers crossed the room, and a stone fireplace covered an end wall. A spinning wheel with carded wool stood close to the polished rocking chair. Comfortable chairs cushioned with colorful quilts edged the room. Jenny was admiring the walnut table and chairs and stroking the tall cherry cabinet when the McBriers came into the room.

The old gentleman had a twinkly smile, and his bright blue

eyes seemed kin to his wife's. He held out his hand. "Mother tells me John sent you. Any friend of John's is our friend, too. You are welcome to stay until it is safe to travel again. My, such carryin' on!" He continued shaking his head sadly as he led her to the fireplace. "We've put your horse up. Now, you just take this chair and let us offer you tea." He paused; looking confused, he said, "I'm forgetting, if you're—"

Jenny hastily said, "Tea! Oh, that would be wonderful."

Before the evening was over, Jenny felt as if she had known these people for years. It seemed they had a story for every treasure in their home. Even the furniture was rich with family heritage. She handled the black-bound Book they held with such reverence and listened to them explain the list of names written on a page in the middle.

While they talked, Jenny was thinking of her mother's black Book. Was her name written into it? Thoughtfuly she thumbed through the pages, recalling how her mother had held that book as if it were precious. And Mark. He had a Book just like this. On occasion he had taken it out and tried to read it to her.

Abruptly the picture of Jenny preparing to shove the Book into the stove flashed across her memory. She cringed as she recalled the fearful time of headaches and oppression that year in Kirtland just before Mark had left. She had blamed the Book for causing them. Just briefly, as she held McBrier's Book, guilt touched her, and she could only wonder why. As she considered that time, curiosity was born in her.

She interrupted Mrs. McBrier's story, asking, "Have you read this Book?"

"Oh my, yes." The woman patted the pages comfortably. "When I was just a youngster I won a medal for reading it through in less than a year. It was hard at times, keeping awake through Chronicles and Numbers, but I made it."

She paused and studied Jenny for a moment before saying, "The Mormons say they believe it is a holy book. Do they expect their young people to read it?"

Jenny cocked her head and thought. Slowly she said, "I don't know. In fact, I don't know any of the young people. I do know the twelve and the first presidency sometimes talk about the things that the Bible says. At times they read it aloud."

"Then you hear it preached about how to know Jesus. About how He died for our sins in order to give us God's righteousness and provide a way for us to be with Him for eternity."

Jenny studied her curiously, "No, that's not the way we heard it. But, then, it doesn't matter, does it? There's only one God; how we choose to worship Him doesn't really matter. It's the worship that's important."

From the far side of the fireplace, Mr. McBrier cleared his throat and with a twinkle in his eyes he said, "Well, I'm not up to talking theology with anyone, especially with a young lady looking as smart as you do. One thing I do know; reading God's Word was like having Him rope me in.

"Just like a rebellious calf, fighting the branding iron and the rope, I was. But do you know, after getting a good exposure to the words, I found out I *liked* it. It made a change in me, sure. Can't read about Jesus Christ without being attracted.

"But, sure enough, the first part of being attracted is being made mighty uncomfortable. You read about all that He went through, the spitting on Him and pulling His beard, the crown of thorns and such; then without complaining He gets killed. I really sat up straight when I found out about Him rising from the dead." He stared thoughtfully into the fire for a long moment before he again faced Jenny and said, "I can remember how I used to feel inside. Reading made me churn around like a creek in spring thaw. I wanted to quit the reading, but by then I couldn't. Now I'm glad."

Jenny waited a moment and then asked, "Why?"

He looked directly at her and said, "Because I soon found out that this man is God, and that He came here to this earth just to die for us."

"That seems like such a waste. I can't understand why He'd do that," Jenny mused as she stared into the fire.

"Well, He did it because He loved us enough to want us with Him forever. See, we couldn't go to heaven on our own, because of sin. Sin, well, that makes everybody squirm just thinking about it. Until we finally accept what God did to get rid of sin." He looked at her while Jenny wished he would talk of something else. "It's like this. Sin's so terrible man can't ever undo it. He can't ever make up for it. So God did. His dying made it possible for people to actually be holy themselves."

"So everyone is holy," Jenny said thoughtfully.

"Only if you believe it and accept Jesus' death for yourself. That's called faith, believing what God says to man in the Book."

Later as Mrs. McBrier led Jenny to the spare bedroom and turned back the colorful quilt, Jenny was thinking about the conversation around the fire. She found herself sighing, and that surprised her.

CHAPTER 16

On October 18 when David Patten and forty men galloped into Adam-ondi-Ahman, the Saints were still spending most of their time huddled around the fire, just watching the snow melt and run down the road. Mark had been thinking how good it was to see the unseasonable snow melting rapidly.

The sunshine inspired hope and confidence, and Mark's secret hope was that Boggs would send his troops back and peace would reign. But the truth of the matter was that the Mormon troops from Far West were still waiting for the Gentile mob from DeWitt, and not with hopes for peace.

Mark was still brooding over the alternatives when he heard the sound of hooves pounding the sodden road. The men around him flew to their stations, and he slowly got up to follow.

When Patten rounded the corner, Lee went forward to meet him. His scowl changed to surprise as he addressed Patten. "What's the meaning of this? Where's the mob we're supposed to be fighting?"

"They're still headed this way, dragging that cannon behind. That isn't why we've come. I could use a few more good men." He paused to look around the group. "You, Tom Timmons. Got a good horse and rifle? Come on."

Patten pointed out other men and waved at them to follow him. Mark watched Tom jump to his feet, glad for activity. As he left the fire, one of the men growled, "Why the secrecy?" Tom looked up; when he met Mark's questioning gaze he shrugged. The fellow muttered, "Don't much care *what* they do, long's they're moving."

Patten got off his horse and the men clustered around him. Mark watched Patten's restless eyes as he looked over the men, saying, "Joseph and Wight sent me out to do a little business. We're headed to Gallatin to give the folks there a little shake-up."

"Wait a minute!" Hansen exclaimed. "They haven't given us trouble."

"Isn't a matter of trouble," Patten said shortly. "The Prophet has said that now is the time for the riches of the Gentiles to be consecrated to Israel. Come on, men."

"So Joseph sent 'em."

"And the riches of the Gentiles are about to be reaped," the speaker chuckled.

Mark turned and saw Phelps watching him. As Mark hesitated, the man dropped his gaze. Mark waited a moment longer before he shoved his hands into his pockets and strolled down the road.

Rivulets of brown water cut down the length of the roadbed, deepening the ruts. Mark eyed them, wondering how the Gentiles would manage to pull their cannon up the hill into Adam-ondi-Ahman. Another horse was coming. From the sound Mark guessed that leisurely trot wasn't threatening. He leaned against a tree and waited.

It was Joseph. Seeing Mark, he wheeled his horse toward him. His grin was challenging, mocking; and Mark realized it was the first time he had seen the Prophet since, along with the other *Oh, don't* men, he had been sent into exile.

As Mark watched the man dismount, he realized his opportunity. He had the Prophet all to himself, and now was the time for his appeal.

He studied the broad-shouldered figure, admiring the athletic stride, the commanding air. But when his eyes met that sardonic grin, he nearly abandoned his mission. No matter that his racing pulse reminded him that it was now or never.

"You're on guard? Where's your gun?" Joseph snapped.

Softly Mark replied, "No. Seems there's no need. Patten rode in with his men just an hour ago. Says you sent him out."

"Did he tell you why?" The grin was still there; his light

blue eyes challenged Mark. But Mark waited. The eyes wavered slightly. "I know your Puritan soul can't accept the way the Lord is working in our midst. I wonder why you haven't gone long ago, like the others." He was moving restlessly, slapping his fine leather gloves against his palm.

Mark's eyes were on the gloves, thinking of the shabby Saints with adoration in their eyes. "Joseph, I think it's time you and I do a little talking. Man to man. Don't pull that prophet business on me." Without waiting for Joseph's reply he plunged on. "Things are bad in the Mormon camp. They are getting worse. You can't hope to continue to hold these people. They are scared, they're hungry, and their children are suffering. At one time you offered these people a beautiful dream. You called it Zion. I call it heaven on earth. But that's not to be, and you know it.

"Now, Joseph, you have a big bunch of people under your control. Have you thought about them? Where does this all lead? Right now they want nothing more than to settle down, have a few acres, and feed their families. You won't let them. Last summer when these people should have been planting their acres, they were preparing to defend Far West. You've a fortified town, but no food. You have people without a heart. You've frightened them with the fear of hell-fire if they think or act for the interests of their families. And if they're willing to risk hell, and head for the state line, you've got the Danites on their trail. Are you going to fight for an impossible dream until the blood of your last faithful one is shed?"

Mark paused to take a breath and pace across his muddy platform. When he turned, he said, "For the sake of these people, be man enough to back down before any more damage is done. For the sake of their very lives, get out." Now Mark raised his head. Joseph's face was white, twisted into lines of suffering and Mark's heart leaped in hope.

Slowly Joseph turned and paced the muddy road and Mark waited. When the Prophet returned he lifted sorrowful eyes. "Mark, my friend," he said heavily, "you break my heart. Will you be another Judas? You know I dare not deny my God. What you are suggesting is impossible. We'll all die if we refuse to follow the commands placed before us. To obey is the only recourse we have."

"Joseph," Mark asked slowly, "where's love? Since I've been a Mormon I've heard a great deal about cursing our enemies, revenge, damning to hell. Now I'm hearing we're to plunder our enemies, steal their cattle and furniture, burn their houses. I'm seeing men with their faces contorted with rage lifting arms against a people we should be able to live with in peace. It's beginning to look as if wherever you are, Joseph, there is no peace. In every place you have gone there's been strife.

"I've been reading my Bible, that Book which you say is all wrong because it hasn't been translated by the power of God. I like what it says. I don't have to shed my blood in Missouri for a cause that any thinking man realizes is all wrong. Jesus Christ shed His blood for me. For all my sins, I only need to accept that gift, humbly, recognizing there is nothing I can do to earn salvation. It's by grace. My Bible says God loves, forgives, restores, guides, makes holy with a righteousness that has discernible fruits of righteousness. Joseph, if you are close to God, where are your discernible fruits of righteousness?"

The sorrow on Joseph's face had disappeared. Now his eyes were alight and his face glowed. Softly he said, "Wait around, Mark; you'll see."

As they cantered toward Gallatin Tom's thoughts were in turmoil. He soon discovered others shared his feelings. Beside him Arnold Johnson shot a quick glance his direction. In a low voice he said, "I'm having feelings inside telling me this isn't right, even though we're taught to accept Joseph's word like God himself."

"You can't question," Tom said roughly; "that isn't faith. You make up your mind to do what Joseph says or be an apostate."

"Just try to leave," the man said bitterly. "It's our neck if we do. It's beyond a man having a chance to talk or think for himself."

Patten halted his men in the last grove of trees before they reached Gallatin. Tersely he explained, "I don't know what we'll find here—maybe the DeWitt bunch, maybe nothing. All right, men, go to it."

With a yell echoing through the ranks, the men galloped through the town. Tom deliberately slowed his horse. Under cover of the shouts, he yelled, "Johnson, ease up and give the people a chance to escape."

When they reached the main street of Gallatin, Tom saw that not a soul stirred. Patten shouted a command to halt and dropped from his horse. When the men clustered around him, he said, "Fresh tracks, but the place is deserted. All right men, get busy." Tom hesitated, bewildered by the strange command.

Patten turned back and said, "Timmons, get in that store and start carrying the goods out. Check out the post office; could be money there. The fellas will be pulling up wagons. We want them filled double time, with everything of value." Tom started to speak, but Patten turned his flinty face to Tom and waited. Tom shrugged and headed for the store.

When the men finally rode out of town, Patten turned to survey the scene behind them. Tom saw the satisfaction on the man's face as he looked from the blazing store and post office to the still-smoldering ruins of a log cabin. He waved toward the wagons his men were driving and said, "Pretty profitable day."

"What are we going to do with all this stuff?" the man riding beside Tom asked. Pointing toward Adam-ondi-Ahman, Patten said, "We're taking it back and putting it in the bishop's storehouse. We've plenty of poor people who could use the spoils of the Gentiles."

They had nearly reached town when Patten wheeled back and said, "Timmons, you know the Millport road. Head down that way and see what you can find out. Don't go into town without cover. There could be a skirmish."

As Tom pulled away from the group, Hansen asked, "More of the same?"

Tom saw Patten's grin and heard him say, "Yes, the fur company's been out that way today."

Tom had just turned down the road leading to the little town of Millport when he met Lyman Wight and a group of men heading toward Adam-ondi-Ahman. Wight hailed him and waved his men on as Tom approached.

"Where are you headed?"

"Patton directed me toward Millport to see what's going on."

"Not a thing. We've come from there. The place's deserted. I'm headed into town to report to Joseph. Come along. I'm thinking we'll need you to carry a message before the night's over."

"Joe wasn't in Adam-ondi-Ahman when we left this morning."

"Well, he and Hyrum should be there by now." They rode the rest of the way in silence. When the two reached town, Tom discovered changes had been made during the day. The Gentile store was now the company headquarters for the Army of Israel.

When Tom entered the building, Joseph and Hyrum were there. But, more surprising, he found Mark talking to the men.

Wight sat down close to the open fire and stretched his feet toward the blaze. "Millport's deserted. I get the feeling the Gentiles are running like scared chickens. Sure seems like the fight's gone outta them all of a sudden."

Hyrum said, "God's put the dread of the Israelites into them."

"Well, they're sure gone," Wight continued. "Left everything, but there's not a soul around."

Joseph leaned forward, "Left their goods, huh? We'd better see to it."

"Never mind," Wight said getting to his feet. "We'll have a private council and take care of the whole situation." Tom saw the look the men exchanged before Wight turned to him. "Come along, Tom. I've a job for you."

It was dusk as they left the building. Wight turned abruptly and cocked his head toward the road. "There's a bunch of wagons coming up that road," he said slowly. "Guess we'd better mosey down and see what's up." At that moment Joseph, Hyrum, and Mark came out the door.

"Wagons?" Joseph questioned.

A lone horseman cantered into town. He circled around and came up to the group. It was John Lee. "Met these men down the road a piece; they wanted me to find out what you want done with the goods."

"Who are they?" Hyrum asked.

A sardonic grin creased Lee's face, "They said to tell you they were the fur company."

Joseph laughed and said, "Tell them to head for the bishop's storehouse."

As Joseph turned aside, Lee turned to Mark and said, "Met your wife yesterday. She was heading this way. Said she had to go to the house. I told her it wasn't safe and directed her to go over to McBriers' and stay until the worst of this mess is over."

"Jenny out roaming while this is going on?" Mark muttered, distressed. Tom saw him clench his fist and bang it against the hitching post. Watching him, Tom was remembering all the tales of horror that had been surfacing. He swallowed hard and took a step toward Mark.

Joseph turned back and said, "Might be you could be spared to hunt for her." He paused and there was an awkward silence as he studied Mark, still smiling that strange smile. Tom guessed Joseph was recalling the reason Mark was up here. The smile became cold as Joseph added, "But then, 'twould be better to send Tom once he gets back from Far West."

Mark opened his mouth, but abruptly he turned away, his shoulders sagging.

Tom muttered, "Seems a decent man'd trust his friend enough to let him go find his wife."

CHAPTER 17

Tom and Lyman Wight rode to Israel's camp where Wight called out a youth to accompany them to Far West. The trio left immediately, riding hard for the meeting.

They splashed across Grand River at the shallow ford, and cut away from the gorge, out onto the open prairie. As they rode, Tom was wondering just what Wight would expect of him. He had to admit to the awe he was feeling. This would be his first meeting with the Danite leaders.

"Don't much like hob-nobbing with the big shots," he muttered to the silent fellow beside him. The youth shrugged and didn't answer.

The road became hard-packed, smoothed by the passage of the settlers. The only sound in the night was the thud of hooves and the clink of harnesses. As the horses settled into a steady lope, Tom found himself caught up again in thinking about Jenny and Mark. His own fears for his sister seemed feeble compared to the pain he had seen in Mark's face. He shook his head in bewilderment. "Sure don't make sense, her takin' off like that," he muttered. The youth beside him grunted and nodded.

It was a clear night. A scythe-shaped moon was rising, outlining the clouds with slices of brightness. Frost was beginning to spread a diamond gleam on bare branches and grass still crushed and matted by the snow. Just beyond Gallatin the trio paused to rest their horses and let them drink in the last fork of the Grand River. As they waited they ate a cold supper of bread and meat.

Only once did Wight bring up the subject of the meeting. He said, "A wise move it would be to keep the details under your hat. You two are young in the Danites group, and there's those who will have your neck if you can't keep the secret paths and the mission of the Danites to yourselves." He turned in his saddle to look squarely at the two. "We're pledged to support the presidency and obey them under penalty of death. We're not called upon to agree, only obey, don't forget that."

By the time they reached Far West, the meeting was well under way. Wight and Tom eased themselves onto the crowded bench in the rear of the building while the silent youth took charge of the horses. Avard, the Danite leader, was pacing back and forth across the front of the room. He paused briefly, saluted Wight and continued with his speech.

"For you who just came in, this is my word to you tonight. Even this very day the word to you has been put into action. You are commanded to take to yourselves the spoils of the Gentiles. It is written, given by the Lord himself to his servant Joseph, that the riches of the Gentiles are to be yours. You will waste away the Gentiles by robbing them and plundering them of their property. In this manner we will build up the house of Israel, the kingdom of God, and thus we'll roll forth the little stone of Daniel's time, which he saw cut out of the mountain. It will roll out until it fills the whole earth. My men, this is the way God plans to build up His kingdom in these last days. If we're seen, what does it matter? We will defend each other, lie for each other. If this won't do it, we'll put our accuser under the sand just as Joseph did the Egyptian. And I promise you, if one of this society reveals any of this, I'll put him where the dogs can't bite."

Abruptly he whirled and, pointing his finger, he said, "If I meet one of you cursing the presidency, I'll feed him a bowl of brandy, get him into the bushes, and be into his guts in a minute."

The murmur of voices ceased and Avard continued, "Now, we are here tonight to appoint a committee called the Destruction Company. The purpose will be to burn and destroy. You will go against any people who would do us mischief here in

Caldwell. If the people of Ray and Clay move against us, you are to burn their towns of Liberty and Richmond. This will be done secretly."

After Avard had appointed the chosen twelve, he turned back to other matters. "I have a decree I want you to vote upon. This statement reads as follows: *Be it resolved, no Mormon dissenter shall leave Caldwell County alive. All such ones who attempt to do so shall be shot down.*" Carefully Tom controlled his shiver as he recalled the advice he had given to Mark.

The formal meeting was called to a close. Some of the men left the room, while Tom and Wight joined the others pressing toward the front.

As they elbowed their way forward, Tom could hear Avard saying, "I propose to start a pestilence among the Gentiles. I have in mind poison. We'll do their corn, their fruit, anything else that grows. We'll say the Lord done it."

There was another question and Tom heard Avard say, "The plan of the Prophet is to take this state, the whole United States, and finally the whole world." There was a murmur with Avard's reply cutting through it. "Joseph's prophecies are superior to the law of the land. I have heard him say that if he was let alone, he would be a second Mahomet for this generation. He would make a gore of blood from the Atlantic to the Pacific."

Each day since the afternoon Jenny met John Lee and had been sent to the McBrier farm, there was evidence of new fires. Often during the day, Jenny heard distant gun shots. Mr. McBrier would emphatically shake his head when Jenny mentioned leaving. Although she was impatient to be on her way, secretly she was relieved at his insistent "just one more day." She knew he had been visiting with neighbors, and she saw his concern and frustration continue to grow.

One evening as he hung his hat and coat behind the door, he said, "I can't pretend to be hopeful about the situation. Since the state militia's pulled out, the Mormons and the old settlers are acting like they're trying to outdo each other in devilment. First one side burns a barn, the next does one better—he takes the cattle and burns the barn."

He snorted in disgust as he sat down to the table. Bowing his head, he prayed, "Bless, O Lord, this food. We thank You for the bounty of this good land." He cleared his throat, "Please set Your hand upon these people and restrain the wicked one. Thy kingdom come, thy will be done. And help our good sister here to be guided by Your Spirit. She has a need to know about You. Supply her need. In Jesus' name, Amen."

As Jenny looked curiously at him, he sliced the meat and held out his hand for her plate. "Not a bit better." He was answering her unspoken question. He said, "Riding toward Gallatin today I saw at least ten fires over the valley."

"Oh." Jenny took her plate and slowly said, "I *must* be going home. Just being there, well, it might help. Surely they wouldn't burn it down while I am there."

Mrs. McBrier shook her head, chiding, "Child, you don't realize how dangerous it is. The stories rollin' in here don't promise a thing for the strongest man, let alone a little woman like you."

They ate in silence, and then Jenny broached the subject which had caught her attention during the prayer. "Sir, you said I had a need to know God. I do know God, perhaps even better than you."

"Why do you say that?"

"Because we have Joseph's book and he has the keys to the kingdom. Besides that, I've been studying out the secrets and the power through—" Suddenly she stopped.

Looking around the room she was seeing it as if for the first time. By the glow of delicately shaded china lamps, she was seeing things she had missed before. The comfort of the surroundings was more than material. There was a serenity about the home; she saw reflections of it in the polished wood and colorful quilts. She also noticed the black-bound Book on the table beside Mr. McBrier's chair. Her thoughts overlapped it with the picture of the green and gold book, and unexpectedly she saw the garish contrast. She looked at the McBriers; they were still waiting.

While Jenny fumbled for words, Mr. McBrier said sharply, "And I suppose you've decided to join the Protestants and the

Catholics as well as the Mormons. Jenny, wee girl, it's reading God's Holy Bible and letting God himself have a dwelling place in your heart that makes you know something about himself." He studied her face for a moment and the twinkle came back into his eyes. "Besides, I've been on the way of following Jesus for these past forty years, and I know myself less learned and less worthy each year I live."

Two days later Jenny decided to take matters in her own hands. In her restlessness, she felt that these good people were determined to smother her with kindness when there wasn't a need.

After breakfast she packed her valise and headed for the barn. With her horse saddled and wearing her cloak, she searched out the McBriers and announced her intention. "I do appreciate your goodness to me, but I simply must push on. Don't worry about me."

She could see from their expression that they realized the futility of arguing further. With a sigh, old Mr. McBrier said, "Then go, we pray, with God's blessing and His care." At the end of the lane, she turned to wave to them.

Jenny knew the direction she must ride to reach Adam-ondi-Ahman before pressing on to the farm. First she headed toward the main road and then turned north. Between the McBriers' home and the road the trees were thick and tall. A screen, she thought, between herself and the rest of the world.

As she started out, Jenny realized sight was blocked, but not sound. She had not yet reached the road when she began to hear gunfire. Pulling on the reins, she hesitated. Suddenly there was the sound of pounding hooves. But only when Jenny heard shouts and the crash of horses, only as her own mount snorted with terror, did she wheel her horse and slap her with the reins. Jenny dug her heels into Patches' ribs, forcing her into the undergrowth beside the trail.

Before Jenny had time to dismount the riders galloped past her hiding place and disappeared. She saw they were going in the direction of the McBriers' home.

She hesitated, wondering, yet not believing those gentle people would suffer at the hands of these men.

At the moment she heard the crack of the whip, Jenny's horse was rearing, snorting with pain.

Over her shoulder she saw the man as he lifted the whip again. "Be off, you Gentile! The Army of the Lord is here and the wealth of the Gentiles is ours. Begone, or we'll have your horse, too!"

Jenny vainly tried to control the fleeing animal under her; she clung to the mare and was conscious only of the roar of wind in her ears. At last the horse stood quivering and snorting. Jenny realized they were in a clearing looking down over the McBriers' homestead.

As she swallowed the dryness in her throat and pressed her hand against the pounding of her heart, her attention was drawn to the activity far down the hill.

She watched a wagon being drawn close to the house. Soon men were running in and out of the McBriers' house, carrying bundles. She caught the gleam of dark wood. The dining table. The pile of brightness was Mrs. McBrier's colorful quilts. The sun glinted off a shiny lamp. Jenny pressed her hand against her mouth and moaned. The words that man had yelled were still with her.

Powerless, Jenny watched from her lookout. After the cattle were led from the barn, it was set ablaze. She was numb with shock as she watched the fire. In a short time, the wagon pulled away, leaving the house burning in an explosion of flame and smoke.

The last timber had crashed with a shower of sparks flying up from the blackened ruins before Jenny tore her fascinated gaze away from the scene and rubbed life into her numb arms and face. The McBriers—where were they? Had they perished in the blaze?

Jenny dug her heels into the horse's ribs and wheeled back the way she had come. When she rode up the McBriers' lane, she found the couple standing in their yard, shivering under wraps too scanty to cut the chill of the afternoon. Throwing herself from the horse, Jenny rushed to them.

They moved like wooden figures. Mrs. McBrier said, "Why, Jenny, you're crying."

It was the old gray-haired gentleman who wiped the tears from her face and listened as she screamed, "I hate them for what they've done to you! Hate, hate, hate! They are animals!"

"Come, child." They both drew her close and the three of them settled on the log beside the watering trough. Jenny saw bits of charred wood floating in the water. At her feet a hen pecked listlessly as if she must concentrate on that tiny portion of her world.

The tears had dried on Jenny's cheeks. She had wrapped her cloak around Mrs. McBrier, and now the old gentleman patted his wife's hand and said, "There, there, Mother. It's going to be all right. God's in His heaven and He's never failed us yet."

Mrs. McBrier pressed her face against her husband's shoulder. Jenny was surprised to see serenity in the midst of tragedy reflected on those old faces as the couple rested on the log. Mrs. McBrier spoke slowly, heavily, "I guess I can't complain; we're no better than the others, and many have lost as much."

"Our men have been guilty, too," Mr. McBrier said slowly. "I just can't reconcile the causes. Seems people ought to be able to live in peace, regardless."

Jenny watched his boot push at the charred wood and needed badly to say *live where*? but the fearful question wouldn't come. Suddenly he lifted his head and smiled. It was like a ray of sunshine in the dark, and Jenny watched him wordlessly wondering how it was possible.

Mrs. McBrier squeezed her husband's hand and he smiled down at her, saying, "One good thing has come out of this." They waited patiently and finally he continued. "Seems every man who's ever searched for God ends up desiring more of Him. Makes a body prone to *not* want to wait for eternity. Right now we're wanting new visions and glimpses of heaven. Some claim to have them.

"I've not envied a man's horses or cattle, but I've wanted to be one of those privileged to sit in God's presence. For a time, listening to them talk about the visions of glory, their calling to build a city for God; hearing about the gold plates and the angels, well, my heart went yearning. Almost I was ready to run after these Mormons.

"But even while looking at this, I recall hearing that Joseph Smith said these people are the most righteous people who ever lived. And no other religion has the keys of the kingdom. Then, sitting here, I got to thinking about what the Holy Bible says about love. You know, Jenny and Mother, God's Word is full of love. It says without love even the prophecies are nothing. Even if we give up ourselves to be burned, if we don't have love, the sacrifice is nothing. And the Bible says God *is* love, that He loved us so much He gave His Son for us."

He was silent a moment; then he lifted his head and looked at Jenny with his gentle blue eyes. "Sister, I guess it was worth losing everything to find out that love isn't in the Mormon camp." He shuddered slowly, shaking his head. "I came close to being enticed into making a terrible mistake."

Jenny was pondering his statement, wondering, ready to ask her question when she heard the sound of hoofbeats. A lone horseman was coming fast, and Jenny slowly got to her feet.

Dread filled her as she faced the road. When the man jumped down from his horse and hurried toward them, Jenny recognized the man who had sent her here, John Lee. Still waiting beside the McBriers, she watched his face twist with disbelief, then settle into a mask of grief.

Going to Mr. McBrier he said, "I'd heard. I just couldn't believe they'd do such a thing after the way you've befriended so many of 'em."

Crossing his hands behind his back he paced restlessly back and forth across the yard. When he stopped in front of them he said, "This trouble-making is wrong. I've told Joseph this has got to stop! It can only lead to disaster for the whole camp. You can rest assured that your neighbors will avenge you for this."

Mr. McBrier was shaking his head even as Lee spoke. "I don't want revenge. I want to see no more hurt on either side. Oh, God," he murmued, "what will be the outcome?"

Lee paced again and when he stopped, shoving his hat back on his head, Jenny saw the sadness in his eyes. Slowly he shook his head. "I don't understand, but I see clearly that religion hasn't the power to subdue this passion in man. It ought not be this way. As soon as the church takes its thumb outta their backs, these men become beasts. They're as bad as if they'd spent all of their lives being the most degraded of criminals."

Lee's words sank deep into Jenny's mind—confusing at first, then shaming her with a nameless guilt. Later she helped John Lee gather up the small bundle of belongings the McBriers managed to salvage and the two of them took the McBriers to the nearest Gentile neighbor.

Late in the afternoon Jenny and John Lee turned their horses toward Adam-ondi-Ahman.

Lee said, "Your husband was quartered in town until two days ago. Joseph called for him to go into Far West. It was something to do with legal questions."

Jenny's heart sank, but she bravely said, "No matter. I'll just ride up to our farm. You might tell him I'm going there when you see him."

"You'll be safer in town. We'll find a place for you to stay."

Jenny shook her head. "I'm not afraid. I'll be doing what needs to be done up there, pack up a few things and go back to Far West."

Finally he shrugged and watched as she turned her horse off the road and headed up the trail to the cabin over-looking the Grand River.

CHAPTER 18

When Tom pushed open the door of the general store in Far West, the first person he saw was Mark. His brother-in-law was sitting close to the fireplace, his leg propped high on a stool.

"What's the matter with you?" Tom stopped in front of the leg and studied it.

"Got it banged up a bit fooling around with the horses. What are you doing back in town?"

"Called back. Them up there insisted they don't need all the troops. Mostly scared of having so many to feed. So they sent a pack of us back here."

"Could I get you to hunt for Jenny?"

Tom raised his eyebrows, "You here all this time and haven't seen your bride?"

Mark's grin was twisted. "Don't forget, I've a bad name, they're calling us the *Oh, don't* men. That's as bad as being a dissenter; they just didn't have the evidence to hang *that* on me. Meanwhile, I'm being shunned. Twisted my leg bad enough I can't take sitting on a horse right now, and I can't get a soul to ride out to the McBrier place and bring Jenny back for me."

"Sorry, old man. I've a little job to do, so Jenny'll have to stay out there another day or so."

Tom grinned at Mark's frown and then asked, "I'd heard you were here. What's Joe got you up to?"

"I don't know yet. He sent me ahead, promising he'd be back here in a couple of days. He mentioned law problems. Seems to feel his friends Atchison and Doniphan don't understand the ramifications of the war problems. I'll worry about that later."

"Worry? Sounds like you aren't too sold on Joe's problems and the need for a body to counsel him."

"Tom, you know that." His voice was low. "A fellow wanting to make it in the legal profession would find plenty here to make him squirm if his intentions were to play the game fair and square."

Tom said slowly, "You know they captured the cannon taken out of DeWitt. Found it over in Livingston County."

Mark sighed wearily. "That's just one more in the catalog of wrongs, on both sides. It's an offense to carry arms from county to county, and it's pretty hard to overlook a cannon."

It was the next day that Corrill came into the store and found Mark. "Well, you've pulled a soft assignment," he joked. "Almost as soft as the Prophet."

"What's he doing?"

"When I left Adam-ondi-Ahman he was wrestling in the mud."

Mark snorted, "Corrill, even I won't swallow that one."

"It's the truth. I was there; just ask him."

"When's Joseph coming back? When he sent me down here, he said he'd be along shortly."

Corrill looked surprised and then he frowned. He shot Mark a quick look and said, "Did Lee tell you that your wife has gone back to your place?"

Mark sat up straight, "Jenny in Adam-ondi-Ahman? Lee mentioned that he found her out on the road and took her to the McBriers' place to stay until things settled down. I'd no idea she had left. When did she leave for our place?"

"Well, I overheard Lee telling Joseph to pass the message on to you. I expected him to be here by now." Corrill paused for a moment and then said, "Sorry, old man."

The door closed behind him. Mark sat staring at the door while the man's words rolled through his thoughts. What did Corrill mean? Abruptly Mark heaved himself to his feet and tested his weight on his lame leg.

Wincing, he walked slowly around the room and then he approached the counter where Mike was polishing glasses and watching him. "If someone asks for me, tell them I had to take a quick trip to Adam-ondi-Ahman."

"Anyone? Even Joe?"

"Particularly Joe." Mark knew his voice was bitter as he pushed open the door.

It was late when Jenny approached her own front door. For a moment she sat on her horse, feeling the quiet and thinking that the forest stillness seemed to have taken possession of her home.

In another moment she realized the silence meant the chickens and cow were gone. "Tyler was to be caring for them," she whispered. "Could he have taken them?" The door of the makeshift barn hung open. It was evident the bags of grain were missing from the rafters of the lean-to.

Filled with dread, she slowly slipped from the mare, led her to a grassy spot, and then went to the house.

Surprisingly she found the one-room cabin as she had left it—with one notable exception. Standing in the middle of the room was a handsome walnut grandfather clock. She moved slowly toward it. Was it another spirit trick?

The polished surface was cool and real under her fingers. As she ran her fingers over the wood, the clock chimed out the hour. Six o'clock. "That must be pretty close to accurate," she murmured. "Whoever brought you here was interested in seeing whether or not you still worked."

She frowned in the effort to think through all the implications of the clock's being there. It was John D. Lee who had told the McBriers that stolen goods were being spread around in order to avoid any one person being blamed should they be discovered. Jenny lifted her head. Slowly she said, "If that is so, Mark Cartwright, attorney-at-law, could be charged."

Jenny slowly sat down and studied the clock. Obviously it was costly. She sighed and tried to find a solution to the situation. Of course, it would be too heavy for her to lift. She cringed, thinking of the neighbor's reaction were she to ask for help. Finally she got up and shrugged off the problem. She found flour, several eggs and some moldy bacon in her larder, and went to start a fire in the fireplace. After sliding Mark's shutters into position and fastening them securely, she prepared her supper. While she was frying the bacon she addressed the clock, "I think it is a very good thing I came up here. You are beautiful and I would love to have you, but, too bad. I think I need to find some way to shove you into the Grand River."

As she ate her lonely meal, Jenny's thought was full of the unbelievable events of the day. The memory of the McBriers' faces knotted her throat into a miserable lump; but at the same time, she was accepting the conviction that once she left this house, she would never see it again.

Would she see Mark? For a moment her spirit plunged and then soared: there was Joseph's prophecy and there was her commitment. Only by obeying the Prophet completely would there be a surety of having her wishes granted. Too often she had heard him remind the Saints that there was no safety except in obeying the Prophet. But there was another thing, too— all the promises of power through the green book. And she intended to use every one of them.

Jenny spent a restless night tossing in the bed which suddenly seemed too big and very cold. Her dreams were filled with dark shadows and Jenny running, searching the sky as she ran, looking for the first star of the evening, the wishing star. And in her half-waking state, she was murmuring, "Star light, star bright, first star I see tonight—"

She sat up. "I should be praying for power instead of chanting childish wishes." Silently she searched her heart, wondering if she were failing the Prophet. Her guilty conscience informed her that she was. As she sighed and settled back in bed, she couldn't help wondering how much her sins were dragging down the cause of Zion.

When morning came, she threw back the shutters. As the giant clock again pounded out the hours with an intensity that reverberated from the walls of the tiny cabin, Jenny greeted the dawn eagerly. She studied the line of coral rimming the sky beyond the trees which marked the distant bluffs of the river and wondered how many of these lonely nights she could endure without going mad. She shivered.

Quickly now she flew about, stirring up the fire, boiling

water, and stirring in a meager handful of meal. By the time Jenny had finished her breakfast, she knew she must find the green book and the talisman.

With a sense of finality, she knew she must go through the cabin searching out each valued item. Had Mark not left behind another rifle and ammunition? What about his Bible? She could tie the extra shawl behind the saddle. It would cover the green book, and if she were to see Mark in Adam-ondi-Ahman, then there would be no need to explain her strange trip.

Late in the morning, Jenny was nearly ready to leave. She wrapped the book in the shawl and was ready to pin the talisman in her frock when the pin-prick of alarm touched her. At that moment the clock gonged out the hours. Ten. In the silence, with only gentle seconds ticking off, her world pressed in. The scenes of yesterday's fire and those stricken faces held her for a moment, and then the heightened sense of need sent her flying to the door.

Jenny guessed what she would find before she reached the spot where she had left the mare tethered. As she stared at the bare pasture, her heart sank. She was totally alone.

There was a broken branch. Jenny fingered it. In dismay she declared, "Since when have you forgotten horses aren't above breaking a dry limb when they're looking for something to eat?" She kicked at the grass chewed down to stubble, and turned to trail the mare.

The sun was directly overhead when Jenny gave up in frustration. "A thief. Right now I wish I could take a gun to that fella!" she cried, smacking one palm with the other as she kicked at a crumbling log. The words she muttered under her breath would have more nearly suited Lyman Wight than the wife of Mark Cartwright; and despite her fear and dismay, she was instantly seized with shame.

For reasons she couldn't guess, she leaned against a tree and allowed bitter tears to flow. As she cried, John Lee's face flashed across her thoughts. She was seeing the sadness in his eyes as he looked at the charred ruins of the McBriers' house and said, "It seems religion's not got the power to subdue the animal passion in a man."

She shoved her head against the tree, pounded her fist against the rough bark and said, "And the passion's taken my horse." But a quiet finger underlined the soul-deep anger she was feeling toward that nameless man, and at the same moment she murmured, "Why, Jenny, that makes you no better'n the bunch that burned out the McBriers."

Again the tears began. For a long time, Jenny leaned against the tree and cried without understanding the reason behind her tears.

Finally Jenny slumped down to rest against the tree. The sun had burned out the last of the night's chill and she rested in the warm spot. When the last of her sobs ended, she heard a gentle nicker nearby.

Raising her head, she listened for a moment, then with a glad cry she jumped to her feet and crashed through the bushes to throw her arms around the mare. Rubbing the horse's neck as she wrapped reins securely around her hand, Jenny looked around, trying to get her bearings. "Old girl, you've wandered a far piece from home. I'm thinking we'll have a time getting back there."

At midmorning Mark took the cutoff outside Adam-ondi-Ahman and headed up the road to his home. He was riding fast, as hard as he dared push his horse, but despite his anxiety, he was seeing things that sent disturbing signals to him.

There was an air of neglect and desolation around the cabins he had been passing. The smell of charred wood and the acrid scorch of burning grass lingered in the air. More frequently now he was passing bands of people heading south and east. Several times he met a wagon, but most often he was seeing women and children walking. He discovered that as he approached, the groups turned and scattered into the bushes. After one attempt to search them out and ask questions, he gave up and pressed harder for home.

When Mark turned down his own lane, he slowed his horse to a walk. The pricked ears of his mare had already alerted him to the presence of another horse. He eyed the gelding as he circled the cabin and stopped at the door.

A sound caught his attention, and before Mark could move, the man, still in the shadows, called, "Well, Mark, I'll ask you into your own house." Joseph Smith stepped through the doorway.

Mark's tumbling emotions held him motionless. When he got off the horse, he took time to pull the saddle from the mare and lead her to grass. Inside the cabin he faced Joseph Smith and tersely asked, "Where's Jenny?"

"I have no way of knowing, Mark. And what gives you the idea that I came here to see your wife?"

For a moment Mark studied the expression of complete candor and his resisting the impulse to squirm like a youngster caught with his hand in the cookie jar. Deliberately he held Joseph's gaze with his own and said, "Let's not play games, or I'll be tempted to do some prophesying on my own."

Joseph's eyes began to twinkle. "You're taking liberties."

"I was ready to say the same about you. There's just too much talk going around about you and some of the womenfolk. First it was Fannie Alger, then Nancy Johnson. Now they're talking about Lucinda Harris. I don't want it to be my wife next."

Joseph chuckled. "Look, Mark, you're a nice-looking fella, don't tell me the girls haven't cast eyes at you."

"Cut it out, Joe, this isn't about innocent flirtations and hero worship. If it is all foolish gossip, why do you feel called upon to denounce the rumors? A prophet ought to be above having to answer these kind of questions."

Now Mark noticed the walnut clock. Jerking his head toward it, he asked, "Where did that come from?"

"If you can't answer that question, then ask your wife."

"No doubt someone's stashed it here with the intention of returning. Joseph, it's all for naught."

"What do you mean?"

"Any sympathy you might have gained in a search for religious freedom has been swept away by total anarchy. You might justify it to your men, but that attitude won't prevail with either Governor Boggs or Washington."

"Are you prophesying again?"

"I'm warning," Mark growled. "These are the things I've been waiting to say all week. Are you taking into consideration the before-Joseph and after-Joseph climate of the state of Missouri? Since I talked to you last, I've had numerous Jacksonites come to me and beg me to get you to back down. They're not mincing words when they say you'll bring down the government on all our heads."

"You forget, Mark, I am above the law. You've seen the revelations. You've heard the promises. God has ordained that we possess the land either by purchase or by sword. That is a *command*. It is only through complete obedience to God through his Prophet in these last days that we can expect to see the promises fulfilled.

"If you or any of the others fail to obey the least of the commands, you'll bring disaster upon the people. I warned you of this before. Mark, don't blame me if this group of people fails to occupy the land. Blame those who are too weak and feeble to stand upon His Word in these latter days."

Joseph took a deep breath and paced the room. As he circled the clock again, he shot a glance at Mark and said, "Mark, I need your help and your loyalty, but right now you are close to apostasy. You've heard the counsel against the dissenters."

Mark watched Joseph's lips tighten as he continued, "Since the very day you entered Missouri, you've been fighting against the presidency."

"What do you mean?" Mark asked, already guessing.

"You've been a troublemaker. You shielded the dissenters, siding with the Whitmers, Cowdery, and Johnson."

Mark didn't bother answering, but he was fully aware of the position Joseph was forcing upon him as he spoke again. "Do you realize I could have shot you when you walked up to the door? And I would have been justified, because you left Caldwell County without permission. I am willing to forget the ugly accusations you've made against me in the past and today, but in return I'll expect more of you."

"Or," Mark said with a tight smile, "it will be like Avard says. I'll be in the bushes with a knife in my guts."

Softly Joseph replied, "You said it, Mark, I didn't."

And then after a moment of quiet reflection, Mark raised his head with a start. "Joseph, Far West is rumbling with all kinds of trouble right now. And in the midst of it, the men are milling around like lost sheep saying 'where's Joseph?'" He moved about the room restlessly. "I think you'd better quit your womanizing and get back to Far West this afternoon before that hot-headed Avard does us all in."

Joseph stared at Mark and Mark returned the look without flinching. He had nearly decided he was the victor in this round when Joseph said, "If that is the case, my trusted attorney, Mark Cartwright, will need to come with me. Seems Atchison and Doniphan aren't being of much help right now, and I have a *compelling* need for all my men to be close at hand."

Mark sighed and surrendered, "Much as I wanted to see my wife, I'm thinking you're right. Let's be off."

Just as the two men started out the door, Mark noticed the pair of blue mittens lying on the mantel. Beside them was a strange medal. He reached out to finger it. Seeing the unfamiliar symbols, he frowned and bent closer to study them. Finally he replaced the medal and examined the mittens again. Surely those were the mittens Jenny had been wearing the last time he had seen her. She had brushed them lightly across his face just before he had marched away from her.

Outside, Mark looked at Joseph standing beside the gelding waiting. He felt his throat tighten.

In the bushes beside the lean-to Jenny watched in amazement. From the moment she had heard the impatient horses stomping beside her door, she had been hiding in the bushes, fearfully expecting to see the thief who had deposited the clock in her cabin.

The sight of Joseph had frozen her beyond voice or movement. While her thoughts had churned out reasons for his being there, Mark had come out the door.

But Jenny still hesitated, wondering and fearful. When the men disappeared from sight, reason returned and Jenny jumped to her feet to run after them. Then suddenly she remembered her purpose for coming to the cabin. The book and the talisman.

She stood poised for flight. There were all those reasons why she needed power, but the most pressing reason was Mark.

While her heart still yearned after him, she rushed into the cabin and began to gather her precious bundle together. "Hurry, Jenny," she ordered herself, as she prepared to ride after the men, even then anticipating their surprise. But Jenny knew nothing of the messenger who met them just outside of town, nor of the hurried conference that sent them pounding down the road, beyond chance of being overtaken.

CHAPTER 19

"Where's the Prophet?" Tom turned to face the agitated man. For some time, Tom had been leaning against the door of the stable; in this position he was able to see down the main street of Far West. During the past week he had been watching men and their families pouring into the town. Every nook and cranny in the place was crowded, and still the people continued to arrive.

Tom looked at the man and sighed. "I don't rightly know. If it's lodging you want, you'll just have to—"

The man interrupted, "It's Joe I want. Our men caught a fella comin' out of Liberty. Seems he was carryin' a letter to Boggs."

"Militia?"

"Naw. Jest a ragged Gentile."

Slowly Tom said, "A fella could get into trouble snitchin' letters bound for the governor's office."

"We just wanted a look-see. He could be bought, and after we read it, he went on his way. That's the problem."

"Well, tell me the problem. I might be motivated to go take a look for Joe."

"It was from Atchison." He paused to let the import of that name sink in.

"Joe's good lawyer friend," Tom said slowly. "Well, what was the gist of the letter?"

"It were a letter of complaint. First off he listed a bunch of stuff. Talked about the goings on up in Daviess County. He were fair, that I gotta say for the man. He mentioned the old settlers doing damage to the Saints, too."

"And?"

"Atchison was sounding like we were doing mob violence, and said he won't disgrace himself by being part of a mob, too. Therefore he wouldn't lead out the militia. Sounds like he was suggesting the governor take his hands off, look the other way, and let us and the mobs cut each other's throats."

"In other words, we don't have a lick of protection anymore."

"On top of that, there's more of them than there is of us."

"Sounds like we need to be tightenin' up the ship." Tom chewed at his lip for a moment, pondering the situation. Getting to his feet, he reached for the bridle, saying, "Guess I'll mosey up Adam-ondi-Ahman way and see if I can round up Joe."

As he started out the door, the man said, "Ah—tell him the Gentile fella said he'd heard General Atchison order out a bunch of his militia to guard the line between Caldwell and Ray counties. He was saying they'd heard the Mormons were fixin' to attack Richmond. Tom, are we fixin' to fight out there?"

"Not that I'd know anything about, but then I don't know everything going on." Tom didn't look at him as he led his horse out and reached for the saddle. He was muttering to himself, "I'm guessin' things are boiling up to a full head of steam; seems it's time Joseph starts actin' like a prophet again."

He turned his horse toward the north and slapped her hard with the reins.

Tom met Mark and Joseph Smith just outside of Gallatin. He delivered the information and the three men headed for Far West at a hard run.

After Jenny left her cabin and turned onto the main road, she hurried her horse along as fast as she dared, hoping to catch up with Mark and Joseph Smith. Just beyond Gallatin she met a group of women and children walking along the road toward her.

Sliding from the mare, Jenny approached the group. "Please, can you tell me," she asked, "have you seen the Prophet and another man riding this way?"

"Were three men," came the terse answer. "The way they

tore outta here I'm guessing it's meanin' more trouble."

Jenny studied their tired, worried faces. "Why are you walking along the road without your menfolk?"

"Just like you—they've run off and left us." The woman gave a bitter snort and added, "The Missourians have had enough of the thievin' and burnin', and they're riled up. The menfolk are running for their lives, and we're left to make do the best we can. The Missourians won't do nothin' to a bunch of women alone. They're after the men."

Another woman joined the group. After listening quietly, she said, "I've been against this squabble all along. Don't make sense to go in and disrupt." She squinted at Jenny. "Seems people learnt their lessons in Jackson. We found we had to keep still about Missouri being Zion, and just go on like common folk." There was an accusing note in her voice, and Jenny began understanding how the Jacksonites were viewing the newcomers from Ohio.

The first woman took up the conversation again. "Like a bird in the hand, most of us were willing to shelve the Zion idea if they'd just leave us alone and let us homestead."

The wistful words remained with Jenny as she rode on toward Far West.

It was dusk when Jenny reached town. Holding her horse down to a walk, she studied the changes which had taken place in the week since she had left. Now Far West was filled with people and wagons. Campfires dotted the town square and children played in the street. On every corner people teemed restlessly about.

Jenny pulled on the reins. Looking around, she tried to guess where Mark and Joseph would be.

A woman stopped beside her. "You be lookin' for someone?"

"Joseph Smith and another—no, two more men."

"Well, things are rilin'. I expect you'll find all the men at the general store."

Jenny thanked her and gratefully slid from the horse. With a tired sigh she tied the horse to the hitching post and entered the store. Spotting the cluster of men gathered around the bar, she headed for them.

Joseph, leaning close to the men, was saying, "Now, fellas, here's what we'll do," he stopped and lifted his head as she approached. Mark turned, jumped up, hobbled quickly toward her.

"Jenny, where've you been?" his voice was strained and his hand grasped her arm until she winced.

"Oh, Mark, I'm so glad—"

"Never mind. I can't leave now, but Tom'll see you back to the Morgans. This time, don't leave until I come after you. Promise me?" She looked up into his face, seeing the lines of strain, the pale circle around his mouth. She nodded and he turned to beckon Tom to them.

When Jenny and Tom stood on the street, he studied her with narrowed, suspicious eyes and asked, "Where you been?"

"Oh, Tom, don't look at me that way." She tried to speak lightly. "I'm not a spy."

"I wasn't thinking spy," his voice was slow, deliberate. She paused with her hand on the saddle horn and turned to look up at him. "Oh, please, Tom. I am so tired."

"I think a lot of Mark," he continued, stressing each word. "And I won't let you make a fool of him."

"Tom!" she gasped. "I love that man with all my heart—why did you say such a thing?" She watched the frown clear from his face as he continued to study her.

"Lee said he met you on the trail a couple of days ago, with you saying that you had to go to your place. He said you were pretty insistent, but that he talked you into going to the McBriers' 'til things settled a mite. Mark went up there looking for you and found Joseph instead."

She thought about that for a moment and then pushed aside the questions. "I did go to McBriers'." Tom continued to study her. Realizing he wouldn't be satisfied until she told the truth, she said, "Come on, I'll explain as we head toward Sally's."

They were out of town when Jenny reined her horse and waited for Tom. "I guess no matter how long we live, I'll still be 'little sister,' won't I?"

"You want it otherwise?"

"No, Tom. I can't get along without you, especially now. I

need you to be my friend, too." She frowned, wondering how much she should reveal. After all, Tom was a staunch member of Joseph's church. She slanted a look at him and discovered his frown was returning.

"Tom," she said hastily, "no matter how badly you think of me, I must admit it. I was on my way to the cabin to get Pa's green book."

His jaw dropped and he stared. "What—you have *Pa's book*? Even after all these years it's meanin' something to you?" He sighed and scratched his head. Suddenly he leaned forward. "That's *all* you went after?"

"All? Of course *all*." She dared not admit having a talisman, even to Tom. "Whatever else could pry me away from Sally's place with the turmoil going on?"

A happy grin took over his face. He wiped it away with a shaky hand; frowning again he said, "It's a surprise to know you've had the book all these years. What does Mark think of it?"

Jenny gasped. "Oh, Tom, I'd never tell him about it."

"Why? He's your husband."

"Because, because—" She stopped and could only visualize the horror and the disillusionment on Mark's face were he to find out about the book. "Can you imagine Mark understanding all we shared in South Bainbridge?"

"No. But that's in the past. Jenny, even Joseph doesn't believe like that anymore."

"Yes, he does. No matter what he says, it keeps cropping up. If it were otherwise, then why does he carry a talisman?"

"It's probably just a good-luck piece. Besides, how do you know?"

"I've seen it," Jenny answered shortly. "I'll just make a bet with you about the craft. I know for a fact that his pa was looking for money with the witching stick while we were in Kirtland."

"What his pa does has nothing to do with Joe's having the book and the keys to the kingdom."

"His pa is patriarch of the church. That's pretty holy."

"Jenny," Tom warned, ignoring her statement, "if you don't

start exercising faith, there'll be no success for the people."

There was her sin again, and she faced it bleakly before saying, "I am. In my own way I'm exercising all the faith and power possible. If there's a way to win out over all the bad things that's happening in this place, I'll find it, even if—" She stopped and searched his face. Even to Tom she dared not say the word that rolled around in her head: *sabbat*.

As they rode on down the trail, Jenny was thinking of Adela and the strange vibration she had on the day Mrs. Martindale had walked out of Joseph's office. Deep inside Jenny the conviction was growing that Adela Martindale was *her* Adela.

When Tom and Jenny reached Morgans' cabin, Sally rushed out to meet them. Weeping, she threw her arms around Jenny, and the terror of the past days suddenly swept over her. Jenny found herself clinging to Sally, trembling and crying.

Tom followed the two women into the cabin. Tamara, seeing her mother's tears, began to cry. While Jenny was mopping her eyes, she discovered Tom looking embarrassed while he thumped both of the Morgans on the back.

"Oh, Tom, you've missed your calling," Jenny said with an attempt to appear lighthearted.

"No, I haven't; I'm heading back to the smithy." He said, looking relieved when Sally managed a smile.

Jenny got to her feet and wandered around the cabin. "I don't know why I'm acting like this. It's silly. Never once was I in danger, yet—" She stopped, remembering the man with the whip. He had called her a Gentile.

After Tom left there was Sally's storm of tearful questions. Didn't Jenny know how dangerous it was? Daily the stories were pouring into Far West, and as often as Andy was able to be home he carried his own tales.

Sally knew all about the Gentiles torturing the Saints, killing their animals and ravaging the crops. She knew of the mass of Saints moving out of their homes, rushing into Adam-ondi-Ahman or Far West, rushing to save their very lives when all other hope was gone.

And when Sally was calm again, Jenny told her story. Sharp memory of the gentle McBriers made her give an honest assessment. "Sally, those people had befriended the Saints. They were willing to be good neighbors, and they were trusting."

Now Jenny's question was for herself. Slowly she said, "How do you measure their story against the other stories we're hearing? I'm thinking there's a lot of wrong going on—on both sides. It troubles me, but also I feel as if just seeing all this forces me into admitting I'm a part of it. Somehow I'm less proud to be a member of the church."

"Jenny," Sally was whispering, grasping Jenny's arm, "don't give up on your faith. You've accepted the revelation in these latter days. You know Joseph is a prophet of God. You also know our only hope in these times is to obey the Prophet in everything he says."

"Sally, you keep reminding me of my duty. But do you really believe what you're saying?" Sally dropped her head. Jenny watched Sally's trembling fingers pick at a fraying spot on her dress.

That night decisions were made that started the battle of Crooked River.

Mark had gone out to walk the streets of Far West. The crisp, clear air hinted of another hard frost before morning, but the sting of cold was preferable to the damp, musty hay that was serving as his bed in the loft of the livery stable. He knew he was brooding over the situation, perhaps feeling sorry for himself. He tried to concentrate on Jenny's lonely state. But there were painful implications if that chance encounter with Joseph Smith at his cabin meant what seemed to be obvious.

Mark limped along, kicking at the clumps of freezing grass and wishing that faith had visible strings which he could yank up tight. He was deeply conscious that the most important decision he could make right now was to do nothing except hang on to his confused, limp faith. He tried to find joy in reminding himself that Jenny was in his Lord's hands.

But there were other things to think about. He watched the sentry walking off the measured limits of his post. The night seemed serene, but he felt it was only an illusion.

Mark hunched his shoulders against the cold and reflected on the nebulous sensation of danger moving closer with each tick of the clock. He knew he wasn't alone in this feeling. He was seeing the troubled frowns, the dark eyes of fear staring at him every day.

From out on the prairie the cry of the night owls went up. Then came the warning call of the wolves as they stalked their territory and terrorized their enemies with their heart-stopping howls.

Even the hair on the back of Mark's neck stiffened in response as he stood in his lonely place, listening to the wolves' message that chilled the blood with its threat.

Peering out across the pale prairie, he was conscious of a parallel between the animal world and the little town of Far West. Wasn't the little town a hedge, staking a claim against the wild; marking with a threat that was all too similar to the wolves' territorial claim?

The wild call and the threat seemed the same. He moved uneasily, suddenly conscious of threat moving closer, just as those roving wolves now sniffed at the outskirts of Far West.

Shaking off the mood, he turned. The only visible light in Far West came from the window over Joseph's work table. For a moment Mark stared at that bright spot. Then with a sigh of surrender, he began to walk toward the store.

Joseph was hunched over the table; he glanced up in surprise as Mark walked into the circle of his lamplight. While Joseph waited in silence, Mark realized he was being forced into position. Aware of the irritation in his voice, he said, "Look, Joseph, I've been thinking. We're all in this together. One falls, we all lose.

"I meant everything I said to you, but then you're a man. I guess you can handle a person liking you even while disagreeing with just about everything you believe in, can't you?"

He could see Joseph struggling. Mark sensed that he knew, even better than Joseph himself, just how far the Prophet would have to come down to accept Mark's terms.

Finally he spoke. "Of course, Mark. I need your help pulling these people out of a bad spot. Someday you'll realize how badly you need me. Until that day, we'll forget the past. Right now—" He paused, and as Mark stifled his one last urge to correct the man, the front door banged.

"Joseph, you there?"

It was Wight. He charged into the enclosure, spewing words as he came. "Long-faced dupes, hob-goblins, devils, what have you. The whole lot is to be damned and sent to hell." Joseph was on his feet and Wight explained. "The Gentiles."

"What now? Calm down and give us the facts."

"Mob. Gentile mob. Sent to Boggs, they did, reporting lies about us. Comes out that in fact it was them. They won't stay away from that county line, when they've been ordered just as much as we have. Came over the county line they did, and snatched three of our men. Now we're hearing they're fixin' to shoot them at sunrise."

Mark watched Joseph's face turn deathly pale. Quietly he asked, "Mob you say; are you certain?"

"Mob."

"We've got to recover our men. This is a job for Patten." He turned to Mark. "I have two things for you to do. First, get Patten and send him here. Then," he paused to take a deep breath, "we've got to have intelligence from behind their lines. We've got to know just what we're facing. Mark, I want you behind those lines, finding out who's where and what they are doing. Get a lead on whether or not the state's behind them, and how many men are milling around with guns."

Immediately Mark got the clear picture. He needn't see the challenge in Joseph's eyes to be reminded that despite their truce, Mark was still a Saint in disfavor. But he must justify with one last word. "Mark, your face is unknown. Being laid up with that leg's kept you out of sight. That's a big advantage to us right now."

In the livery stable Mark aroused Patten, and the other men crowded around. He delivered Joseph's message. Looking around at the other men, he added, "I guess you'll all be called out before the night's over."

Tom was at his elbow. "What about you?"

Briefly Mark explained his mission and Tom exploded, "That's foolish! Doesn't make no difference now. We just fight regardless. You'll be a loser no matter which way you go. I'm sayin' just split, Mark."

There were averted eyes around the circle. Patten was dressed and pulling on his white coat. His voice was hard as he said, "Tom, that's going against counsel. I'll forget I heard it this time, but don't *you* forget that God is protecting us. There's no bullet, no knife can touch those the Lord is protecting. We may be small in number, but we shall expect the holy angels to fight our battles for us. Don't fear, Cartwright. You'll come back safely."

"Captain Fearnought!" exclaimed a youth affectionately. "You cheer us all with your faith!"

Tom was to recall that scene vividly just a few short hours later. He followed as the men scurried along behind Patten striding toward the store.

Joseph was pacing the floor in front of the fire. He lifted his head, gave a short nod of approval as the men clustered in behind Patten. "Here's the information I have now," he said tersely, moving behind his table. "There's a Gentile mob just south of here on the line between Caldwell and Ray counties. From what we can determine right now, they are down in this draw, holding three of our men. Their intentions—the poor devils—are to shoot our men at sunrise. Need I say more?"

Tom found himself adding his growl of rage to the chorus around him.

It was nearly dawn by the time Patten and his sixty men reached the slough at Crooked River. They had spent the pre-dawn hours creeping soundlessly through the rough terrain. Now nerves were taut with strain as eager men, confident of victory, pressed to the battle.

With his men around him, Patten pointed out the final hill. "Just over this rise is the mob's camp. We've smelled their fires, heard their dogs. Now, before it is daylight we rush over the hill and have them in our hands before they can think." There was a ripple of excitement through the troops.

"Captain, sir," a cautious voice whispered, " 'tis nearly dawn. I suggest you remove that white coat. It gleams like a flag of truce, and we don't want them making a dreadful mistake."

There was a choked howl of mirth and Patten responded, "Well said, my lad. However, we've nothing to fear, either of being taken too lightly or too seriously. The coat? Well, the Lord's on our side. His angels wear white. Perchance they'll see me as another angel."

When they reached the last hill Tom saw that hickory trees blanketing the slope made an unexpected obstacle, dragging at the Saints and slowing their progress. Tom realized the threat immediately, and looking at the sky felt his first uneasiness. But there wasn't time for fear; it was too near sunrise.

Flat on their bellies, the Saints squirmed into position. Patten's word passed down the line. The Gentile camp was safely ensconced behind a sheltering line of thick oaks. But daylight was already upon them, and Patten's strategy was in disarray. Reluctantly the order was given. There was no recourse but to dash down that hill.

Patten's men were on their feet; then came that cautious change of position. Muscles tensed, rifles readied.

"Halt! Who goes there?"

"Friends," Patten yelled.

"Armed?"

"Yes."

"Lay them down."

"Fire," Patten snapped. He was on his feet, leading the men, surging with them down the hill.

Tom heard the shots. In the next second, there was return fire. He heard a startled grunt. The Saint in front of him dropped and rolled limply down the hill. With a growl Tom was on his feet, shooting as he ran; but that scene of the rag doll figure, rolling away with arms like useless ropes, stayed with him.

When the Saints charged into the Gentile camp, Tom was still on the hill, bending over the man, knowing suddenly the reality of war. Nothing but that man was important. But his help was useless. As he got to his feet he saw the Gentiles fleeing their camp, running like startled partridges.

He was still staring at the scene when he saw the one Gentile who didn't flee but instead ducked behind the tree. When the crack of the rifle came, Tom was looking at Captain Fearnought and saw him fall.

They carried him back to Far West to die. Tom, in the frozen emotion of the moment, could only focus on the white coat smeared with blood.

It was late morning when Jenny and Sally learned of the battle. Jenny and Tamara had gone for a walk, with the toddler happily leading the way. They had circled through the woods, following Log Creek nearly to the settlement of Haun's Mill. When Tamara was tired, her tearful face won a ride on Jenny's shoulders.

Homeward they went, with Tamara sagging against Jenny, and Jenny feeling every vibration of the forest, drinking in every fragrant whiff of moss and wood, seeing every shade of green, brown, and dampened gray.

There they met Andy Morgan, sagging, white-faced, and bone-weary from battle. Jenny led him home, but before he could rest, they found he had to relieve his soul.

He described the battle. "Patten died early this morning," he added. "I was down there with the others. Danites. It was a lark. Nothing could touch us." His voice was bitter, his eyes bleak. Jenny and Sally clung to each other, shivering.

"Patten, foolish man. He'd heard so long that we were invincible. Didn't take ordinary precautions. In his white coat, he yelled, 'Charge, in the name of Lazarus!' I could see we were outlined against the morning sky."

He got to his feet to pace the floor, and when Jenny tried to comfort him, he said, "I'm ashamed. I could have reasoned with the man. But it's hard when you've been taught not to question. Not to even think they mightn't have all the right answers." Later his voice was bleak as he said, "I'm the one who'll have to live with my uneasy conscience. It's too late to change what has happened."

And then Jenny remembered. She could only say, "Mark?"

Andy turned quickly. "Oh, I'm sorry. Mark was sent on another assignment."

At that moment Mark was facing Joseph in the office behind the shelves and barrels. Did Joseph seem surprised to see him? Mark rubbed a weary hand across his face. "I found out that all of Richmond is running like scared rabbits. They're moving the women and children out, preparing for siege."

Mark was seeing the pleased smile on Joseph's face. "But that isn't the most significant fact I discovered. Sorry I didn't find out in time to warn you, but—"

"Warn?" Joseph was leaning forward now.

"Yes. That wasn't a mob Patten and his men attacked; it was men sent out by the state militia."

Joseph Smith leaned back in his chair and the smile disappeared from his face.

Mark had to say the obvious. "Joseph, there's bound to be trouble over this."

CHAPTER 20

The day was cold and moisture hung in the air like the draperies of mourning. *Fitting*, Jenny thought as she left Morgans' cabin to join Andy and Sally for the ride into town. She commented, "Looks like the eternities themselves are mourning for Captain Patten. The sky seems ready to weep."

Sally pulled her shawl close, shoved the black bonnet more securely on her blonde hair and turned a tear-reddened face to Jenny. Jenny shivered. Sally's sad, hopeless face was the epitome of the collective emotions in Far West today.

There were a few wagons moving into town for the funeral. But when they reached Far West, Jenny saw the mass of people swarming into town from the cluster of campsites on its fringes.

Tom and Mark joined them as they stepped out of the wagon. Jenny clung to Mark and tried to believe his unresponsiveness was related to the occasion.

Jerking his head toward the group just driving into town, Tom said, "That's the bunch from Haun's Mill. I was at the store earlier today when Jacob Haun came in to protest Joe's order to evacuate all the settlements and move into Far West. Seems he doesn't want to give up the mill. Can't say I blame him. The Gentiles won't grind our grain for us, and we can't live on dry corn all winter."

"Joseph did hear him out," Mark said soberly. "He left the decision up to Haun, saying it was better to lose the mill rather than their lives. He told me later that he was confident they'd sacrifice their lives for their decision."

Jenny shivered. "Why didn't he insist they come?" And when

Mark didn't answer, she asked, "Will those from Adam-ondi-Ahman be coming for the funeral?"

He was avoiding her eyes as he answered tersely. "Most of the men are already here, called in to guard Far West. It's best the remainder of them stay there." He looked squarely at her for the first time, and she saw the shadows in his eyes. "Since we've left they've been building siegeworks in the middle of town."

"Then it *is* bad," she said slowly.

Again he met her eyes and said, "Jenny, we're getting very close to being in a real skirmish. The men Patten attacked weren't a mob. They were militia sent out by Boggs, part of Atchison's company. Do you realize this is part of the company sent out to make peace?"

Jenny shivered, "Mark, what is going to happen next?"

His voice was weary as he slowly said, "I don't know. I've tried to get Joseph to come to his senses. I—"

Abruptly he stopped. Jenny searched his eyes and what she saw there made her shiver again. "Are we really safe at the Morgans' place?"

"Andy insists so. But he did promise me that he'll make plans to move you and Sally out by the first of November. I'll try to be free to join you then." He pressed her fingers and her heart lifted, but in the next moment, the somber notes of the bugle drew their attention to the crude coffin in front of the schoolhouse.

As Joseph took his place beside the coffin, a pale wintry gleam of sunlight pierced the clouds and shed a glow about the dark-suited man. Jenny looked curiously at Joseph, wondering briefly why he had stopped by their cabin.

The light against his hair seemed momentarily to bring back its youthful brightness. Although his features were heavy with strain and sorrow today, she was reminded of the long-ago boy. For a moment her heart yearned for that peaceful yesterday, filled with foolish, girlish dreams. Abruptly his words began to filter through her thoughts.

"The missiles of death will cut down a Saint, just like any other man," he was saying. "You have not the right to believe that just because we are the Lord's chosen, we will never escape the judgment of the Lord. We have not got a magic circle drawn about us, protecting us from what folly we have chosen to bring upon ourselves."

He paused and the group standing before him shifted restlessly, and Jenny was piercingly aware of the wooden coffin. She clung more tightly to Mark's arm while Joseph's words continued to build fear in her.

His voice was sad as he continued. "I have been communing with the Lord these days, seeking wisdom. Now I must advise you that the Lord is angry with these people, yea, even the chosen of the Lord. They have been unbelieving and faithless. A stubborn generation this is, refusing to give to the Lord the use of their earthly treasure. How can any one of you expect the blessings of the Lord in the face of disobedience?

"To expect the favor of God, we must learn to blindly trust Him. I tell you, my people, if you would do so, the very windows of heaven would be opened and showers of blessings would be poured upon you. All that the people could contain of blessings will be the reward of obedience to the will of God given to mankind through the prophet of God. Verily, I say, when you are obedient, you will enjoy all the wealth of the world. God will consecrate the riches of the Gentiles to you."

The mood of the crowd changed from outrage to excited hope. When the flutter of excitement passed, he added, "I have been charged with the restoration of the house of Israel in these last days. Called of God, I have been given the power and authority from God to accomplish His purposes. I can help that power to rest upon all who will do His will. Again I remind you that Saints from the four corners of this earth will be gathered to Zion, this holy land. We shall set up the kingdom of God, ready for the second coming of Christ in these last days. This is the word of the Lord to you."

Jenny and Sally went home with the chastisement and the future promise of blessing still swirling in their thoughts.

Briefly Mark and Andy lingered before returning to their posts. As they were preparing to leave, a wagon stopped beside the cabin door. From the conversation, Jenny realized it was a man who had been at Crooked River. She could see a bandage showing under the rim of his hat.

Carefully tilting his hat, he nodded as Andy introduced Sally and Jenny, still standing in the doorway. Then addressing Andy, the man, Byman, said, "Hyde, Tom Marsh, and a couple of others slipped outta Missouri during the night. Joseph sent a bunch after them, but they never did catch up with them. Had their families with them, but they were sure traveling light to have slipped the bunch trailing them."

"Fortunate for them," Mark said heavily. Jenny pressed her fingers against her eyes, trying to crowd out the memory of Rigdon's face and the words he had shouted from the steps of the schoolhouse.

Byman nodded soberly. "And after Joseph's threat today, there's not many men who'd dare. They were brave."

Andy added, "I don't know. Things are getting sticky enough around here; maybe it's worth the chance." His brooding eyes studied Sally and Tamara.

Mark and Andy Morgan rode away together. Mark was shaking his head soberly as he said, "It makes me uneasy to leave the women there alone."

"Well, if yours would just stay put, they'd be safe enough," Andy drawled.

Mark threw him a quick glance, saying, "She's promised. I don't know what got into her, but I think she's convinced it isn't safe."

He was thinking about the mittens and talisman when Andy added, "That Gentile mob out there is crowding us close. And Doniphan's not far behind. 'Tisn't that I'm really fearing him, but that's the reason I'm reluctant to move the women at this time."

Mark added, "Haun's Mill is a mighty attractive target. I keep hoping the Gentiles don't take it into their heads to latch on to it. Maybe it hasn't occurred to them that they'd about starve us out if they controlled the mill."

The next morning, like a chess game subjected to a gentle, seemingly harmless maneuver, the whole scene started to change. What had been a contest of will and power had begun to develop into open war. That which had seemed insignificant had become strategic. Strangely, dissenters from the Mormon camp made the move.

Mark and Tom were with the men in the town square when the fellow rode in. Mark recognized him as the man sent out to spy when he had returned from Richmond.

Tom grasped his arm and spoke softly, "Mark, something's wrong. Tucker looks half-dead, and that horse is lathered. I'll take care of his mount; you get Tucker in to Joseph."

In Joseph's office, Tucker drained the mug of water, wiped his hand across his face and gasped, "Joe, it's bad. Soon as I found out Marsh and Hyde had dispatched a message to Boggs, I tried to intercept it. Couldn't catch up with the kid carryin' it. Musta had a twenty-mile start on me.

"I laid around Boggs' stable, hopin' to have a little chat with the fella later. Found out he'd left before I got there. But the whole place was buzzin' with the talk."

Mark interrupted impatiently, "What makes you think they leveled with you?"

"They weren't talkin' to me. 'Twas all between themselves as they were preparing to move out."

"Where?" Joseph's voice was taut.

"Here. Seems troops were layin' over near Jefferson City, and their commander was called in to confer with Boggs when he got the dispatch."

"So it was from Marsh and Hyde. What did they pass on to Boggs?"

"First off, they gave him the details about the Danites. Told about spoilin' Gallatin and backed up their comments by giving the details of your Mahomet talk, when ya said you'd take your sword and make a gore of blood from coast to coast. Seems they also said something about the Danites planning to burn Richmond, 'cause they mentioned that and something about them poisoning the wells of the old settlers to start a pestilence."

When Tucker finally got to his feet and headed for the door, he turned. "Joseph, I forgot to tell you—Atchison's real mad." He hesitated and then left.

Mark was watching the play of expression across Joseph's

face. When he spoke, his voice was bitter. "So even my friend Atchison has turned against me."

But in another moment, Joseph started for the door, saying, "Come on, there's lots to do. Spread the word that all the Saints from all the outlying areas are to move into Far West as quick as they can get here. Could be their lives will depend on it. I'm going to start those lazy fellas around the fire building a fortress in the middle of town, even if they have to tear down every house to get wood."

It was the next day, the Sabbath, before Mark finished contacting the outlying communities and put in motion the exodus to Far West.

When he rode back into town, he was feeling the effects of the gloomy day and the cold drizzle of rain; he was also brooding over Jenny and dismally accepting the sense of loss which was slowly wrapping itself around everyone. He had seen it on the faces of the men and women, and he had been unable to offer hope.

He stopped first to warm himself at the fire burning feebly in the center of the square. He noticed that in just a day's time the fortification had grown to a haphazard, rearing chunk. Looking at the barricade, feeling the message of hopelessness it transmitted, Mark shook his head and turned his back.

The men grouped around the fire looked as dismal as their handiwork. Shifting from foot to foot, they blew on their reddened hands and kicked at the embers. Mark's terse greeting was acknowledged by a grunt. He rubbed his hands and searched for something to say.

"Hey, you fellas there!" Mark heard the angry growl and recognized the Prophet's voice. Joseph strode up to the fire. Like the others, his coat was damp and his hands red, but he didn't slow his stride. Moving from man to man, he grasped them by the shoulders and spun them away from the fire. "Come on!" he roared. "Move, jump, run! Anthing but mope. Let's wrestle! A soldier will win at anything."

Joseph was still moving, shoving the men into a ring. Stepping into the middle he threw back his head and laughed. The challenge was out. Within seconds, Joseph was the center of a laughing, brawling group.

With a smile, Mark stepped back to watch as the men, one by one, tried to throw Joseph.

"Stop, stop!" Mark turned and watched Sidney Rigdon charge into the midst of the wrestling match. He was waving his sword. Astonished, Mark noticed the man's face was contorted with rage. "You will not break the Sabbath in this manner! I forbid any more of this! I will not suffer it!"

Instantly the men were subdued, scuffling their feet and glancing at Joseph from the corners of their eyes. A braver one exclaimed, "Brother Joe, you put us up to this! Now clear our names."

Joseph moved. "Brother Sidney," he said in a low, deliberate drawl, "You best get out of here and leave the fellas alone. It's my orders putting life into them. You are an old man. Go get ready for meeting and leave them be." Suddenly he moved. Mark had only time for a choked protest as he watched Joseph knock the sword from Rigdon's hand, spinning him around. A pleased grin swept across Joseph's face, and with another quick movement, he swept the hat from the smaller man's head, and dragged him bodily from the ring. Now grasping his fine coat, he gave one quick yank, ripping it in two.

Rigdon's voice rose in protest, but Joseph turned to his men. Breathing heavily, he said, "My lads, don't ever say I got you into something that I couldn't get you out of."

On that day when the first of the troops stationed outside of town trickled back, Mark was in the square. He saw their crestfallen faces and asked, "What's happening out there?"

With a dejected sigh a young fellow said, "We've been called into retreat. We were guarding the county line. Captain said, 'Head for Far West'; and we did." Even as the man spoke, Mark saw the picket guards and scouts coming into town. From their drooping shoulders and slow steps, it was easy to guess that the rest of the men had been ordered in.

The men were still milling around in the town square when a scout and Joseph came out of the grocery store. "They're mobbers," the scout declared as the men began pressing around Joseph.

"Are you certain?"

"Couldn't be no other. Every Gentile in the state's gathered out there, just waitin' for us to make a crooked move. Chased us in here. I wanted to stay'n fight. The Lord's promised—"

An angry voice rose, "There's a multitude out there. We've only a handful. Don't even have sufficient arms."

Excited voices rose as the restless crowd jostled the men about. Joseph abruptly turned and leaped upon the line of barricades the men had been erecting. The silence of the crowd caught Mark's attention, and he turned to study the faces of the men as Joseph addressed them. Those hungry faces devoured every word their leader said.

But Mark's despair grew as he watched their emotions change to hope.

Someone cheered, and Mark turned to listen to Joseph's charge to valor. "We must fight for everything we hold dear— our homes, our Zion. God is for us!"

While Joseph was speaking, Mark's attention had been caught by the dark line of the Gentile mob moving slowly across the prairie toward Far West.

When the final cheer was over, Joseph's men took formation and moved to the edge of the prairie.

Mark climbed to the top of the breastwork to watch the confrontation. Cautiously the Saints moved across the prairie toward that dark mass of Gentiles waiting for them.

Mark winced and started to jump from the breastwork when something caught his eye. It was a dot of white being hoisted.

He could hardly believe his eyes as he watched the flag of truce waving in the Gentile ranks. Frowning, he strained to see, trying to comprehend the significance. "Surely that big bunch of Gentiles isn't giving in to Joseph's men without a fight. There's something very strange going on," Mark muttered to himself.

Mark had only begun to limp his way toward the store when some of the men started to trickle back into town. He called to the nearest soldier. "What's going on out there?"

Joseph came out of the store in time to see the man's stricken face. Together they heard the words. "Them's not the mob we've been after; it's Doniphan's militia. Won't be easy straightening this out, taking after the state militia when we thought it was mobbers. I'm feelin' like we got our hands smacked good."

Mark followed the Prophet back into the store. He watched Joseph drop heavily into his chair. Head in hands, he sat beside his fire. Mark held his silence, waiting.

Later, when the scout came, Mark was there to listen as Joseph received the news. The man spoke heavily, "It's Doniphan's troops." He ran his finger along the crude map spread on the counter. "He's positioned them between Haun's Mill and Far West, just one mile out of town."

When the ragged soldier turned and left the store, Mark wheeled, "I'm going to the Morgans' for the women."

Joseph stepped in front of him. "No, you are not. If one Saint sees you leave, he'll shoot without asking questions. Simpson's said every Gentile in the state has surrounded the town, and they're all holding their guns on Far West. Maybe that's so, maybe it isn't. But I'm not making a move until I figure out what's going on. If you want activity, then start praying." He paused, then added, "I'll shoot that lame leg out from under you just to save your life if I must."

Mark turned to leave and collided with a man standing in the shadows behind a stack of barrels. "Beg your—" He saw the uniform. Instantly Mark grabbed the man. "Spy!" he cried, and Joseph was towering over the man, gripping the dirty uniform around his neck like a noose.

The man gasped, "Doniphan sent me. Message."

Joseph released the man and shoved him against the wall. "Hand it over."

The man trembled as he smoothed out the sheets of paper and handed them to Joseph. While Mark kept his gaze on the soldier, Joseph moved close to the lamp.

Mark heard the exclamation as Joseph whirled around, smashing the papers between his hands. His voice was thick as he yelled, "Get out!"

The youth trembled. "No message?"

Joseph shook his head and paced the floor until the soldier had disappeared. Stopping in front of Mark, he shoved the papers at him. "You are a lawyer; read these. Tell me what it means."

Mark scanned the letter from Doniphan. Slowly he said, "He's enclosing an order from Governor Boggs and he's suggesting that you take action quickly since Lucas and General Clark are headed for Far West with six thousand men, and with instructions to enforce this order."

Mark sat down and spread the second paper across his knees. "The order from Boggs is dated October 27, 1838, from Jefferson City." He glanced up at Joseph, "It appears he's had a change of mind from some previous decision—"

Joseph interrupted, "Previously he'd ordered troops to Daviess County to reinstate the Gentile residents. I'd received word that Doniphan's men were to be the ones sent to Daviess County."

Mark glanced at the paper he held. "Well, now he states that he has information just received that has changed the whole face of things. This new information indicates to him that the Mormons are in defiance of the laws of the state. He accuses us of 'having made open war upon the people of the state.'" Mark was silent for a moment and then said slowly, "he advises that the Mormons are to be treated as enemies and must be exterminated or else driven from the state."

Looking up at Joseph, Mark winced. "Exterminated. That's an unusual word. Do you suppose he's planned revenge, using the very word Rigdon proposed in his Independence Day speech? I remember hearing him use it."

Joseph shook his head and sighed. Mark watched him again drop his head into his hands. With a strange sensation of detachment, Mark wondered if the whole scene, even the alarming papers Joseph still held, were real. But he couldn't help measuring the reaction of Joseph Smith, and he decided he was seeing a defeated man.

As he hesitated, a conviction gripped him that it was no accident he was sitting here beside Joseph in this one quiet moment before a decision must be made.

On the far wall of the long, dimly lighted building, a clock ticked off the minutes. For a moment Mark recalled the unexpected sight of the walnut clock standing in the middle of his cabin. Immediately the impulse to warn Joseph was overlapped with the memory of Jenny's blue mittens and the talisman. He stopped.

His jaw tightened as he stared down at Joseph. *The man deserves whatever Boggs plans to give him.* Mark clenched his fist and then relaxed.

Pushing aside his own angry feeling, he squatted in front of the Prophet. "Joe, there's the people to think about. You've got to save them; it's your responsibility as leader. Do you see? Joe, it's starting to look tough out there. I think you'll have a chance if you get out and level with your men. Admit you've no heaven-stamped guarantee that your troops will be victors. Admit that God's not playing favorites with you. The riches and lands of the Gentiles aren't going to be handed to you on a silver platter. Pull your men in. I saw them facing off out there on the prairie. They're still thinking they're obligated to fight because God's ordered it. You know there's only a handful compared to Doniphan's men. Plead with Hinkel, Wight, Avard, and the rest to get back here, and then surrender. Admit—"

Joseph jumped to his feet. "Mark, I'm not seeking advice. I'm a prophet of the Lord, *I* give the orders."

"And you haven't a chance in the world to succeed if you follow this track. Joseph, in God's name, can't you see what your childish play-acting has led you into? You have no more audience with God than—" Joseph turned away and stomped toward the bar at the end of the building. Heavily Mark followed him. His voice was controlled and low now. "I could say all the things like repent, accept God on His terms, quit trying to be God; but I don't think you intend to listen."

Mark started for the door and Joseph called, "You might stay around to pick up the pieces. One of these days, just maybe—"

The door burst open. Lyman Wight and Colonel Hinkel charged into the room. "You've got communication," Hinkel said. "Let's see it."

Joseph clenched the papers and glared at Hinkel. "Who's in command?" he snapped. The men dropped back and Joseph stepped forward. "What's going on out there?"

"It's Doniphan. His troops have moved closer. Don't think they're more'n a mile outta town. We're using the breastwork down the middle of town. The men are lined up, just dancing with excitement, daring Doniphan's bunch to get close enough so's they can take a shot at 'em. Joseph, our men are straining at the bit. When do I give them the word?"

Joseph's voice was deliberately slow as he said, "Not until *I* give the word. We're going to play hell with their apple carts."

Mark grabbed up his coat and left the store, shaking his head in dismay. For some time he walked around the camp, watching the men, listening to their subdued conversations. More than once he saw their quick glances his direction. It was easy to guess they were seeing him as a spy for Joseph. No wonder they turned away, with expressions very nearly like fear on their faces. Mark sighed heavily.

Later when he picked up his tin plate and joined the others around the mess fire, he discovered that the men were silent, but the air of depression was real. In the absence of conversation, he found himself mulling over all that had happened that day. Measuring events against the feeling that Joseph's decisions were wrong, he picked at his food and admitted the obvious. Not only were Joe's decisions wrong, Mark's legal mind admitted uneasily, but the decisions must be challenged or the constitution of the state, as well as law and justice, were impotent vessels.

One statement Joseph had made still rang in Mark's ears: "I am above the law."

Mark sighed, gave up on the plate of cold food, and headed for his bunk.

Mark knew it was late when the armed guard touched his shoulder. He knew it because he had known how long he had tossed on his mat before going to sleep. When he raised himself to one elbow, the man's grip tightened. "Mr. Cartwright," he said respectfully, "Joseph bids me tell you that you are under arrest. Please, sir, this is for your own protection." The man's grip had become steely. "Come with me; Haun's Mill has been attacked."

CHAPTER 21

October 30 dawned with the promise of being a nice day, and Jenny immediately seized on the promise. "Sally, let's get out. We've been cooped up here like a bunch of chickens. Let's walk over to Haun's Mill; it's only a good stroll down the creek. You've made friends over that way, and there's a woman I want to inquire after."

Sally lifted dull eyes and moved restlessly on her bench. "I suppose so—anything's better than sitting here, fearing what's happening to the menfolk. We haven't heard a word for days."

"I suppose I should have walked into town," Jenny said slowly. "But they say no news is good news. With Mark riding Sammy, and Patches with a lame foot, it's been easier to sit and wait on the fellows."

"I did promise Mrs. Harris I'd visit," Sally added.

After breakfast, Jenny bundled Tamara into warm clothing and hurried Sally along.

The heavy, unseasonable snow earlier in the month had broken branches and stripped leaves from the trees before they had completed their cycle of autumn glory. Snow still lingered in the heavy shadows, and the leaves were a soggy cushion underfoot.

While Sally shivered, Jenny enjoyed the pungent forest smells—the pine and the acrid odor of ancient foliage. She gloried in the scurry of squirrels and the raucous complaint of jays. With Tamara beside her, she was seeing with new eyes the wonder of twigs and shiny rocks. They followed Log Creek into the settlement.

218

Haun's Mill was a tidy circle in the midst of forest. In addition to the mill and a cluster of cabins, there was the blacksmith shop and corrals. Over all lay order and neatness. Jenny studied the garden patches, saying, "I like it here. It would be a pleasant place to live. Seems there's such a haphazard air to Adam-ondi-Ahman."

Sally lifted her head and looked surprised. "Why the difference?"

Jenny shrugged, "Probably because up that way the settlements are new." Abruptly she changed the subject, "I've been hearing things about Far West that surprised me. Mrs. Harris said everything's topsy-turvy. She was blaming most of it on the disorder of the breastworks they're putting up for defense in case the fighting gets into town. She was telling me she heard one woman complaining that Joseph has had them building block houses for defense for such a long time, they didn't even get a chance to put in crops. She told Mrs. Harris, confidential-like, that they'd all be thieving for their grain before spring— and from what she says, there's plenty of that going on right now."

Sally poked at a pile of leaves with the stick she carried, saying, "What difference does it make? The Prophet's promised that the cattle on a thousand hills belong to the Lord, and that means it belongs to us, too. Why worry about planting when there's more important things to do?"

As it turned out, both Sally and Jenny found many of their Kirtland friends living at Haun's Mill. The day passed quickly as they visited from cabin to cabin. Women, as isolated as they, were eager to talk. Jenny was only vaguely conscious of how quickly the time passed as they worried together over the latest news and the fearful things taking place.

Jane Laney shivered and said, "I'm right grateful we settled down here in Caldwell County instead of in Daviess. I don't think the Gentiles will ever give in to the Saints up there."

Later on their way down the lane they met old Thomas McBride. He leaned on his cane and waited until they reached him. There was concern in his eyes as he said, "Now don't you young ladies linger until dark. I've been listenin' to the troops all day."

"They're just shooting rabbits," Jenny said with a laugh. "The McLaughlin boy crept up on them. It's just a bunch of men from down the way. They're not the militia, and they're not any more serious about this business than we are."

"What makes you think that way?" His eyes were piercingly intent. "You're too young to know war and suffering and you're thinking it can't happen to you. I fought in the Revolutionary War, and I know it's not that way at all."

For a moment Jenny was caught by the memory of the McBriers' home—both before and after. She shivered, saying, "Yes, I know it can happen." Suddenly sober, she added, "Sally, perhaps we'd better go."

The always-present fear settled back down over Sally's gentle face. As her eyes darkened, Jenny added hastily. "Oh, it can't be that bad. We'll finish our walk to Matilda's and then go home."

She turned to wave at Mr. McBride and then took Tamara's hand.

The afternoon was far gone when they left Matilda's cabin. Jenny said with a sigh, "We've still not asked about the Martindales."

"Martindales?" Sally said wrinkling her nose. "Why do you want to visit that stuffy old lady? She's the biggest bore I've ever met."

Jenny stopped abruptly. "She is?" she said slowly, thinking back to the whirling red-clad Adela with her sparkling smile and mysterious lilting voice. "I wonder if I'm mistaken—" She looked at the heavy clouds overhead and sighed. "It's going to darken quickly tonight. Those clouds promise a storm."

They were still hesitating in the path when the gunfire began. At first Jenny thought *rabbits*, but then she heard the screams.

For a moment she could almost dismiss it as a bad dream. Looking around the clearing at the solid cabins and rustling cornstalks, she thought, *It seems so ordinary and peaceful.* Then she heard Tamara's whimpers and felt Sally's frantic hands grasping at her.

Turning slowly, Jenny looked at the scene behind them. The

gunfire was coming again. She saw people running; women and children streamed toward the woods, while men with guns were running, shooting, and running again toward the blacksmith shop standing in the middle of the clearing.

In the space of one hard breath, Jenny saw men swarming up the creek bank toward them—strangers, dirty and ragged. Jenny caught a glimpse of their faces, some leering, some contorted in rage, waving rifles over their heads.

Still with a sense of idle detachment, Jenny saw them turn on the running figures, chasing the women and children, herding the silent racing figures into the woods.

Until the screams penetrated Jenny's confusion, she didn't comprehend what was happening. But even while Jenny watched, she saw them kneel and lift their rifles. Dust pricked upward in puffs.

Once again the men laughed and aimed their rifles at the women fleeing toward the trees. In the brief silence after the women disappeared, the men turned back.

Hands were shoving at Jenny and she moved in response. Now aware of gunfire coming from behind her, Jenny forced her numb body to move, stepping backward into the sheltering trees.

Now she could see a ring of men gathered around the blacksmith shop, shooting, waiting, and shooting again.

Then Jenny realized that she and Sally were clinging to each other. With every blast of gunfire, Sally cringed, her body jerking as if she felt those bullets. In a brief, silent interval, she cried, "Will it go on forever?" Jenny could only shake her head.

Darkness was nearly upon them when the rapid volley trailed into an occasional burst of gunfire. Jenny became aware of Sally's strangling sobs. They were still clinging to each other with Tamara wedged between them. Jenny found mind enough to be glad the child stayed motionless and soundless.

Later Jenny began to breathe easier. A few shadowy figures pulled themselves upright and came to huddle in the trees. The silence was alive with fear. Once more men pounded past, circled, and returned. With every sound of their searching feet, the women cringed deeper into the trees.

When the footsteps faded and the eerie quiet grew, Jenny began to realize that their total, mindless fear had saved them. In the trees she discovered others had survived too. Much later, like Jenny and Sally, they came creeping out of the woods. Together they huddled in the clearing, stunned and wondering.

That gunfire. They saw the silent shop and remembered the men and boys who had fled into the blacksmith shop. Finally Matilda spoke, and for moments Jenny could only compare the strong, confident woman she knew with this trembling, weak creature who was clinging to the tree beside her.

Jenny spoke out of memory she didn't know she had. "Those—those, they knelt down and shot through the spaces between the logs. It was like—they didn't have a place to run."

The women continued to huddle on the edge of the clearing. The last gun had long been silent. The final shadowy figure slipped away, and the scent of gunpowder disappeared. They were still motionless when a lone shadow moved hesitantly toward them, stood, and stumbled to fall again.

One of the group, braver than the rest, said slowly, "It's a woman." Her voice unshackled the others and slowly they began to come forward. They surrounded the trembling figure and waited, powerless to act.

She spoke in a faltering voice, "I was hiding in the wagon. Old Thomas, he surrendered his rifle, and one of those men—" she choked and they heard her ragged breath—"one of those men hacked him to pieces with a corn knife." Her voice became shrill, "The others—" She shook her head, but it was enough.

They turned and faced the blacksmith shop. First one and then the others began moving hesitantly toward it.

Mark pulled on his clothes. As the guard instructed, he picked up his rifle and coat. The man's voice had been heavy; that should have been enough to alert Mark, but even now the information, still seeping into his mind, seemed unreal.

When they reached the store, the facts began to add up and make sense. Joseph was sitting behind a table. His arms rested on the piles of paper; his hands clasped the base of the smoking oil lamp. When the guard spoke, Joseph sighed and got to his feet. Now his face was shadowed, and Mark found himself leaning forward to peer into his eyes.

Joseph spoke as if stunned. "We've just received communication from Haun's Mill. One of the wounded made it in with the information that they had been fired upon this afternoon. Seventeen are dead and fifteen wounded."

"But why am I arrested?" Mark questioned.

"I need you and I can't have you running off to Log Creek to be shot like a hero."

The final fact sank in: Haun's Mill was fearfully close to Morgans' cabin. He had to moisten his lips before he could ask, "Then you think the outlying cabins were attacked too?"

"It's possible." As Joseph paced the floor, Mark watched him, his heart thudding; but he dared not allow his thoughts to probe further.

The door opened. Corrill and Reed Peck entered the store. When they walked into the circle of lamplight, Joseph returned to his chair behind the table. He pulled a pile of papers toward him and said, "I've a mission for you men. I want you to find Doniphan and beg like a dog for peace."

The three men facing him stood motionless, silent. Mark moved first, and with a puzzled frown, glanced at the other faces. Then the realization struck him. Joseph had chosen dissenters to carry his message. He was speaking again and his voice was level, emotionless. "Yesterday it was Haun's Mill. God knows what it will be tomorrow. I'm getting new information almost every hour. The militia is moving in from all directions. We're outnumbered five to one. By this time tomorrow there'll be ten thousand men surrounding the town."

And Mark knew why they had been chosen. Wight, Avard, and all the other men who had been brainwashed by Joseph's doctrine would never back down now. He could almost hear Avard's cry: *Charge, Danites, charge! The Lord will fight our battles for us!*

Dawn was breaking over the horizon when the three saddled

up and pointed their horses in the direction in which they believed Doniphan's camp lay.

Already Israel's army was stirring, moving toward the town square. When Mark heard the cheer, he muttered to Corrill and Peck, "Wait up, fellows; let's hear what Joseph has to say to the men."

They watched the lithe figure vault to the top of the breastwork and face the men. "The Gentiles are coming." His voice rang through the crisp morning air. "I care not a fig. For years we've tried to please them. Their lawlessness spells out their belief that 'might makes right.' And mighty they are. But we have God on our side. They are a damned set and God will blast them into hell."

Corrill shivered and said, "Come on, fellas."

As they wheeled their horses, Joseph's voice followed them: "All we lack in number the Lord will match. He'll send angels to fight."

When they reached the road, Reed Peck looked at Mark. "Lee told me confidentially he doesn't believe that Joseph has the least conviction that his little band of men can stand off the army coming against him."

"Then we'd better get going before Joseph's battle cry leads his men where his faith can't take them."

At noon, Peck reined in his horse and waited until Mark and Corrill halted. "Men, we've seen plenty of evidence that Doniphan's been traveling this route; but at the rate we're trailing him, we won't catch up with him until midnight."

"Any suggestions?" Mark asked.

"We're under orders!" Corrill snapped. "There's not one thing we can do except continue to trail him and hope we reach his camp before it's too late."

"From the way this trail is leading, I suspect he's received communication and is going in the back door of Far West."

"Then let's stretch these horses' legs."

The light of supper fires in Doniphan's camp informed the three they had reached their destination. Peck stopped and scratched his head. "Well, I'll be—look at that, we've ended up in our own backyard, just like you said, Cartwright. As late as it is, Peck, I suggest you pay Joseph a visit, tell him where we found the camp, and ask if there's a message. We'll keep our eye on the place."

When Peck returned, Mark and Corrill had a small fire burning and supper simmering in a pot. Corrill heard the horse first. He looked up from his work and cocked his head. "If that's Peck, he's not riding the horse he left on."

They stepped back in the trees and waited until they could identify Peck. Corrill stepped out. "Whose horse?"

"Joseph's."

"You sure? If you ride into camp on some Missourian's horse, there could be trouble."

"I asked Joe if it were consecrated property and he said no."

Later, as Peck held out his bowl for the stew, he shook his head and said, "In Far West there's men lined along the edge of town, facing the militia. They looked ready for a fight."

"Still?"

He nodded. "But then, before I left, I met men on the street wandering around looking like they'd been kicked in the stomach."

"I'm trying to figure out whether that means Joseph's leveled with the fellas and told them what's going on, or if they're just looking at the bunch out here, scared to death of what could happen."

He shrugged, and Corrill said, "Well, finish up that stew and let's get on down to camp with Joseph's message."

When they were close to Doniphan's camp, Corrill said, "Get those white rags up high before they decide to shoot first and ask later."

They had gone another fifteen yards when a guard challenged them. Stepping from behind a tree, he waved a gun and yelled, "Halt!"

Peck called, "We're from Joseph Smith with a message for General Doniphan."

"Well, he's not taking communications tonight."

"I've an idea if you tell him that Reed Peck is wanting to see him, he'll be mighty glad to know about it."

The guard spoke to someone behind him and then addressed

Peck. "Might as well settle down and stack your arms. Could be a while, if ever."

To the tired, impatient men it seemed a long time before the guard stood in front of them and nodded, saying, "Follow me."

As they walked through the Gentile camp, Mark was aware of Peck's heavy mood. He tried to ponder the meaning of it, but it wasn't until they stood before General Doniphan that he began to understand.

Peck handed over the folded paper bearing Joseph Smith's message. Mark watched the change of expression on Doniphan's face as he read and slowly refolded the paper.

Then Peck spoke, hesitantly at first. Soon his words began to tumble over each other eagerly.

There was a thoughtful expression on Doniphan's face, Mark watched him nod in agreement. Stepping closer to listen to Peck, Mark took a deep breath and felt the burden on his heart grow lighter.

Peck was saying, "We're not all the way you've been seeing us. Don't forget we're under obligation to obey the Prophet, but there's some who's been doing a little thinking for themselves. Many of the people are warmly opposed to the wickedness taking place in Daviess, the plundering and slaughter and burning. They're also opposed to the oppression being put upon them by the church. Just as much as any man in your army would be. But they're compelled, even to the place where they must stand and let their blood be shed for measures they don't approve."

General Doniphan jumped to his feet. With a muttered oath, he linked his hands behind his back and paced back and forth in front of the fire. When he stopped and faced the three, Mark could see the line of pale faces circling the far side of the fire.

Now Doniphan's words caught him with their intensity. He was saying, "I promise you that these people will not be endangered when they turn to us for protection." His voice rose to a subdued roar. "Without a doubt, society must be restructured within this state. It must be the people who will determine whether or not they will be governed by priestcraft. If the people are too weak to fight off the oppression which surrounds them,

I promise you they will be protected in their flight out of the state."

As the three men prepared to leave, a shadow of a smile softened the face of the white-haired general. "We're here to enforce peace, not to destroy a helpless people. You realize, don't you, that our numbers make the Mormon force look ridiculous. You might say our strength is only a statement designed for wise people." As he turned to go, he spoke over his shoulder. "I want to see the leaders of these people early in the morning."

Mark could hold his tongue no longer. "Sir, Haun's Mill—"

"Unfortunate," Doniphan rumbled. "That mob wasn't under orders. You must believe that."

Mark, Reed Peck, and John Corrill mounted and headed back to Far West. The men rode silently, each busy with his own thoughts. Mark was feeling a new appreciation for Peck and wondering if his statements would swing the tide of feeling for the Saints.

Corrill turned to Mark, saying, "I know you share the good feelings of the Prophet. I can't bind you to silence about what was said this evening."

"No, you can't," Mark answered thoughtfully. "If I felt Joseph needed to know, I would tell him. Right now I see it would serve no purpose whatsoever. Both of you are to be commended for your concern for the people."

Far West seemed to be sleeping as they rode through the streets. Silently they separated. They didn't need to remind each other of their early morning meeting with Joseph.

CHAPTER 22

In the morning Joseph's men were waiting. It was very early as Mark walked down the street toward the store and their meeting with Joseph.

He noticed how the November frost rimmed the mud puddles as he passed the group of ragged soldiers pacing before their breakfast fires. Their faces turned toward him; he saw the questions in their eyes, the lines on their haggard faces.

As he walked, he reminded himself that these were family men. They had children and wives waiting for them, and, without a doubt, they were going to lose everything they owned. His heart squeezed with pity and he turned his face away, lest they asked the questions he dared not answer.

Later in the morning, when Joseph received a dispatch from Doniphan, Mark was there to hear him read it. "Says, 'No settlement can be approached until the arrival of orders from Governor Boggs, which we expect immediately.' That's that." His voice was filled with despair, "We know how those orders read. He said exterminate."

Mark watched him crumple the paper and pace the floor of the store. A fire burned, cheerfully crackling under the spider on the hearth. Joseph faced Reed Peck and said, "A compromise must be made, honorable or dishonorable."

Peck's gaze met Mark's, and again Mark recalled Peck's statement to Doniphan. He was also remembering his own heartening reaction. Just now he felt his heart lift in a wordless prayer, and at the same time he was accepting the calling. Those men out there must be warned, rescued.

Now Mark could no longer hold back the question. "Have you heard any more from Haun's Mill?"

"A woman was injured; it wasn't your wife. I believe Andy Morgan has gone looking for them. I'll send him to you at first convenience." He turned impatiently away.

Late in the afternoon the lookout passed the information down. Mark hurried back to the store as soon as he heard the shout. Joseph turned when Mark entered. Slowly he moved and sighed. "I know," he said heavily. "A runner brought the news ten minutes ago. I guess he expected me to duck out the back door." There was a touch of bitter irony in his voice. "It's Lucas out there. That won't help our cause in the least."

Mark thought of all the things which could be said, but he knew he was looking at a beaten man and he turned away as Joseph added, "There are several other generals out there too. Boggs is going to make certain his order is delivered and enforced." He nodded his head toward the door. "I've sent Corrill, Phelps, Cleminson, Peck, and Hinkel. I hope they'll use their heads."

There was a stir at the door. "Sir," the youth said timidly, "I have a request here from General Lucas. He requests that Joseph Smith, Sidney Rigdon, George Robinson, Parley Pratt, and Lyman Wight present themselves as hostages until tomorrow morning." He took a deep breath and lifted his chin. "At such time, if a treaty is not forthcoming, these men will be returned. Also I am sent to inform you that if such men are not forthcoming, the army will be forced to march into Far West and take them."

Joseph winced. "Kindly inform Lucas that we shall be there shortly."

They watched the door close softly. Mark sighed. "You realize that the first term of the treaty will likely call for the immediate removal of the Saints from the state."

Joseph turned and said, "I don't care. I'll be most happy to get out of this damnable state." After a pause he added, "There's not much point in resisting the militia acting under Boggs' orders. The church is over a barrel, and it'll have to comply."

Mark stood at the window, watching the men mill restlessly

about the streets, but again he recalled Joseph's brave words, *I am above the law.* He turned. "Joseph, those men out there don't know what's going on. How much longer are you going to leave them in the dark?"

Joseph didn't answer. Neither did he move from his position at the table. Uneasy now, Mark sat down and waited. When Mark finally spoke again, he tried to keep his voice light. "It's getting late; do you want me to round up the men?"

"No."

At the sound of footsteps, Joseph raised his head and waited. Mark was relieved to see Corrill and Peck, but he also saw they looked as worried as he felt. "Joseph, Lucas is getting mighty edgy. He meant what he said. They're prepared to march in here and take you if you don't come along."

Joseph's grin was ragged, and Mark turned back to the window. He was busy thinking, and it was a moment before the flurry of activity began to have meaning. When the drums and bugles sounded, he sprang away from the window. "Joe, the fellows are preparing to fight. That means the militia's heading this way."

Corrill whirled, "Haven't you told the men what's going on?" When Joseph didn't answer, Corrill and Peck ran out the door. Mark watched them dashing toward the oncoming troops.

He took Joseph's arm and snapped, "Get out there right now before there's more bloodshed. I'll round up the rest of the men."

As Mark ran into the street, he collided with George Robinson. "Get Rigdon and head for Lucas' camp. Where's Wight? Bring Pratt. He's got to come, too."

When Mark reached the conference grounds with Pratt and Wight, Joseph was still talking to Lucas. Mark winced as he heard Joseph pleading for permission to stay the night with his family. He saw the general shake his head, and immediately the troops surrounded the men. As they were escorted away, the militia began to shout.

Slowly Mark walked back to Far West. He was aware of the silent, staring men as he entered the store. Mike was behind the counter. "Wanna stiff one?" Mark shook his head and wandered aimlessly about the store, worried and confused. Mike, his sleeves bunched above muscular arms, stopped in front of him. "Have they included you in on it?"

"I'm not certain I know what you're talking about."

"The bunch who fought at Crooked River are running scared. Have been since they found out they were fighting Doniphan's men. Avard, too." Mark frowned and Mike said hastily, "They're gone."

"Just pulling out, leaving?"

Mike nodded and said, "Joe told them to head out."

Slowly Mark said, "They're family men. How are they getting their women and children out?"

"They aren't. Sounds like they're leaving their families to take care of themselves. Might be it's the only way," he said apologetically. "By the way, Andy Morgan was in last night and said to tell you the womenfolk are all right. They'll be coming in as soon as they can safely pass the troops."

"Jenny, she's safe?" At Mike's nod, Mark turned away with a deep, thankful sigh.

The next day, after another sleepless night, Mark was back in the store office at dawn.

As he had walked toward the store, he realized that Far West had become a restless camp, bearing the marks of fear and discouragement. For the first time, he noticed that the tidy cabins and gardens looked neglected, while wagons and cattle still crowded the streets. It seemed the breastwork erected about the town was the only sign of real activity. He studied the block houses Joseph had ordered built. As he marveled at the extensive fortification, he couldn't help thinking that the breastwork had become the most significant landmark in the town.

"Mister?" Mark turned to face the woman picking at his sleeve with nervous fingers. "What's going to become of us?"

He took a deep breath, "Ma'am, I don't know. There's to be a meeting between our men and the generals in charge. Right now there's nothing I can tell you."

She swallowed with difficulty and whispered, "What's going to happen to Joseph?"

"I don't know." Mark saw the darkening of her eyes, the

fear. Hastily he added, "All you can do is hope that Governor Boggs will be compassionate."

She wrinkled her brow, thinking. Slowly she said, "Some's saying we'll be sent out of state, losing our homes, ever'thing we've worked for. Mister, I've been here since '32. We've been pushed around for so long. Seems the revelations about Zion are amiss. Begging your pardon. But could you just tell Joseph we're tired of it all? Please, just let us go home."

She started to move away and then looked back. "We can stand to lose our homes, Zion. But how'd we ever get along without Joseph? We'd not have much to hope for. Seems we'd be adrift, not knowing which way to turn."

"But you'd still have God."

She looked blank. "That's true, but we did before, too. Seems kinda pale to go back."

At midmorning Colonel Hinkel came into the store carrying a sheet of paper. "Since you seem to be the only one around with a part of his mind left; here, read it."

It was a copy of the treaty. Mark ticked off the items. The Mormons were to deliver up their leaders for trial. Those who had carried arms were to surrender their property in payment of war debts. Arms were to be surrendered immediately, and the Mormons were to leave the state.

Thinking of the people, Mark sadly shook his head. Hinkel said, "It could have been worse. Lucas turned out to be fair-minded. He said he thought treaty could be had instead of the route Governor Boggs had advocated. It was fortunate for us all that he was willing to overlook even Joseph's last high-handedness."

Mark looked at the man and remembered the talk of the men. They had called Hinkel a fair-weather Saint, saying that in the thick of battle they had seen him turn his coat inside out. Studying the man, Mark saw only the elegant figure, the charming smile. He seemed every bit the southern gentleman. "What a motley group we Mormons are," he said softly and watched Hinkel blink in surprise.

Hinkel moved toward the door. Then he stopped and turned, "By the way, the charge against Joseph is treason."

"Of course, it must be," Mark murmured, "I—" he stopped, realizing that he had been hearing sounds of activity, and suddenly he understood. The militia was moving. Those were shouted orders, the thud of feet. He started for the door, and Hinkel said, "They've come."

Standing on the steps, they watched the army of Israel march out of town. Slowly they followed. Out on the prairie, where November had left the landscape a blank page, the army of Israel stopped and the state militia surrounded the men on three sides.

Distance blurred the shouted command, but Mark saw the men slowly surrender their arms. Within a short time, the men were marched back into Far West and placed under guard. "Well, that's that for the day," Hinkel said. For a moment Mark wondered if he detected a note of satisfaction in his voice.

Jenny had no clear remembrance of the walk from Haun's Mill back to Morgans' cabin. But sharp images had been etched on her mind: a mass of people, suddenly all kin in tragedy; the wounded and the dead. And she had found it impossible to shrink away from the ugliness and the need.

Much later there was the sensation of stumbling through the darkness with someone leading the way. And now, with soiled frock and blood-stained hands, Jenny knelt on the hearth in Morgans' cabin and blew life into the slumbering coals.

Intently, patiently, she fed bits of bark into the fire. When there was a glow and a touch of warmth, she got to her feet. Sally still stood beside the door with the sleeping toddler in her arms.

Jenny found she must ignore those haunted eyes and concentrate on Tamara. Slipping her arms under the wonderfully warm, limp child, Jenny carried her to the cot tucked back in the corner. There was a streak of dirt on the child's cheek, marked through with the water-course of tears.

As Jenny pulled the coverlet over her, Tamara curled one hand across her forehead. The blood on her hand must have come from Jenny's own. She winced as she looked down at herself and wondered whose blood it was.

Sally knelt beside the fire, shivering and weeping silently. The kettle of water was beginning to steam, and Jenny went to her precious store of herbs. Mindlessly she murmured the chant, stirred the herbs together and poured the hot water over them.

When Sally had drunk the last of the pungent mixture, color returned to her face. She placed the cup on the table and whispered, "What's to happen to us all? Will we be next?"

"Laney said no, that they have gone."

Sally shivered again, and from the horror in her eyes, Jenny knew she would talk. "I'll never forget the smell of blood, those cold, limp bodies. Why did those men shoot that little boy?" Jenny shook her head and closed her eyes against the memory of the backsmith shop and the smell of death. Her spirit shrank in horror even as taunting voices bound her thoughts and sent prickles of meaning into the scene at Haun's Mill.

The words had to be said, and Jenny gave them voice. "Good and evil. The one is wrapped in the other, and never can they be escaped. The spirits laugh with glee. How can I believe in anything good when such horror abounds?"

Jumping to her feet she dashed for the jar of herbs. Pouring a handful of the mixture into the skillet, she bent over the fire and waited until the dried leaves began to smolder and smoke. Shivering with fear and urgency, Jenny began the chant against death and disaster. When the leaves spiralled into flame, she slowly stood and, holding the skillet high, walked about the room, lifting the purifying smoke into every corner of the room.

From her place on the hearth, Sally watched. When the last wisp of smoke had dissipated, she whispered, "You really believe those charms work, don't you?"

"They are working on you—see how calm you've become?"

"I thought it was the drink." She paused and then asked. "What will the smoke do?"

"Dispel the bad spirits and give us peace."

"If that is so, why does your hand still shake?" Soundlessly Jenny shook her head. With new horror, she felt the tears rolling down her face.

Later, when the fire had burned to coals and Jenny slept,

the dreams came. She awakened in terror. Sitting up in bed she stared at her hands in the pearly light of dawn. In her dream they had dripped with blood. Everything she touched became tainted with human blood, even Mark. And he had slipped from her grasping hands, disappearing in darkness.

As she huddled in her bed, trembling at the memory scent of blood and wondering why the herbs hadn't dispelled the spirits, she recalled the rest of the dream. Jenny had been wearing the crown of a high priestess. It had been shiny, glittering with jewels, but when she had stretched out her regal hand to confer blessings and power, the hand dripped blood. Looking down at her robe, she discovered it filthy and covered with blood.

Jenny and Sally dragged themselves about their morning tasks, and then at high noon, Andy came.

Seeing their faces, he slowly sat down and pulled Tamara to his lap. After listening to their experiences, Jenny saw their own horror reflected on his face. She saw the concern as he looked from her to his wife. It was an expression she couldn't understand.

It was several days before Andy began to talk about all that had been happening. Jenny learned about the siege in Far West and Adam-ondi-Ahman. He described that final disheartening scene when the men yielded their arms and their Prophet was marched away under guard. "It makes a person wonder and question. Especially when all the promises seem to be failing."

Sally's reaction forced Jenny to grasp the seriousness of it all. "No!" Sally cried, clasping her hands against her face. "That cannot be. He is the Lord's anointed in this dispensation. God's will and promises to him must not fail. Oh, where have we failed the Prophet?

"We must not allow his hands to be tied. He assured us that if we were faithful to obey, then the blessings of the Lord would shower upon us. Blessings from heaven!"

She dropped her hands and lifted her chin. "I have not failed him. I shall be obedient to the Lord's anointed until death." For a moment her face flushed and her eyes sparkled, but Jenny was caught by the expression in Andy's eyes. It was disturbing to her, but she did not understand why until much later when she was to see that same expression in Mark's eyes.

CHAPTER 23

"Tom Timmons, Lyman Wight's sent for you. Hurry, they're rounding up the men right now." Tom dumped the handful of horseshoes he had been holding and turned. Mike looked at him curiously, "What have you been doing? Folks were beginning to think you'd left with the rest of the fellas."

"Trying to salvage this bunch of old shoes. A body's got to have something to do to keep from going crazy." Mike nodded sympathetically, but Tom knew his concern was only skin deep. Mike was a Gentile, an easy-going fellow who liked everyone and refused to side with any.

Mike continued, "Joseph and all the other Mormon big shots are being pulled in. Wight sent me to find you. He wants you to be sticking as close to Joe as you can. Says follow the bunch, bend an ear and, whatever you do, watch out for Avard."

Tom frowned, "Why did you say that? Is Joe fearing Avard will turn traitor?"

"I'm in the dark," Mike said with a shrug. "I only know what Wight said. He was talking about a paper Avard didn't dispose of. Joe had told him if the Gentiles got a hold of that paper, it would give them information about the Danites that would be grounds for charging him with treason." Mike studied Tom thoughtfully before adding, "Looks like your bunch is knee-high in hot water right now." He was still shaking his head when he left the stable.

Late in the day, following the orders he had been given, Tom eased through the militia lines and nosed around until he discovered the open area where the prisoners were bedded down.

236

It had begun to rain about the time Tom left Far West. The cold drizzle continued all night.

Crouched close to the guards placed around the men, Tom shivered in his wet clothes. He couldn't help wondering who was more miserable—Joe and the other prisoners, the guards, or himself.

Late that night, he heard the low murmur of voices coming from the guards. Cautiously Tom crept closer to listen. The rumble of conversation was punctuated by an occasional word and a mocking laugh. As Tom listened, he realized the guards were betting each other on the outcome of Joseph's trial. Tom moved restlessly in his hiding place. Only his promise to Wight kept him quiet. All instinct demanded he attempt to rescue the Prophet.

He had nearly dozed when the clink of metal stirrups startled him. Inching forward, Tom immediately recognized General Lucas' cold voice speaking to Wight. "You are sentenced to be shot to death at eight tomorrow morning," he was saying. "You and the rest of the men."

Just as Tom moaned and ducked his head into his folded arms, Wight's voice thundered back, "Shoot and be damned."

And Lucas admonished, "We were hoping you would come out against Joseph Smith. It would save your hide. I fear your fate is settled."

When Lucas turned and strode away, Tom moved back in the shelter of the willows; the rain was dripping down his back. All talk had ceased, even the guards were silent except for sober monosyllables. Tom was left to his thoughts as he crouched, shivering, under the willows. He tried to imagine the Saints without Joseph, and could feel only despair.

Without a doubt, every person in Israel's camp would feel the rending. Tom tried to analyze his faith and compare it with some of the strong ones. His gloom deepened when he finally acknowledged his feelings. Without Joseph there didn't seem to be anything to have faith in. Shaking with cold, he waited for the dawn.

The sky was just beginning to lighten when Tom managed to mingle with the men around the corrals. Later he discovered he had a ringside seat. When the restless milling of the crowd ceased, there was a roll of drums. General Doniphan and his brigade marched in and took formation.

Slowly the crowd parted. Tom watched the bedraggled prisoners being brought to face Doniphan. Tom studied the impassive faces of the dark-clad Joseph Smith and his tattered men. Remembering Lucas' statement last night, he felt his heart tighten in horror and pity. He felt that somehow all life had been suspended. Even the early sunlight touching the faces of the men seemed to pause before moving on.

There was silence and a hushed expectancy as Doniphan walked regally toward the line of prisoners. For a moment his figure outlined against the dawn seemed larger than life. His roar filled the arena. "You have been sentenced by court-martial to be shot!" He paused until the echo of his voice died away. "Your actions have not been the actions of honorable men. But I have indicated in the past that I will not disgrace myself or my men by sinking to mob tactics, and that is just what I deem today's order. My brigade is here, not to carry out those orders, but instead to take up a line of march out of this camp. I refuse to be a part of cold-blooded murder."

General Doniphan turned and held out a white paper. For a moment a vagrant pencil of sunlight touched the paper, and Tom was filled with a sense of good omen. With awe he watched the orderly run across the field carrying the paper, which he thrust into General Lucas' hand. Tom watched the confusion of expression and sound as General Lucas quickly gathered his men about him and retired from the field.

Stealthily Tom made his way behind the line of tents, seeking a place to listen as Lucas called the court to order and read the paper to them. In addition to the declaration which he had made on the field, Doniphan had included his instructions, which Lucas slowly read aloud. "If you follow through with the execution of these men, I promise you I shall hold you responsible before the courts."

Before Tom had a chance to bring his news to Far West, the message was carried by Lucas and his men. When Tom reached the town square, it was packed with Saints. He studied the tired, careworn faces gathered to listen as General Lucas delivered the verdict in a cold, passionless voice.

Tom was watching the people as the man delivered his speech in ringing tones that filled the square and echoed back, underscoring the finality of the situation.

It took another Saint to understand the quiet expressions on these faces—the softening of the men's furrowed brows, the tears on the faces of Joseph's parents, Emma's tightly closed eyes. These things might not seem like high emotion to Lucas; but Tom knew what it meant.

These people were not only hearing that the lives of Joseph and his men had been spared, but they were hearing a vindication for themselves. Once again they were to be given an opportunity to pick up the staff of their religion; and through obeying their Prophet, they would give God a chance to fulfill His promises to them. That was hope reborn.

Tom turned away. Most surely there would be prison and trial, but that bridge would be crossed later. He grinned. Joseph had survived the death sentence; didn't that prove the Lord was on his side?

Before the glad tears had dried on the faces of the Saints, there was another order. All of those who had participated in the war were to surrender their arms and prepare to yield their property to pay for the expenses of the war.

When Lucas paraded the prisoners through the streets of Far West, Tom was there. He had spotted Mark in the crowd and edged close. Together they watched the prison wagon move slowly through the streets, carrying Joseph Smith and his men.

Right at the last, in the confusion created as the wives and mothers of the prisoners pressed close to the wagon for a final word with their loved ones, Tom hissed in Mark's ear, "Get Jenny and head for the state line. You won't be in the wrong; that leg kept you out of the battle. But if you don't leave, they'll find some way to get to you. Be off, get my sister, and go."

"Since Haun's Mill I've been trying to reach her. Once Joseph's men broke and ran, we were placed under heavy guard, and I can't get out of town. But Andy's been with the women nearly all the time, so they're safe."

"You don't understand, Mark. It's for you I'm fearing."

"I'll see," Mark answered slowly. "You know Joseph asked me to keep a hand on the affairs around here until Brigham Young can help out. I'm about the only one of the bunch left. Brigham and Heber Kimball have left the state. Avard and most of the other Danites who didn't get caught have left, too." He paused and then asked, "What about you?"

"Right now I'm the only smithy around. I'm better known for hanging around the stable than for my Danite activities. If I'm lucky they'll be concentrating on their list of names and leave me alone."

Despite Tom's warning, Mark lingered on, trying to reassure the bewildered people. But within the next week the town of Far West crumbled. With the surrender, rioting mobs freely entered the town, destroying and looting. Tom couldn't help wondering if the Gentiles had gained new confidence since they knew the remnant of the army of Israel—those who had been forced to yield their arms and surrender property—were being held prisoner in Far West.

A committee had been assigned to investigate the affairs of the Saints, to determine what property would be assigned to them in order to enable them to leave the state. But for now rioting intensified, and the spirit of lawlessness grew.

In the end, in the midst of the confusion, Mark simply walked out of Far West. He was only one more restless prisoner managing to escape.

That evening when he walked through the Morgans' door, Jenny stood staring at him, unbelieving and without hope. When he held her, he knew the difference. With his hand under her chin, he lifted her face. "My dear, we are going to leave this place as soon as possible." Studying her face, he saw all the horror of Haun's Mill reflected in her shadowed eyes.

Mark turned and led her to a bench. She sagged helplessly against him. "Tell me all," she said. "I know only Haun's Mill and Andy's view of the troubles. It isn't that bad, is it?" He couldn't understand the expression in her eyes. Had she lost all hope?

He was silent a moment, thinking of his hope and wishing

desperately that she would listen to him. He sighed restlessly, trying once again to be patient.

"It is total. Jenny, Missouri has crushed us. All Joseph's people are paupers. If we escape with our lives, it will be a miracle." He couldn't withhold the truth of the situation; Jenny was too intelligent to stand for anything except the truth. But at the same time, he clung to her hand and tried to reassure her with a smile.

"All because we would not obey the Prophet," she said. Mark looked deeply into her eyes and saw still another shadow but could not name it, except to say that it resembled failure.

Their flight was aborted before it began. Andy brought the news. "General Clark is in town. Tomorrow every Mormon man is to be in Far West to receive orders." He eyed Mark disapprovingly, knowing his plan to leave.

Mark saw that look, but there was nothing he could say. In Andy's eyes he was apostate, another Judas to deny Joseph.

The next day Jenny, Sally, and Tamara went with Mark and Andy. While Andy drove the team, he told them that General Clark was the commander and chief of the Missouri Militia. Andy faced the women and said, "You see, this is getting to be very serious."

"It's snowballed," Mark added. "The whole situation has just been getting bigger since Joseph moved to Missouri. First it was the run-in with the local justices; then it became an unpleasant game with the militia. That built until now we have the commander and chief of the state militia out against us." Mark saw Jenny shiver, and knew she was beginning to understand the seriousness of the situation. Mark himself began thinking of Tom's advice. What possible evidences of guilt could be brought against him? Then he remembered the walnut clock at the cabin and winced.

In town there was an additional stir of excitement. Avard had been captured as he attempted to flee the state. When Mark heard, he carried the news back to Andy, saying, "Every man here is shaking in his boots. No one has the slightest idea what'll happen now."

"I don't understand," Jenny said slowly.

Mark said, "Rumor's such that it's looking like Avard had Joseph wrapped around his finger. It's Avard who's supposed to be responsible for the Danites. If they manage to pull out all the information about their activities, there're many men who could be ruined."

The air of dread and excitement was rising in the town as the people waited. All the Caldwell County Saints were in Far West, crammed into the town square when General Clark and his men arrived.

While their families huddled miserably, shivering in the cold wind, fifty-six men were separated from the others. Now prisoners of the state, they were advised they were to be sent to Richmond for trial.

As the charges were read against the group, General Clark paused to look out over the town. "The citizens of Daviess County are faced with the task of trying to restore a measure of order to their lives." His voice was dry. "It has been ascertained that prior to his surrender to General Lucas, Joseph Smith ordered that the plunder taken from the citizens of both Caldwell and Daviess counties be gathered and stored in one area in order to avoid any one person being charged with the particular crime. This attempt to shield his people has expedited the recovery of goods. It has also enabled us to honor the request of some of your past churchmen, now referred to as dissenters. We have been able to recover some of the household goods belonging to David and John Whitmer, Oliver Cowdery, and a Mr. Johnson. These goods will be returned to them." There was a stir among the people and for a brief moment, Mark grinned.

The final business of settling the disposition of the Mormons' property was handled before General Clark rose to address the people. His stern voice rang with authority, and his message settled into the hearts of the people. "This state has suffered irreparably because of the character, conduct, and influence of these Latter-Day Saints. We have endeavored to restore our state to the best of our ability by the actions we have chosen to take against you. As you know, the orders of the governor of this state were that you be exterminated and not allowed to remain in the area. Had your leaders not surrendered, we would have, of necessity, been forced to follow through. Now I say you must leave.

"I don't ask that you leave before spring, but do not delay for another season. The doom of your leaders is sealed. You have been the aggressors; these difficulties have been brought upon you by yourselves. I advise you to take it upon yourselves to become citizens of decent standing wherever you choose to live. To follow any other course will bring ruin upon you."

Tom lingered beside Mark and Jenny while the Saints wandered about the town. There was confusion, disbelief and, on several faces, relief.

"Yes, people do look stunned," Mark remarked softly to Tom. "I can hardly believe it myself. But it feels like the end of an era to me. Joseph's church can't endure this punishment and survive."

Tom looked slowly around, studying the faces of his friends. He was thoughtful as he spoke. "Mark, religion aside, these people are fighters. They're where they are today because they have no better sense than to dream big and not think about the consequences. Sure, they're confused, but change?" He was shaking his head, "Once you pick a way to live, it becomes mighty hard to change. If by some fluke Joseph manages to survive this, he'll land on his feet. Might come up with a better idea to make the whole promise of Zion even more attractive." He paused for a moment, then added, "Joe's still my friend, and I'm bettin' on him. Right now I feel mighty sorry for the fella. I guess I'll go sympathize and give him the latest news."

Tom rode away as Mark and Jenny, Andy and Sally climbed back into their wagon. When Andy picked up the reins, Tom circled back to them. "By the way, Mark, don't bother going back to your place. Them Missourians aren't gettin' much outta you."

"What do you mean?"

"Burnt. Was up there last week and everything's a big ash heap." Tom turned his horse toward Richmond. "Going to visit the jail; gotta see the Prophet."

When Tom was led into the enclosure which served as home and office to Joseph, he remarked. "Sure's not many around;

what's happened to the others?"

Joseph stood up, saying, "Some had bailable offenses. I understand they posted bond." He grinned slowly.

Tom said, "I'm guessin' the state'll see no more of them, right?"

"I 'spect." After a moment, Joseph added, "We'll be moving on to Liberty jail pretty soon." Again he was silent, and Tom watched his features settle into a countenance of defeat.

"You're thinkin' this is the end of the road, no matter what you said in your brave speech?"

"It hurts to see men I trusted turning from me to save their own hides. I should've known I couldn't trust a man as bloodthirsty as Avard. He told everything he could think of in court. All about setting up the Danites, even showed around the constitution. There's things in it that makes the lawyers think they have grounds for charging treason against me. Judge King's trying hard to prove we're setting up a kingdom. A man without a speck of religion can't even think like a man of God," Joe said, moving restlessly about his small quarters.

Tom admitted, "There's things we talked about in meetin' that an outsider wouldn't understand. Like how we swore to protect the secrets of the society."

"He charged me with being the prime organizer of the Danites, and went on to say they were set up first to take care of the dissenters, then to fight the Gentiles and take over their property."

"I can see where if a man wasn't in the kingdom, he wouldn't understand the Danites bein' necessary." He shot a glance at Joseph and continued, "I suppose he told all about how the first presidency was made up of all the officers, and how in your blessing you prophesied that the Danites would be the means of usherin' in the millennial kingdom with God's help. I'm supposin' they wouldn't be understandin' a man feelin' so strong about all this that he would swear his life to be forfeit if he was to reveal the secrets of the society?" Joseph didn't answer, but Tom knew it wasn't necessary.

Tom had a question that had burned in his mind for weeks. "Joe, mind if I ask you something? I've been strugglin' with my faith. It seems the spirit's tellin' me to ask you. You've been preachin' how the Lord's askin' us to set up Zion, and how we're goin' to be successful and how the Lord's goin' to be fightin' our battles for us." He paused to take a deep breath; looking up at Joseph he said, "Joe, we've had one big pile of failure. How are we to believe now?" Tom watched the big man sitting opposite him. He was slumped forward, resting his arms on his legs and staring at the floor.

When Joseph lifted his face, Tom saw the despair. "Tom," he spoke slowly and carefully. "I want you to understand what all this means. Simply, I've been betrayed. These men—not just Avard, but Wight, Pratt, Robinson, Marsh, Stout, Rich—you name them, from one end of the roster to the other, they've betrayed me. The church has betrayed me just like Christ was betrayed by Judas."

Tom got to his feet, standing awkwardly and wondering how to take his leave. Joe looked at him. "Remember, Tom, no matter how you judge me, God intended for the army of Israel to be victorious, but these men were just not perfect enough to withstand so large an army."

Joseph followed Tom to the door. "You know some of the things that contributed to the failure. There were those who wouldn't consecrate their property, who wouldn't obey council." He added, "Come back. The Lord's still working. I have a feeling that there's still important things ahead for us." A half-smile lit Joseph's face, and Tom saw the dreamy expression in his eyes. For just a moment a tingling excitement, a promise of hope reached out to touch Tom, and he nearly forgot his disappointment.

CHAPTER 24

Mark pulled Jenny's hand through his arm and cuddled it close to his side. The day was clear and pleasantly warm for November. "I'm glad you agreed to a walk this Sabbath day," he murmured. "Seems the Morgan cabin is getting more crowded every day. Jenny, we need to be pushing out of the state."

She raised troubled eyes and studied his face. "Mark, what did you think of all we were hearing this morning?"

"Are you talking about the letters Joseph wrote to us from prison?"

She nodded and then added, "Brigham Young is being a good fill-in for him. But he admitted he'd carried news to Joseph. I wish he hadn't told him that some of the Saints are calling Joseph a fallen prophet. I wish he hadn't troubled him with the news."

"And you didn't care for Joseph calling Hinkel a traitor, saying there was a parallel between him and the way the Savior was led into the camp of enemies? I saw you frown."

"Well, something about it made me uneasy. I keep wondering who he will denounce next." She was thinking of the label *Oh, don't* men as she looked up at Mark. But he didn't seem uneasy, and she sighed with relief. Then she added, "It couldn't help Joseph to be spreading information about Isaac Russell's setting up a little church of his own. And it's too bad Brother Young had to admit to defending the Prophet before the high council of the church. Seems right now it would be best if we didn't have to be airing our linen in front of the Gentiles." She sighed.

"Well, there's not much being aired, compared to what could be—" Mark abruptly ended his sentence and headed Jenny down the trail, away from the turnoff to Haun's Mill.

"Do you suppose Brigham's let Joseph know how his brother William's going around telling people that if he'd had his way, Joseph would have been hung years ago? What ever does he mean by that? I know there's been trouble. William's just jealous that Joseph is the Lord's anointed."

Slowly Mark said, "There's some whisper of talk that Joseph has the position William was to have held."

Jenny was silent for long minutes. When she spoke it was slowly and thoughtfully. "Are you saying that William was supposed to have been the anointed one instead of Joseph?" She turned away. Her shoulders drooped and Mark wondered what she was thinking.

They continued their walk, quietly, arms linked together as they wandered down the winter-crushed path. When Mark pulled Jenny to a halt under the spreading branches of a giant oak, he lifted her chin and studied her eyes. When he bent to kiss her, there was only a sad, dutiful pressure from her lips. He wrapped his arms around her and snuggled her close, but it was minutes before she relaxed against him.

He found himself wondering if repeating the gossip about Joseph had hammered a new wedge between the two of them. He thought of the cabin they had shared, and immediately the memory of Joseph standing in front of their fireplace intruded. Mark pressed his lips tightly together and tried to shove the picture out of his mind.

"Jenny, let's go now, before the rest of the Saints start trailing out of here with their wagons. I'll get a buggy to take us to the river. From there we can take a steamer to Saint Louis. I've a mind to look around Springfield, Illinois."

She pulled back and looked up at him. Her eyes seemed to probe the very depths, making him uneasy with all his unspoken thoughts. He was aware that both of them were carrying problems they dared not discuss with the other. Mark found himself wondering if there would ever be a day when all of those questions could be faced.

She spoke, but she was ignoring his plea. "Why did Joseph say those things in the letter Brigham Young read today?"

"Well," Mark said hesitantly, "I suppose he was apologizing, but he was also defending himself. I'm glad he had the manhood not to deny responsibility for the Danites. I suppose saying Avard was responsible for teaching erronous things is justifiable."

Jenny interrupted, "But why did he bring up the subject of polygamy? No one has accused him of any such thing."

Mark was surprised to hear sadness in her voice, not the indignation he expected. He studied her open, questioning expression. "Because," he spoke slowly, deliberately, waiting for a change in her eyes, "there's talk. Always the taint has followed Joseph."

Jenny frowned slightly but she was still gazing steadily at Mark. "I don't believe it. I can nearly assure you those are lies."

He must push one last time. "Do you know Cowdery has stated that you visited Joseph in his office on more than one occasion?"

She reacted, but before the flush touched her face, astonishment flooded her features. "The office! I went there to get books, to—" She paused and then said, "Did he talk about all the *old* women who went in there too?"

"Jenny," he caught himself, but he had her attention. When she looked up, he said, "Then you won't mind settling in Springfield, will you?"

Mark's question stayed with Jenny during the weeks that followed. But even more than the question was the dark expression in his eyes.

The little cabin was crowded. Its one room offered not the slightest privacy, and as winter settled in, even the quilt serving as a curtain between the bunks was discarded in an attempt to keep the occupants warm.

The pressures of living under those circumstances forced a routine on the two families. During the day the men were gone, mostly listening to the latest news from the state legislature concerning the Mormon problems. Just lately they carried back tales of Corrill's attempt to win concessions with a petition to the legislature from the Mormon people.

Andy added, "After all the trouble Joseph and the people heaped upon Corrill, I'd have expected him to be gone without troubling himself anymore with the woes of the Saints. But he was right in there, bending the ear of anyone who would listen to him. It didn't do any good, though, and the restrictions remain. We must all be gone before another spring planting."

Mark retorted, "In his plea he was rather rough on Joseph and the Danite leaders, but all the talk didn't do much. However, from reports drifting back it's beginning to look as if there's a good chance the legislature will grant a little stipend to help the Saints get out of the territory. I'm thinking it's starting to look as if we might as well pull out as soon as we can."

"Might as well," Andy replied. "I intend to go as soon as I dispose of this place, and for what they're offering, I'd be well off just to dump it."

Several days later, while the men were in town, the two women were sewing. Their conversation had dwindled away and Jenny was busy with her own thoughts. While half-heartedly stitching together scraps of cloth to mend a torn quilt, she recalled the Sabbath walk and Mark's conversation.

She was still remembering how he had looked at her. She was sure he believed she was lying to him. Her heart was sore. But, then, it had been for a long time. To discover he doubted her was only the capstone on the troubled feelings she had been having for months.

Never would she be able to explain to him all that was on her mind. One thing was very certain—she had discovered it in the cloudy, jumbled thoughts. There was no hope. Joseph's dream of Zion had failed. Not even in the green book had she found one concrete evidence of hope. Looking back, she realized that since the day she had retrieved the green book from the cabin, life had begun to crumble around her.

She had not quit trying, but everything she had attempted had failed. All the herbs and charms, all the incantations and chants had failed. Even the final promise of contacting Adela for help had disappeared. Adela Martindale was not Adela of the red chiffon.

"Ouch!" Jenny stared at her pricked finger and watched the blood drip onto her sewing. Blood. Sabbat. Was she receiving a message? The memory swirled before her. She hadn't thought of the event for many, many months. But suddenly without warning the sickening memory of the sabbat made her jump to her feet.

For a moment she stood paralyzed as the remembered smell of blood overwhelmed her. Against her closed eyelids she saw the silver chalice floating in front of her.

"Jenny!" Sally's needle was poised. "It isn't fatal," she said dryly. Her attempt at wit didn't touch Jenny, and she added, "Jenny, what's the problem? I've been watching you and Mark for a week now. You won't even look at each other."

Jenny sat down and squeezed her finger. She tried to think of an answer, but there was only truth. "Mark thinks I've been unfaithful to him."

Cautiously Sally asked, "What has made him say that?"

When she lifted her head, their eyes met and Jenny whispered, "Sally, don't look at me like that. I've done nothing. It isn't what he said, it's the way he looks. There's Cowdery's story about my going to the office in Kirtland. I saw then that Mark believed me unfaithful. Sally, before all this, we would have laughed. Now everything is twisted and ugly."

Sally's hands were limp and motionless in her lap. Slowly a strange expression crossed her face. She focused on Jenny and said, "You mustn't let it discourage you. Regardless of what Mark says, you must be true to your religion. Your whole eternity depends upon that."

Puzzled, Jenny studied the curious expression and tried to pick sense out of the pieces of information being thrust at her. "Sally, you know Mark's apostate from the one true religion, but he didn't bring religion into it. It was us. Me—he was doubting me. I love Mark with all my heart. It hurts terribly to have him treat me this way."

Abruptly Sally crossed the room and knelt beside Jenny. Clasping her arm in a surprisingly strong grasp, she said, "Look at me, Jenny. You must give him up. I've heard him pressuring you to go to Springfield. He's trying to get you to leave the

church. He's thinking that now's the time to force you to go."
Abruptly she dropped her hands and rocked back on her heels.
"Or do you?"

"Do I what?"

"Believe, like some of the others, that Joseph is a prophet
fallen from grace, that he no longer holds the keys of the kingdom. You know what his letter said. The Lord himself assured
Joseph that he still holds the keys of the kingdom, and, furthermore, Zion is not dead but alive!"

Sally's voice rose in a cry of triumph that sent prickles of
excitement over Jenny. She searched her friend's face. "Sally,
if only I could recapture my faith. I'm so dead inside. After
Haun's Mill I didn't believe you would ever be happy again.
Now I'm the one whose faith is faltering and whose hope is
gone."

Sally threw her arms around Jenny. "Oh, I will pray for you
that the Lord will make you strong enough to do His will, even
if it means you must renounce Mark himself."

Jenny leaned back and slowly asked, "Do you remember
what Joseph has taught? That God has put the right way within
us, and that it is natural and easy to follow along the way we
should go, that God will make us have a witness to the way?"

Sally leaned forward, her face was shining as she whispered,
"Yes, Jenny. I remember. I really believe it. We are to follow
that inner light. Sometimes it comes across only as a big desire,
but I know it is right."

Jenny looked at her curiously for a moment. Now cocking
her head, she was lost in a response that surprised herself.
Slowly she said, "Sally, I don't think that's totally correct. At
least right now, this moment, I'm feeling some strange tuggings
taking me every which direction.

"For a moment, mostly because I loved so much and because
I know Mark is so wrong, I believed that I must give him up,
run forever from the pull he has on my life. But there's something else."

She paused and lifted her face. It was Sally who said with
awe in her voice, "Your face is shining like an angel. I didn't
believe before that you could see things. Now I'm sure of it. Tell
me, what do you see?"

Jenny's eyes were wide. Slowly she said, "I'm seeing, I'm remembering. Our wedding. There were yellow roses and—" now she was whispering, "so much spirit feeling there. I'd never experienced it that way. I still smell the roses, I still know those promises I made to Mark were the most important words I've ever said. Sally, it was like the whole heaven and earth witnessed our vows. But there was more, someone or something that transcended every influence I've ever known. I know it was there when I said, *Mark, I promise you*."

Now Sally whispered, "Was it God?"

Jenny opened her eyes wide. "Oh no. It wasn't God. I know the god influence." Unexpectedly she shivered and looked at Sally. "God is fearsome. This was like love with eyes. Do you know what I mean?" Obviously Sally didn't.

Thinking hard now, trying to understand her deepest feelings, Jenny said, "Well, I'm believing that my inner self is telling me to follow Mark. But it isn't easy to decide that. It's as if there are two Jennys inside arguing that out. I want badly to be here waiting for a miracle to happen to Joseph, but that isn't to be. Somehow, I know that the only right way is to go with Mark. Perhaps he will be won to the only true church through my going with him now."

"Jenny, that's not possible. He's taking you away from the church!"

But Jenny wasn't listening. She hugged herself and sighed with relief. For the first time in months she had a strong, sure sense that she was making a right decision. She couldn't wait for Mark to come.

"Sally!" Jenny jumped to her feet and tossed aside the sewing. "I want to go meet the men."

She was nearly to Far West before she saw the lone horseman. It was Mark. When she ran to him, he slid off the horse and stood waiting. His face was clouded with worry, but when he saw her open arms and lifted face, he began to grin.

"Oh, Mark! I'm ready; let's go now!" His arms were tight about her and Jenny sighed with contentment. Nothing else was necessary. She didn't see his lips move or hear the whisper, "Thank you, Lord Jesus."